TORTURED SKIN

The Paul Isaac Vampire Series

JAMES C. GILLEN

Hydra Publications

ISBN: 978-1-942212-94-2

Hydra Publications
Goshen, Kentucky 40026
www.hydrapublications.com

"To my grandmother, Alma, for giving me an electric typewriter to support my habit."

CHAPTER ONE

The evening sun had already fallen below the horizon, but there was still a pastel glow of sunlight blanketing the city. A palette of pinks and baby blues painted the cloudless sky, giving way to the rapid pace of darkness only minutes away. The moon already glowed above like a huge spotlight.

It was also that time of the evening when the neon begins to step out of the anonymous clutter of signs and lights up all things around it. Headlights glowed on the streets. On-lookers and sightseers began to stir, waiting for the macabre world of unimaginable gothic horror. Tourists and natives of the city alike crowded the sidewalks in groups, eyes taking in the circus of a world only found in their childhood nightmares.

Still, it would be hours before the first vampires or cockroaches, as I call them, would be walking the streets. The humans were already here. Waiting for the sunlight to be swallowed whole, allowing the dark world to rise again. Thanks to the bleeding-heart liberals and politicians, the humans no longer feared the bloodsuckers, but embraced them, welcomed them, worshipped them. You see, our own government now endorses the vampires as historical artifacts, has put a lot of money into vampire awareness, and how they are simply misunderstood. I'm no longer allowed to stalk and kill them without a court order of execution from a judge or the Vampire Council. I'm only allowed to kill if the daisy-pusher rose as a monster instead of being born as one. This is our way of not being overrun by them and the cockroaches' way of keeping the race pure. And evil.

I got the call from Detective Zeke Kansas. A young woman had been found dead in Bat Town, which is what we call the vampire district of Orlando. Kansas told me that she had the markings of a bloodsucker attack. He needed me to come down and confirm. Oh yeah, then there's the usual tag line of "Keep this quiet. We don't want the tourists to freak out." Sick bastards. We are actually protecting the murderers. Heaven forbid the city lose a tourist dollar due to such a trivial thing as murder.

The dead woman had been found in a vacant lot on Jackson Street, just east of Bat Town. No pun intended, but this was the dark side of the vampire district. Most attacks on humans happened back here, where witnesses were few and those few had fangs. I swear I can smell the blood in the air, vile and sour. I know, I know, it is all in my head, but still...

As I rounded the corner, I saw the usual set of cars parked along the street-police cruisers and Detective Kansas' Ford Explorer. Silhouettes gathered around a yellow-taped area. Two large lamps illuminated a white sheet on the ground, under which I assumed I would find our unfortunate soul.

I parked my black 1970 Plymouth 'Cuda and took a deep breath. I grabbed my crucifix, an ax, a stake, and a vial of holy water from the floorboard next to me. I had an arsenal in the trunk, but this should do it for now. I also carried a Magnum with customized ultraviolet bullets in a shoulder holster and a 9mm in a hip holster. I am Damage Incorporated to the blood maggots. I get off on it.

If I had one wish right now, it would be that Kansas was wrong about this one and I wouldn't have to do anything, but chances of that were slim. I took a deep breath, lit a cigar, and got out of the car. The smoke encircled me like a shroud as I caught Kansas' attention. He nodded and began to move toward me through the crowd of police.

"Good evening, Saint Avenger." The words struck like an ice pick.

"Dieter Procnow," I said to the five-hundred-year-old vampire behind me. "I was in a relatively good mood until I heard your voice. How'd you get here so quick after sunset? I hadn't expected to see your dead face for hours."

"It is my job to make your life miserable", he said telepathically.

"I am here to protect the rights of vampires from the likes of you. It is up to me and my associates to make sure the victim is not tortured in a way unfavorable to a vampire." This was said aloud, for the benefit of the bystanders.

"'Torture in a way unfavorable to a vampire,'" I quoted. "Dieter, can you tell me a way torture is favorable?"

"Apparently our killer has found a way to make it most favorable; otherwise, we would not be at one of these things."

"One of these things? Is that what this is to you? Your compassion overwhelms me."

"It is the least I can do to help my community, Avenger." Dieter looked at me with eyes black and dead. He tried to trap me with them, but I was too slick for that trick.

"If you really want to help your community, why not allow me to put a bullet through your black heart? I know it would make me feel safer at night." I faked a smile. "It's a shame I didn't find you before the new laws came down. I'd have given a whole new meaning to spreading the ashes of the dead."

"Still bitter, Avenger?"

He calls me Saint Avenger because he knows it gets under my skin. What does it mean? Don't worry about it. It's not something you need to know right now.

"I'm gonna take a great deal of pleasure in killing you one day," I said, looking just short of his eyes.

"How can you love life so much, and hate those of us that never die?"

"Because you do things like this. You've declared it open season for my kind." I looked over at the draped body. "This is what happens when we allow your kind to walk freely around on the streets."

"All this time and energy being wasted on a common street whore. It is a shame, is it not, Avenger?"

I moved toward him, anger building at his lack of compassion. "She someone's daughter, not some nameless body. And yeah, she might have been a street walker, but that doesn't mean she should end up a Happy Meal for the undead."

"Paul!" Detective Kansas shouted. "Don't let him get under your skin. We have work to do." Looking at Dieter, he added, "He's not worth it."

Dieter smiled as I backed off. "See, Detective Kansas, I told you Mr. Isaac has anger-management issues. He is a loaded gun, ready to go off at any moment. The Vampire Council is very concerned with his behavior."

"Dieter, if the Vampire Council has issues with Mr. Isaac, they need to settle them through the proper channels. To be honest, I don't care about the concerns of the Vampire Council right now," Kansas said, his face stern, his eyes nearly slits.

I blew the smoke in Dieter's face, turned my back to him, and began to walk toward Ms. Jane Doe. I could feel the vamp following me, but didn't much care. He really didn't scare me, and I think that was starting to get to him. Intimidation is the name of their game, but if you push back hard enough, they cave.

Around the body I noticed two police officers that I had never seen before. I nodded to them, but didn't speak. Ahead of me, I saw Senior Detective Price and Officer Rook. These two I knew. I acknowledged them, but again said nothing. I'm not exactly in their little clique. To them, I'm a freak because of what I do, much like many feel about psychics. We help the department, but aren't actually in the club. Don't get me wrong. I'm okay with that. I don't want to be in the club.

The white sheet on the ground seemed to almost glow in the artificial light above it. All it needed was a flashing neon sign that read, "Dead body, right here!" Small red spots scattered across the surface of the sheet: blood.

"Save me the speech on how she set herself up for this. I've already heard it, remember," Kansas snapped. His blond hair was thinning; light pink skin glistened beneath it, growing brighter as his temper flared.

I could feel my gut tighten. "Yeah, if she was down here partying, she set herself up. I'll keep preaching until someone starts to listen. But at the same time, no one deserves to lose their life like this. I hate the fact that I have to cut the heads off the victims, but I know I can't look at them as humans anymore."

I took a deep breath as Detective Kansas lifted the sheet, revealing the aftermath underneath from the waist up. "Don't get grossed out on me," he smiled.

"Dead people don't gross me out, but knowing what probably did this makes me want to turn around and choke Dieter simply for what he represents," I said, loud enough for Dieter to hear.

The young woman looked as though she was sleeping, curled up in a fetal position, golden hair flowing across her chest and pooling on the sidewalk under her. She was naked, bruised, and dirty.

"She was a very beautiful girl at one time," Kansas responded.

I leaned down to get a closer look. "Something doesn't fit the classic vampire attack."

"What do you mean?" Kansas asked, bending down next to me.

"Usually, a vampire doesn't take the time to undress you before or after an attack. Still, that doesn't rule out the possibility that she was a freak, you know, likes to fuck fang boys for the thrill of it. If so, it's very obvious that she got in over her head last night."

"Much like a common whore," Dieter said under his breath. I could feel his eyes on me, but I wasn't willing to let him know I even heard him. "Just because someone dies in the vampire district, Detective, doesn't mean that a vampire was involved. She could have just as easily been killed by a human pervert she picked up at one of the bars. Or, more likely, was murdered somewhere else and just dropped here."

I would never give Dieter the satisfaction of saying it out loud, but he had a valid point. Maybe Kansas was jumping to conclusions on this one. I didn't see any signs of a bite. I might luck out and not have to cut her head off tonight. "What makes you think that this was a vampire attack?" I asked Kansas.

Detective Frank Price stepped in the circle. He was about fifty years old, balding, his glasses always perched so close to the tip of his nose that they threatened to slip right off. He had been a cop his whole life, and still hated working the freak-and-monster district. I couldn't blame him. The man had a good life going for him, and now he was assigned to things like this. Sucks to be him.

"This, for starters." Price pulled the sheet down away from the thigh and legs. Things got a little more graphic. There was a lot of dried blood on her lower body, and as my eyes followed the length of her legs, I saw why. "Her right foot was amputated just above the ankle, just like the other ones we found." His eyes looked to me as if I would be able to resurrect her or something.

I set my tools and cigar down on the ground, crouched low, and began to examine the body. I always felt smoking over a dead body and blowing ashes everywhere was disrespectful. Wasting a cigar seemed trivial compared to what this woman had been through.

"Her fingernails don't show any sign of a struggle. They're remarkably clean for a body in this condition," I said as I looked at the fingers and wrists. "She's been bound with something. That's why we don't see any blood or skin under the nails." I moved her head to the side. "No sign of a bite here."

Detective Price spread her legs apart and I felt my heart sink. There it was on the inner thigh of her right leg, the one missing the foot. A set of marks set inside a bruised and swollen area. "I've never been bitten by one of these things, but by the looks of the bite, it has to hurt like a son of a bitch," he said.

I tried to regain my composure. "Our monster has grown a little cocky on his attacks. He's apparently getting his kicks on not only feeding off of young women, but torturing them as well. Looks like a possible sexual assault too."

"There is no way for you to know that, Avenger. Besides, if she was a whore, sexual favors were what she was paid for." Dieter asked. "What I would like to know is how the attacker could cut her foot off while she was kneeling in front of him."

He knows me so well. I have to give him that one. He knows which buttons to push, and he hits them hard. I stood and looked just below his black eyes. "Don't tempt me tonight, Dieter. I'm not in the mood."

Kansas pushed me away from Dieter, his eyes were like a storm. "Look, I know he's a real piece of crap, but I expect more control out of you. I need you to tell me if this attack is consistent with the other bodies we found." He hesitated for a moment. "There's something else I want to show you."

I squatted near the body again.

"I will kill you when you least expect it. They cannot watch you all the time", Dieter whispered in my head. His breath dripping hot on my neck, his words, stilted and formal, almost so thick they could take shape. The old fang-heads never used contractions, an affectation that grated my nerves.

"Look at this," Detective Kansas said as he rolled the girl's body over, revealing her bottom. Dried blood had pooled under her butt, leaving it brownish and sticky. In the maze of blood was a tattoo: the letters TS, and a rose with a barbed-wire stem.

I didn't have to say it. My eyes told Kansas everything he knew I'd say.

He shook his head. "I know. Just like the other ones."

"The tattoo isn't fresh. Our killer didn't do this at the time of her death."

"What are you getting at?" Kansas asked.

"It takes tattoos weeks to heal. If our cockroach had anything to do with the tattoos, he's been stalking the women for quite a while. Chances are, the victims knew the vampire that did this, and possibly knew each other."

"Could be. I'm checking with all the tattoo artists in Bat Town to see if anyone has seen this tattoo before. With four girls having the same tat, it stands to reason it's a local thing," Kansas sighed. "I've talked with friends of the first girls. If they know anything, they aren't talking."

I looked at the truncated leg again. Meat, muscle, and bone cut with great care. "I'm not sure if something like this could cause someone to bleed to death or not, but I would assume that it would cause quite a bit of blood loss. I think the cockroach fed more to cover his tracks than anything else."

"Meaning?"

"Meaning the amputation led to the death more than the feeding. He got carried away with the torture. And just like the others, she's about twenty or so." I looked under the body for anything that maybe the police missed. "Whoever the killer is, he wanted us to find the body. It's his calling card. Usually when a vampire kills, it keeps the body hidden until the turn so there'll be no investigation. No body, no crime. Not our psycho. He wanted us to find his work, wanted us to know what he had done. He wants us to kill her again." I stood and took a deep breath and grabbed the cigar from the sidewalk. "Any ID on this one?"

"Not that we've found," Kansas replied, now standing and lighting a cigarette of his own. Getting information from him was like pulling teeth. He began to pace in front of the body like a football coach. He looked up at Dieter and me. "So this one is authentic?"

"It's authentic," I said. It sounded more like a diagnosis than an answer. I never liked this part of the job. To me, there was still a human element to them. They were still victims. It was after they turned, lost their souls, that I lost my love for them and was able to do my job with no interference from my conscience.

"You agree?" he asked Dieter.

"Unfortunately, your street walker was at the hands of a vampire at one time, Detective. I am not convinced it was her cause of death."

"But she was bitten by a vampire," Kansas finished.

"Yes, but is it not common for the street whores to feed vampires on a regular basis? It is possible, Detective, that this woman fed a vampire, then was killed by a human."

"We have no way of knowing if that's true or not. What we do know is she's been bitten by a cockroach and needs to be taken care of."

"The record shall show this is an unconfirmed vampire killing when I file my report to the Council."

"Do whatever you want, Dieter, but the truth of the matter is the same. She's been bitten by a vampire, and is now dead. We have no way of knowing if the bite killed her or not. Chances are, it is, but it doesn't change anything. She must be treated as though it was a cockroach attack."

"Very well." Dieter waved the debate off with his hand. "Cut the whore's head off; it is insignificant. But my findings are inconclusive as to cause of death."

"Then let's get this over with," Kansas said with a sigh.

"Let me know if there is anything the vampire community can do to help in the investigation, Detective. We are all saddened by this loss of life," Dieter said, shaking Kansas' hand and giving his best "I care" look.

I couldn't help but roll my eyes and let a sarcastic laugh escape. He was part of the problem, not the solution. "You could take her place if you really want to help," I started. "I'll make you a deal. Let me cut your head off and I'll let this one live, a cockroach for a cockroach. We only lose one foot in the whole deal."

"Death will come slow and with great pain, Saint Avenger," Dieter silently said to me, his face showing the anger hidden only skin deep.

He looked back to Kansas. "Let us try and keep this as quiet as we can, please." He reminded me of one of those bad TV preachers, a wide smile with nothing behind it. "The Vampire Council would be forever grateful for your cooperation."

Now you see what I mean by cover-ups for all the wrong reasons. "We have a young girl tortured, mutilated, and killed by a bloodsucker, and all he can say is 'keep it quiet.'" I had to walk away to get some fresh air. Any more of Dieter's mouth would send me over the edge.

I walked to my bag and brought out the ax and a vial of holy water. In a few moments, this would all be over but the paperwork. Authenticating a vampire attack can destroy an entire forest, pink copies to this official, white copies to that official. It can get overwhelming before you know it.

A crowd of policemen still circled the body, but unlike when I first arrived, they now stepped back, allowing me to enter. It's a gruesome sight to see a body being decapitated, but it's human nature to want to witness it from afar. Most of those watching me were seeing it for the first time. They all wanted to watch the executioner do the deed. The more gruesome I made it, the bigger their stories would be. All we needed was for someone to sell popcorn to the show. Classless and self-indulgent, that's what it was. I bet they wouldn't find it so enticing to watch if it were their daughter. They gave me the creeps every time I did this.

Out of the corner of my eye, I saw something. Something familiar. I looked past the officers and into a small crowd of onlookers that had gathered behind us. I hadn't noticed them until now and probably wouldn't have if it hadn't been for that face. Instant recognition for both of us.

Vinnie Gallerani.

Two

CHAPTER TWO

I had been looking for this creep for the last four months. He was a time-share salesman just outside of Orlando until his untimely run-in with a vampire. From what I had gathered on Vinnie, he wasn't the most upstanding citizen as a human, but now he was one of them, and that made him my problem.

You see, I have a database of all suspected vampires in the city: V.A.M.P., which stands for Vampires And Missing Persons. A database compiled from missing person reports, surveillance cameras, sightings, witness reports, and other sources. The police had given the information in this database to me. I am given pictures and information on the subjects, with court orders to kill them. It's really cut and dry.

We made eye contact. I could see him starting to shake already. He was scared, on the run, and from word on the street, pretty much out of friends. Many people believe that all daisy-pushers are these gothic, self-confident, fearless creatures, but that is nothing more than an urban legend. Becoming a blood-lapper doesn't change your personality or your intelligence. If you were a spineless coward as a human, you will be a spineless coward as a blood-sucking cockroach.

I don't know who turned Vinnie in, and I really don't care. The fact remains that he's a confirmed stake donor. I arrested him four months ago and tested him. He failed. Just as I was about to stake his sleazy ass, he was able to get out of the cuffs and hit me with a steel pipe. To say we have a score to settle is an understatement.

I quickly pushed through the circle of cops and began picking up speed. He was still about fifty yards away. I was eating up the distance, coming to a full run.

Vinnie turned away from me in a fury of speed and split through the small crowd of onlookers. His short legs were scurrying quickly, the smooth skin of his scalp reflecting the streetlights as he ran.

The crowd Vinnie was with was smart enough to give me room as I approached. Screams rose from the group as I pushed my way through. Magnum in hand, loaded with cockroach-killing bullets, I gave chase.

"Hey, where the hell are you going?" Kansas yelled from behind me. That question was nicely framed by expletives.

The dead body would have to wait. It wasn't like she was going anywhere. Deal with the greatest threat. That's how I handle things. Vinnie was moving around on the streets, capable of making more of these bloodsuckers. He was clearly a more immediate danger to us all.

I moved past the crowd and tried to keep focused on Vinnie. He made his way to the glowing neon streets ahead. He was wearing a black fake leather jacket and blue jeans, making his movement harder to track in the dark. His dress shoes, however, made him sound more like a horse than a dead man, helping me track him. Every few seconds, he would glance back at me, trying to determine if he was gaining ground or losing it. A series of quick screams escaped his lungs. He desperately tried to find more speed.

I had to stop him before he made it to Church Street, for various reasons. One, he could easily hide in the thick crowd. Two, he could grow desperate and turn this into a hostage situation. I've had that happen numerous times. And three, I'm not exactly welcome down here; friends are fewer for me than for the fang-head ahead of me.

We were on Jackson Street. If I was lucky, I would be able to get off two shots max before he hit the crowds. The sounds of the cars on I-4, which ran parallel to the street, would mask the shots.

I was closing in on him now, thirty-five yards away. I sent a shot blistering toward him. Missed. His screams matched my Magnum note for note. The crowds of people walking along Church Street now started to part as they watched the pursuit coming toward them.

There was probably twenty or thirty of them, running, scream-ing, and gathering their little ones. Eyes wide with panic, unsure of which direction to run, they made way for the two of us. Welcome to Bat Town, my little pretties. If they were lucky, they might make it through this alive. Might.

It was apparent I wasn't going to get another shot off before entering the crowd. Vinnie began to move through the first few humans. More screams rang out in waves. We continued to push through the bewildered crowd.

A rush of sound and energy hit me as I turned the corner onto Church Street. I moved fast through the wake Vinnie was making. Deep bass filtered into the streets from the clubs. Flashing lights from the rainbow of marquees filled my eyes with blinding color. Faces everywhere avoided my eyes as I moved past them. Screams of horror sounded in the night. Everyone was seemingly oblivious to the fact that I was the good guy. Can't really blame them for the panic, though. I was the one with the gun.

I had lost sight of Vinnie in the crowd, but I was still able to track him by the wake of people being pushed aside and the screams that followed. I was gaining on him. He was having a difficult time plowing through the crowd. I moved through the openings he created. Note to self: People get out of your way when you have a gun.

Vinnie made a quick right, dodging through the slow-moving traffic. He bounced off hoods and tried to keep what momentum he still had. I continued toward him, zigzagging through the cars. I debated whether I could get a clean shot off or not. The last thing I wanted to do was shoot an innocent bystander in all this.

With blood racing through my veins, adrenaline fueled my pursuit. Horns beeping. Tires squalling. Drivers yelling. As we hit the far side of the street, we melted into the sea of people. They were paralyzed with confusion, not sure whether to run or stand still.

Vinnie made a quick jaunt to the left, moving down another alleyway. I smiled inwardly at the sudden move. The further he moved away from the crowds, the easier it would be for me to get off another shot. Inside me, it was a battle of wills. Part of me wanted to just get this over with and collect my fee. A darker side of me wanted to kill him slow for the inconvenience of our little chase. Not to mention the pipe to the head. Complete with five stitches.

"Please don't kill me!" he screamed as he ran further down the alleyway, his fake leather jacket flapping in the wind. He glanced back at me, eyes white with fear. Sweat was beading on his forehead, and his fangs showed as he gasped for breath.

I didn't say anything. Truthfully, I needed all the breath I could get just to keep up the pace. Besides, dialogue was only going to be a waste of time. No amount of begging was going to save him. He was going to die tonight.

Vinnie ran to a dock ramp on the right side of the building, grabbed the door handle, and pulled on it hard. The door swung open violently, crashing into the blue handrail next to it. A small light glowed above it, illuminating in dim colors.

The door slammed back shut. Momentum sent my shoulder crashing into it. I stopped myself, backed up and opened the door.

Inside, my eyes strained to see in the darkness. A series of endless shadows lay ahead of me. Rows and rows of shelving units were filled to the ceiling with boxes of various sizes. I scanned the floor for signs of movement. Nothing. I listened for footsteps. Nothing. Great.

I felt myself holding my breath as I moved slowly deeper into the warehouse. I had to be careful. I was in the middle of the vampire district, in a vampire-owned warehouse, and I was certain there was at least one vampire in here with me. There is nothing the fanged cockroaches down here wouldn't do to get a piece of me. I was walking into a death trap.

Odds were still in my favor. Vinnie wasn't smart. He was lucky to tie his own shoes. I have my suspicions that whoever attacked Vinnie did it simply to put a death mark on him. To kill him outright wasn't good enough. This was not about reward money.

I scanned the rows to the left and right of me, looking for anything that might give Vinnie's hiding place away. Smooth concrete floor, roughly ten feet wide, separated the large walls of shelving. He couldn't have gone too far. I came through the door only seconds after he did.

Vinnie's weight hit me hard from above, knocking me to the floor. I didn't have the chance to brace myself. My face and chest took most of the fall as a spider web of pain shot through me. I tried to roll over. He continued to force my body to the floor. I still had the Magnum in my hand, but at the moment I wasn't able to get a clear shot.

I freed my right shoulder and arm, and pushed them into Vinnie's rib cage. He grunted with pain as he tried to remain in control. However, I outweighed the creep by about forty pounds. I began to roll him off in a series of small rocks.

He dug his nails deep into my shoulders, growling as his advantage began to slip away. The growls soon turned into whimpers as I freed myself from his grasp.

I looked into Vinnie's eyes, scared and hopeless. The emotions stuck to his face like glue. "All I can think about is running a stake through your weasel heart."

"You should've stayed away from here." His mouth was almost touching my ear. "Should have just staked Sheri and left me alone."

Vinnie stood and started to run again. I stabbed him in the thigh with the silver-bladed knife I kept with me in case I ran into unexpected shape-shifter issues. I knew the silver wouldn't kill him, but I didn't want him dead just yet. The silver blade would cause unbelievable pain if used right, and that was just what I wanted to happen.

Vinnie screamed as the blade sizzled into his skin. It was all I could do to keep from puking. The smell of burning skin is putrid enough, but when dead skin burns, it creates a whole new flavor of stink. "Get it out of me!" He tried to pull it out, which only caused him additional pain.

"What did you say about the girl?" I asked.

"Didn't say nothin', man. Get it out of me." He looked at the silver blade and then back to me, twitching. He was burning from the inside out; the pain had to be excruciating.

"Who was she?" I now stood above him. "Tell me, and I'll end it quick."

"Sheri. Sheri. That's all I know. God, it hurts."

"How do you know her?"

"She's a freak that comes down to Bat Town all the time. I don't know her personally, just seen her around, man." Sweat beaded his forehead as he writhed on the ground. "Please, take it out."

"Who did that to her? You know I'll get it out of you eventually. You're in no position for negotiation."

He looked up at me, his breathing growing quicker. "Don't know. She was just a freak. Humped a couple of vamps and disappeared again."

"Tell me what I want to know, Vinnie, and I'll end this all with a bullet to the head. Quick and painless." I hauled him to his feet, dragged him to a pipe that ran along the wall behind us, and pulled out a set of handcuffs. They make it a lot easier to interrogate than simply talking. Vinnie screamed as I pulled his arms up to the handcuffs and locked them in place, fear glowing in his eyes.

"You ready to talk yet, Vinnie?"

"You know me. I'd tell you anything I knew if I knew it."

"Why were you watching tonight?"

"Payin' my respects, that's all. Please take this thing out of me. I'm filing charges."

"Paying your respects to a stripper you don't even know? How noble of you."

I tried to catch my breath as I slapped a second pair of cuffs on him just as a safeguard. Remember, this blood-sucking cockroach already cost me five stitches. Fool me once, shame on you. Fool me twice, shame on me. I could feel liquid running down the side of my head, though I was unsure whether it was sweat or blood. All I knew was that I was getting too old to do this kind of running. Note to self: Quit smoking.

"Who killed her, Vinnie? Any information I can get out of you will help this investigation tremendously, and I'm not above bending a few rules to get it."

"Told you, man, I don't know. She was just a freak. That's all I know." He squirmed as the blade continued to sizzle in his dead flesh.

I caught his gaze. "You know something, Vinnie? I think you're lying to me. And if there is one thing I hate as much as a cockroach, it's a liar. Unfortunately for you, you happen to be both."

"I'm not lyin', man. I don't know nothin'. Please, you gotta believe me. Take that thing out of my leg. I promise, I don't know nothin'."

"We're gonna find out if that's true or not, aren't we, Vinnie?" I was now up in his face. I could see those fangs, smell the burning flesh, and feel the fear. I pulled a crucifix from my pocket and dangled it in his face. "Know what this thing can do? Wanna meet Jesus, Vinnie?"

"No! Come on, man, he'll kill me!"

I stepped back and smiled at him as I swung my arms out to the side. "You're a dead man either way."

Vinnie volleyed between laughter and crying as he spoke, "You don't know what you're getting yourself into. He'll literally eat you alive." The look in his face began to change. "He's lookin' for you, Avenger. Says you'll help him or die."

"Who?"

"He says you'll know when the time is right."

I shoved the crucifix in Vinnie's mouth and held it shut. He nearly caught fire when I pulled the chain out of his mouth. Smoke rolled from his face as he tried to regain composure. "Who is he, Vinnie?"

"You ain't allowed to do this to me. They'll get you for this. I have my rights." His voice was now hoarse and his speech mushy from his scorched tongue. "You ain't nothin' without your toys. He will kill you dead."

I had to laugh. Even while being cuffed to a building, a blessed blade in his leg and his mouth nearly rotting off, Vinnie was still able to talk smack. "Who's gonna stop me? I don't see this friend of yours coming to your rescue. Now tell me what you know." I shoved the crucifix down the front of his pants. If you've never seen a blood-sucking cockroach dance, take it from me-they have no rhythm.

"Okay, okay, I'll tell you. Get it out. Get it out!" His voice was almost out of human range of sound.

Again, I pulled the chain, and the crucifix was back in my hand. I didn't even want to think about what virus might be on the thing now. Vinnie would screw just about anything, and don't even get me started on the hygiene of low-life vampires. The thought was too sickening, even for me. I patted his cheek. "Now we're getting somewhere." I stepped back to listen to my songbird. "Start from the beginning."

Vinnie tried to catch his breath. "I want a lawyer or something."

I swung the crucifix in his face again.

"Okay, okay. Forget the lawyer. Look, he hangs around at the Lunatic Moon down at the end of Church Street. It's a sex shop of sorts. Run by shifters. He's using runaways down there for some sort of amusement, plans on taking on Quinn Rubio for the whole district. He thinks since you hate the vampires as much as he does, you'll help him. He wanted me to meet up with you tonight to talk about it."

"Is he cockroach or shifter?" I asked.

"Shifter, sort of. I ain't never seen nothin' like him."

"And he killed the girl?"

"I don't know. I just know I saw her around there a lot. One of his girls, I guess. He pimps them out to the vampires and others that come in. They feed off the girls, then leave them on the street."

"Who was with her last?"

"I ain't sayin' I know who killed her or nothin'. She was into some kinky things. She was a vampire freak." He was struggling to remain calm despite the blade in his leg. I could have removed it, but why?

"I need a name, Vinnie."

"I need this thing out of my leg!" Panting.

"Not gonna happen. Now, I need a name, or you become my personal torture toy." I gave him a cold smile.

"You ain't no cop. I don't have to tell you nothin'. I already told you more than I should. If he finds out I snitched, he'll dig me up and do a lot worse than what you can."

"Don't count on it. I have plenty of ways to hurt you enough to make you wish you were dead. Now, I need a name."

He eyes bulged like a Pekingese. "You don't know what you are getting yourself into. You hurt me, and he'll take it as a sign of hostility. This guy is not like anything else here. The vampires are afraid of him and what he can do. He can shape-shift into anything he wants."

He wasn't bullshitting me. He was too scared to. I kind of liked it. Unfortunately, I didn't know much about shape-shifters-or any of the other creatures down here, for that matter. Vampires are my game. "More girls are gonna die if you don't tell me." I opened a vial of holy water and moved in on my subject. "I'm willing to do anything to save them, and insane enough to enjoy it."

"Stop! Okay, okay, I'll tell you what I know." He swallowed hard, like he was taking a spoonful of medicine. "He is known as Piel. I swear, that's all I know!"

"Piel. Means 'skin' in Spanish. Good job, Vinnie. We're getting somewhere." If given time alone with the fanged cockroaches, I can get the information I need. It's when the police, politicians, and lawyers get involved that things move slowly, if at all. I don't see anything wrong with bending a few rules when human life is at stake. Piel is taking human lives, or at the very least is a link to the killings. Now my only dilemma was whether to go to the police with what I had discovered and wait on them to go through all the red tape, or visit Piel myself and possibly save the next victim. I pulled the knife out of Vinnie's leg. "One more thing. Have you ever seen anyone with a tattoo of a rose with a barbed-wire stem and the letters TS?"

I heard something. We were not alone in the warehouse. It didn't make a difference whether it was vampire or police. My personal time with Vinnie was up.

I didn't wait for Vinnie's answer about the tattoo. I had a bigger piece to the puzzle. I pulled the Magnum around to meet his heart. "Nothing personal." I pulled the trigger. Vinnie never had a chance to beg before he turned to ash.

I was lying. It was personal. I made it personal.

CHAPTER THREE

There is nothing worse than being sucker-punched. The pain struck me like a lightning bolt. I dropped to my knees, disoriented and confused. I knew I couldn't pass out. If I lost consciousness here, to say I'd be put in harm's way would be putting things lightly. Then again, when someone sucker-punches you in the back of the head, there is very little doubt that you've been put in harm's way anyway.

Everything around me was spinning at the speed of light. I felt my body growing weaker. My head felt like it had exploded. Blood trickled down the nape of my neck. Bleeding is something you just don't do in Bat Town if you can avoid it.

I could hear voices above me; three or four of them. I tried to look up when the second blow hit. It wasn't a fist that hit me, but a steel bat or tubing of some sort. My eyes were unable to pick it out with my blurred vision. My shoulders took the brunt of the second blow, causing me to lose my breath. My chest began to tighten.

"Kill him," I heard one of them say.

I made sure I didn't lose grasp of the Magnum. I was low on bullets, so I had to use them with care. I wasn't sure how many more might be hiding in the shadows.

I rolled along the floor, trying to move away from the next blow. With each roll, I could feel my head threatening to explode again. The pain was like doing gymnastics with the worst migraine ever. I was sick to my stomach as each throb of pain hit.

"Not so tough now, are you?" the second voice said, accompanied by a kick to the ribs. Like I needed that.

So that's what the chase with Vinnie was all about. He was bait to get me here, and I bought into it hook, line, and sinker. Son of a bitch!

By the sound of the voices, my assailants were young, maybe twenty, twenty-five at the most. As I rolled away I could see the outline of three men standing over me. They were cockroach punks, trying to make a name for themselves. They began to spread out in a loose circle, each with a hollow pipe in hand.

The second boy, in a Ramones T-shirt, swung at me, missing my face by less than an inch as I dodged and slid near the wall where Vinnie's ashes fell. I grabbed my wooden stake and came to my feet again. I now had firepower in one hand and a death stick in the other. Swirls of colors filled my vision, nearly knocking me back to the floor. Blood rushed into my eyes. I swung the stake wildly, connecting with nothing. I would use the Magnum once my vision cleared, but until then, I couldn't afford to waste bullets. I wasn't sure how many shots I had left. However, the punks didn't know that, which worked to my advantage. Besides, staking them would work just as easily, and in all honesty was more satisfying.

The third punk, in a Billabong shirt, tackled me from behind, sending both of us violently forward toward the other two. I dropped the stake and again landed on the smooth concrete floor. You never realize how hard things are until you hit them with your face. My face slid slightly along the wet blood on my forehead, warm and gooey.

"Kill him!" Ramones yelled from above me.

I was face to face with Billabong, who now had a knife. His eyes glared into mine without remorse. I spit in his face and finished off with a nice head butt. If I was going to have a headache, everyone else would, too.

The first, in a red T-shirt, kicked me in the side of the head. Repeatedly. Nice touch. I kept my eyes on the knife Ramones had. Knowing where it was at all times would help me keep from being stabbed. Light bounced off the blade in the artificial light.

The problem with their plan was that they brought a knife to a gunfight. You gotta love stupid cockroaches. I couldn't wait any longer. I had to use the gun if I was going to make it out alive. I brought the Magnum up to Ramones' chest, whose eyes widened with surprised fear. I pulled the trigger; the explosion nearly lifted the roof off the warehouse, echoing in an explosion of vengeance.

Ramones fell silently on top of me, dead weight followed by a warm pool of blood.

"He shot him!" Red Shirt yelled.

Both ran as I lifted Ramones off of me and tried to collect my thoughts. Something was very wrong with the situation. My heart pounded. The boy I shot was not a vampire. If he had been, he would have exploded into dust, not blood.

Many times, the vampires recruit humans to do their dirty work. The teenage boys in particular hope they will be rewarded with eternal life. But most are only used and discarded for fresh blood.

Another option existed. Quite possibly they were cockroach activists. Like I told you, everyone down here has some kind of cause; some just get you killed easier than others.

I was standing over the dead boy before I even realized it. Adrenaline took over. Killing a vampire is one thing, but when it's a human, death takes on a new feeling. My mouth grew dry as I searched my pocket for the cell phone.

"Shit," I breathed. I felt the panic taking over, like a raging river. "Fuck," I said a little louder as I took a step backwards. He was dead. He was fucking dead. Shit. Shit. Shit!

My fingers refused to dial 911. I simply looked at the phone for help.

"You will not need that, Avenger."

The voice was smooth and deep. I recognized it. Dieter.

"Should've known you had something to do with this." I turned to face him. "You set me up." God, I felt dumb.

Dieter laughed as he slithered across the floor. Behind him were other figures, silent and hiding in the shadows. "I did not pull the trigger, Avenger, you did."

"Who were they? Who was the boy?"

"Does it really matter now, Avenger? The fact is that you took a life. We are all witnesses to what you did. The press and the community will eat you alive. A loose cannon, I believe the local media called you. This was, as you might say, like taking candy from a baby."

It was hard for me to focus on his spew of words with a dead man in front of me. A stream of blood still trickled into my eyes. The situation was consuming me. I shot the boy in self-defense, true, but still, he was just a stupid punk doing the work of the blood-sucking cockroaches.

My mind was made up. If I was going out, I was going in a blaze of glory. I would take Dieter down with me. Besides, it would make bigger headlines and, contrary to popular belief, there were still multitudes of people that were secretly rooting for me to exterminate them all. They just couldn't say it out loud. I'd get to see Dieter die. It was better than rotting away in a cell, while he was still on the streets.

I brought the Magnum up for the last time and pointed it in

Dieter's direction. A needle bit deep into my neck from an invisible hand behind me.

"Sweet dreams, Avenger," Dieter whispered.

I remember seeing the outline of Dieter's smile just as everything went black.

CHAPTER FOUR

When my sight finally came back, it was in tandem with one of the worst headaches I've ever had. The light cut into my brain like a buzz saw. It was all I could do to keep from throwing up. I shivered uncontrollably, disoriented. And most alarmingly, cuffed to a chair.

There were ghost-like images in the room with me. Each time my eyes tried to focus on them, I found myself growing dizzy and sick to my stomach. I wasn't even sure how long I had been here.

Between the swirls of light, I thought I saw something move. I struggled to keep my eyes open, to keep from losing consciousness. Asleep, I couldn't defend myself. Then again, being cuffed to a chair, I really had no option other than wait to see who had me and why.

Dieter's ugly mug had been the last thing I saw when I had been blindsided by the needle. That made me more than just a little nervous. I remembered the boy and the pool of blood. I could feel it, sticky on my skin and shirt. Everything was coming back to me, bit by bit.

I saw movement ahead of me, slow and methodical. I tried again to focus as my vision gathered strength, but the lights only allowed glimpses, like looking into the sun.

"What do you want?" I called out. What the hell? I might as well act as though I could see them and wasn't intimidated.

Nothing.

I half expected that. They would communicate when ready. The smell of blood was thick in the air.

"Who are you?" I tried again.

Still no answer. As my vision cleared, I could see five others with me in the room. They seemed to appear as if by magic. Figures as lifeless as mannequins. They didn't blink. Didn't breathe. But they were alive all the same.

I was sitting at a large table, much like a conference table. I could see shades of lights and darks, but the details were not clear. Light fell from above. Blinding light. Unforgiving. I closed my eyes in pain.

There were two figures to my left, two to the right, and one at the head of the table. At least that's what I think I was seeing. It was all so surreal, dreamlike.

Vision improved slowly. I made out more details. They were all staring at me with empty smiles, silent and creepy. I recognized most of them.

I felt my fists clinch. Fear. The shadows were cockroaches. Dieter sat closest to me, on my right. His black doll eyes, hard in his pale face, made me catch my breath.

I pulled on the cuffs, only to find them snug. Figures. Whatever I was in for, it couldn't be pleasant. Joy. I swallowed the fear lodged in my throat like a large pill.

"Dieter, so pleasant to see you."

"This is no time for you to be rude, Avenger. You are at risk of becoming a dead man."

"You set me up, didn't you? You pathetic fucking corpse."

"You did all the work, Avenger-quite well actually. All we had to do is wait for you to trip the snare."

Unfortunately, he was right.

"Do you mind if we shelve the verbal sparing?" a deep voice asked from the head of the table. He was the so-called Master of the cockroaches, the Big Cheese, if you will, powerful, and dangerous. Quinn Rubio. He was about five-ten, blue eyes, long, flowing hair so black it looked purple. He was quite dapper, even for a blood junkie. If he were human, I would have guessed he was about thirty, but of course it's harder to guess a cockroach's age; probably nine hundred and change. European descent.

He ruled the district with violence. Buying who ever he had to buy. Killing whom ever he had to kill. Nothing personal, unless you were the victim. No one crossed him, from police to politicians. He held the district hostage; devouring, murdering, extorting. Yet the law protected him from the likes of me. A monster of his power wouldn't be an easy kill. If you crossed a coffin roach of his strength, you had a death wish. I was no match for him. I was smart enough to know that, cuffs or no cuffs.

"I would have expected a little more of a challenge in compromising you," a sultry voice said. She was about six foot tall; with long hair so blond it was almost white, thin, deep-red lips, well built in all the right places. She gave me a look that could kill. I avoided eye contact.

"Sorry to disappoint you, bitch," I said without thinking. I was angry, and my mouth usually gets the best of me in those situations.

"Watch your tongue, or I will cut it from your mouth," Quinn snapped.

I glared at the female cockroach, but said nothing. Somehow, I didn't think Quinn was bluffing. Being smart enough to understand that would keep me alive. I hoped.

The other two leeches, like Dieter, were dressed in black silk suits with red ties. I have to admit, vampires are usually snappy dressers. Too bad underneath they are nothing more than walking corpses. The one next to the hottie was Maximilian. As I recalled, he was another powerful cockroach, a politician of sorts, in other words, a double bloodsucker. The one next to Dieter was Virgil. He was just as powerful.

"Mr. Paul Isaac, the great vampire killer. I have always anticipated our meeting," Maximilian said with a fake smile.

I had to watch my tongue. Had to. My situation left me with no options other than to give a façade of respect. I could fantasize about killing them, but my tongue had to behave. Superman has his kryptonite, and I have my tongue.

"Maximilian."

"I do apologize for your inconvenience, and your compromised situation, but for the safety of us all, this seemed to be the best scenario."

"Somehow, I don't buy the hospitality."

"Again, our apologies."

"And why am I in this compromised situation?"

"Let us describe it this way, Mr. Isaac," Quinn explained. "You have pulled the trigger on a young man in the Vampire District. The police and the papers will not find that information in your favor. We want to know who they were and why you attacked them."

"That doesn't explain why I'm here in cuffs, Rubio. Those little punks attacked me. They tried to kill me. I shot in self-defense."

"We all agree with you, Mr. Isaac. But the truth remains: there is a body in the warehouse that must be addressed. Why were they there, and who did they work for?" Maximilian added.

"I was trying to address it when I had a damn needle stuck in my neck. Besides, you're the ones that need to be concerned. They worked for you."

"We know nothing of the sort, Mr. Isaac. They neither worked for us, nor did we have any association with the unfortunate soul."

My anger boiled, but outwardly I remained as cool as possible. "Bullshit."

Okay, maybe not.

Virgil stood quickly and sucker-punched me in the face. My head rocked with the impact. My skin stung and swelled as my headache erupted. God, how many times was I going to be hit in the head tonight?

"Better learn to hold your tongue, Avenger, or you will find this night to be quite uncomfortable," Dieter whispered in my head.

"You miserable piece of shit. You will be the one that I kill first." My tongue was now officially out of control. Dieter always did have that effect on me.

"If I remember correctly, Avenger, it was your finger that pulled the trigger, not mine." This time - out loud.

I took a deep breath, remembered where I was and what I had to lose. "Why the fuck am I here?"

"To be our bitch," the blond hissed.

"Kiss my cockroach-killing ass." This earned me yet another punch from Virgil.

"Enough!" Quinn barked.

All sounds and movement stopped. Quinn glared at my assailant until he was seated again, then looked back in my direction. I immediately dropped my eyes. "Paul Isaac," he drawled. Was it a statement or a question? I didn't know.

I nodded, but said nothing. I could feel a trickle of blood running from my nose. At least my shirt already had bloodstains on it. No harm, no foul. I took another deep breath and got my emotions back under control.

"Someone get Mr. Isaac a towel," Quinn said softly. He floated toward me, ominous, radiating power. His finger touched my lip. It was warm. He had fed.

Quinn licked the finger as though it was ice cream. "I will get right to the point, Mr. Isaac. I, along with the entire vampire community, need your help. The men that attacked you tonight present a great danger to us all. A danger we need help in extinguishing."

I raised my eyes slightly, staring at his chest. "You need my help?"

There was a long pause. Maximilian stood and began to walk along the far wall parallel to where I was sitting. After pacing a few lengths, he spoke. "He has my daughter. He plans to kill her."

"Who has your daughter?"

Virgil returned with a white towel and wiped away the trail of blood from my face with one rough swipe. It stung, but I wasn't going to show it.

"Thank you, Virgil," Quinn said, then turned to me. "The man responsible for the attack on you tonight is known as Piel. I don't expect you to know him. He is new in the city, very dangerous, and a shifter of sorts, but far more powerful. There seems to be an undercurrent of war between our kind and the lycanthropes. He has vowed to take over the district. Greed is the root of all evil, is it not?"

Piel. That was the same name Vinnie gave me. "I don't understand." Which was true. "Why do you want my help on this? You have to know that, given the chance, I'd rather stake your daughter than help her."

"Lyric is a very free-spirited girl." Quinn explained. "She has always looked for adventure, pushing the envelope to see what would happen. Conforming to my rules has been a challenge, to say the least. She ran away about six months ago, and I have confirmed reports that she is under this Piel's control." He looked back at me. "She is caught in the middle of something very dangerous."

"Look, you need to go to the police with this. I don't do search and rescue. Especially for cockroaches."

"We cannot," Maximilian said. He looked at Quinn for a few seconds, and then back to me. "Piel will kill her if we involve the police. Besides, the fewer people involved the better. Piel will never expect you to come for her. If the police or the papers find out we asked for your help, it will tarnish my reputation and Mr. Rubio's, not to mention the impact it could have on the entire district."

"So this is more about keeping your tourist trap squeaky-clean than retrieving the girl?"

"We need to make the tourists feel safe. Give them the thrills they want. If they have the illusion of danger, they will soon believe it to be true. But more importantly, it will make us all look weak and irresponsible. With the growing threat of lycanthrope uprising, we cannot afford the added press. If you go after her, it would not raise any...what do you Americans call them? Red flags. No one would suspect you rescuing a vampire. Besides, death and blood becomes you." He smiled, showing those damn fangs. "I guess we have more in common than previously thought."

"It is a very delicate situation, one that needs to stay private to prevent further endangering Lyric," the beautiful blond added. I could feel her gaze on me, feel the power radiate off of her. I was having dirty thoughts about a cockroach-a new low, even for me. "We are willing to pay you two million dollars if you kill Piel and bring Lyric back to us alive."

"Sorry, Miss..." I needed a name for my mental file. No, not so I could look her up. Get your mind out of the gutter. She was beautiful, yes, but still a cockroach-and all cockroaches are best headless.

"Veronica Powers. I am the attorney for Mr. Rubio."

How ironic. I had the hots not just for any vampire succubus, but a lawyer. Note to self: If I make it out of here alive, step in front of a bus. It's the humane thing to do.

"Ms. Powers, apparently you weren't listening. I don't do search and rescue. I don't take blood money. I kill cockroaches, period. You need to find someone else."

"We are quite aware of what you do, Mr. Isaac. We have seen your work. Trust me, you are truly the last resort for us. If we had no use for you, you would most assuredly be dead by now. You should be more appreciative of that fact alone," Maximilian said.

"With all your connections, I'm sure you could find someone else to do your bidding." I paused to make sure I chose my words correctly. "Unless there is more to the story."

"Piel has taken an interest in you. You would be able to get close enough to him without arousing suspicion. Mr. Isaac, we are willing to make your problem disappear if you agree to help us," Ms. Powers added.

"Meaning the dead body."

"Precisely. We all stand to have our situations simply disappear."

"You think it can really be that simple, don't you?"

"We own you, Mr. Isaac. You just do not know it yet."

"You can threaten me all you want. You can even kill me, but I'll bring you all down with me. I'll let them know just how involved in all this you really are."

"And how is your record with the media and the community, Mr. Isaac? I refer to both the human community and the vampire community."

"Your point?"

"Over the past two years, you have been connected with several reports of violence and questionable killings in our community. Times are changing. We are not seen as the monsters that we once were. You, on the other hand, are no longer seen as a hero, but rather as a menace to both our societies. Juries have not been kind to those that have been violent to vampires. It is no longer politically correct to discriminate against us. All I have to do is file the proper paperwork, and you will be indicted in a heartbeat." She moved behind me, which made me nervous. "Remember when you and the great Father Pablo Manuel Garcia killed that innocent young man, in cold blood, in front of his mother? The city still has a bitter taste on its tongue. They still want retribution."

She was right, every fucking word of it. And there was nothing I could do about it. "Thank you for the diversity and history review, but it does nothing to sway me to your cause. I'd rather die in a cell than sell out to you. Besides, I know there's more to all this than what you've been saying. You went to too much trouble for it to simply be a rescue mission."

Maximilian cleared his throat. "Lyric has been into things that I would prefer the media or the police not know about." He hesitated. "There have been three deaths, prominent vampire businessmen's wives or mistresses, in Orlando that we know of. Threats that there will be more if we do not give up our ownership of the district. The vampire business community of Orlando is up in arms about the killings, afraid for their lives and the lives of their families. There is a delicate balance that must be maintained in the district. Our power is being challenged. I have given my word that the killings would be stopped. I keep my word, Mr. Isaac. I have asked the community to keep this quiet until we talked to you."

"Let us come to an understanding," he added. "I tolerate you and your temperament because in its own perverse way it helps keep order among the community. But if I fail to find use in you, you will die."

"So now you know our dilemma. The lycanthropes are killers of both our kinds. Piel has stirred a pot of violence, you might say. Kill him, and both our problems go away," Ms. Powers purred.

"According to the crime scene I was at earlier tonight, Ms. Powers, I'd say there's a killer among your kind. I have no beef with the fur balls."

"I control all the vampires in this town. None of them would have been connected with such a thing," Quinn snapped. "Not that I give a damn about the prostitute you found tonight. She was a common freak that comes down here and spreads her diseases and tarnishes our good reputation. By morning, no one will remember her." He regained his composure. "We have worked hard to conform to your ways. It is your kind that continues to see us as the monsters."

I looked over to Dieter again. "You knew about all this?"

"We need to remain focused on the reason you are here, Mr. Isaac," Quinn interrupted. He was now walking toward me-no, scratch that, floating toward me. Cockroaches can do that crap. I could tell it was all he could do not to rip my throat and drain me dry, but there was too much in the balance. We both had something to lose. "It is imperative you tend to this. A minute ago you thought you were looking for the killer of common whores. Now you see it is much more."

"How do you see that? After all, mistress is just a sugarcoated term for whore, right? And if that's what Lyric is, then we're still looking for a killer of whores. The girl we found tonight might not have been a Sunday-school girl, but she has a family out there somewhere. She had feelings, knew pain, and became a statistic. You can all suck me dry if you want. I'm not going to kiss your asses while you disrespect a dead girl. She deserves better."

Maximilian stopped just inches from my face. He had a certain power over all living things that I can't really explain-you simply respect him to a certain extent whether you like it or not. "Mr. Isaac, Lyric is very important to me. And I will not allow a quick-tongued human to disrespect any of us. If you do not help us, I will make certain that you die as slowly as possible. You take care of Piel, bring Lyric to us, and you will not be hunted down by the police. There is more at risk here than just a dead body. There is the balance of power between the vampires and the lycanthropes. Do not presume that the bloodshed will not spill out into the streets of the humans. Piel cares about control and power, not consequences."

"Isn't that just the pot calling the kettle black? I guess you're expecting me to trust that this is not a trap?"

"I do not set traps, Mr. Isaac. If I want you dead, you will be dead. I never thought you would help us without persuasion. That is why events had to unfold the way they did," Quinn interrupted. He was careful with his words as well. We both had a lot to lose with the slip of the tongue.

"Meaning?"

"Meaning we knew you would be coming here to kill Vinnie. We have had people throughout the Vampire District waiting on you. Predictability trapped you. We have already explained that to you. The three men nearly compromised it." This from Maximilian.

"So you killed Vinnie, turned him into a cockroach, then had him killed again, just to speak to me about saving your daughter? Vinnie was a scumbag, sure, but are you telling me he died just so you could keep your dirty laundry a secret?

"We had nothing to do with anyone's death, Mr. Isaac. Mr. Gallerani was simply an unfortunate casualty of violence," Ms. Powers added.

"Yeah, violence caused by cockroaches. It's against the law to not report a cockroach attack, Ms. Powers."

"Who do you think reported him to the bureau? It was our civic duty," Maximilian said.

"Oh, so it was just coincidence he died about the same time your daughter disappeared."

"Call it what you will, Mr. Isaac, but the truth is you work for us now." Maximilian smiled wide. His fangs glistened in the dim light. He leaned toward me.

"I don't see how you can think that, Maximilian. I turned down the mission. I don't care if the girl lives or dies. No, I take that back. I do care. If she dies, that's one less of you I have to stake. As for the cockroach girlfriends that you found mutilated, all I can say is welcome to your own world. They probably had it coming to them." I looked at Quinn. "And this battle for supremacy between the cockroaches and the fur balls? Piel can eat you for all I care."

"And what of the young man you murdered tonight? Sounds like you are the danger here, not us."

"It was self-defense, and you know it. You set me up."

"It would be terrible to see you convicted of his murder," Maximilian laughed.

"Better than selling out to you."

"Dieter, you heard Mr. Isaac. He does not want to help us."

I looked over at Dieter and smiled.

"There is one more small detail you should know, Mr. Isaac," Maximilian added slowly.

"I'm waiting."

"You have a situation you need to deal with."

"And that is?" I was sticky with blood, my face had been used as a punching bag, and I had been kidnapped. To say I was a little frayed was an understatement.

"There is a poison running through your veins right now. You will have no symptoms, and the poison cannot be traced. Help us get Lyric back alive and you will be given the antidote. Otherwise, the poison will kill you in three days, turning you into one of us."

I jerked the cuffs in anger. Fuck being nice. "She can rot in hell for all I care."

"The choice is yours, Mr. Isaac. Live or die. But make no mistake, the poison will kill you in three days."

"And what happens if I go to the police with all of this?"

Ms. Powers' answer was cold and calculated. "We deny any wrongdoing. The poison is untraceable. You have far more to lose in this, Mr. Isaac. You killed a man in the warehouse. We will testify that he was shot in cold blood." Just like a woman. "When you come back as a vampire, you will be tried, convicted and executed for it. I will be the one that prosecutes you. Poetic justice."

"You will beg for a quick execution," Quinn snarled. "I only hope you put up as much of a fight as your parents did."

"You son of a..."

For the second time, a needle stuck in the back of my neck, causing me to black out.

CHAPTER FIVE

As I regained consciousness, I struggled to recognize where I was. It was like that sensation you get when you wake up in a hotel room and, for a moment, can't remember where you are. I needed to find out if I was still in the midst of vampires or something even worse. I was literally waking from a nightmare.

Slowly, my vision began to clear. My surroundings, I found, were familiar. I took a deep breath, realizing I wasn't in immediate danger. In fact, I was in as safe a place as a vampire executioner could be. I was in a church. Not just any church, but the church I lived in as a child.

I was in a small room, far away from the grand sanctuary, that had been my bedroom. It was barely big enough for the single bed and the small chest of drawers, which stood at attention in scuffed white paint. The walls were a faded mint green, plain except for the picture of Christ above the chest of drawers. Everything was familiar and safe.

The room's smells of pine cleaner and mold instantly took me back to my childhood. Doesn't sound like a great place, I know, but it was the only home I'd known for years.

"You're going to be all right," a familiar voice said.

I jumped when I heard it. I hadn't seen her at the side of the bed. Sister Mary looked down on me with those charcoal gray eyes.

"Nearly got yourself killed last night, I take it." Her face was like a stone.

"Sister Mary, it's good to see you, too."

"How long will it take?"

"Take for what?"

"Take for you to finally see that this isn't the life for you. Surely you don't want the same thing to happen to you that happened to your parents. You're lucky to be alive. Those things are the devil's children. They will be the death of you one day."

"Nothing happened. I'm okay." I just wanted to see a smile on her face. If I had to lie, so be it. "God won't let anything happen to me."

"God didn't put you in the crossfire of those things. You have done that yourself. He has better things in mind for you."

"I'm still waiting." I believed in God, but we weren't really doing a lot of talking either. "How did I get here?" My throat felt as though it had been through a shredder. My mouth was like cotton. The throbbing headache returned.

"You were found on the lawn this morning."

She poured a glass of water.

"What day is it, Sister Mary?" I lifted myself up into a sitting position, with my back on the wall behind me.

"Tuesday."

I shook my head and filled my mouth with the cold water she handed me. It soothed my throat between sharp jabs of pain as I swallowed. Tuesday. That was another good sign. It was Monday night when I was rudely kidnapped by vampires.

"What time is it?"

"Four-thirty in the evening."

Great. I had wasted an entire day of finding Ms. Runaway while I was in bed sleeping. The clock was ticking.

"What were you doing last night? You had blood all over you."

"I cut myself shaving." I said sarcastically as I sipped on the water.

She swatted me on the back of the head. "Don't you run that smart mouth to me. Just because you're bigger than I am doesn't mean I will allow you to be smart-mouthed. You need to settle down and leave this vampire killing to someone else. You're going to get yourself killed." She handed me a couple of Tylenol. "Here."

I took the pills from her hand and swallowed them together. I closed my eyes, trying to ease the pain from the headache. "I don't see anyone pounding down the door to take over." My eyes remaining closed.

Silence.

"Who did this to you?"

"Quinn Rubio and his damn cockroaches."

She slapped me again. "Don't swear in God's house."

I smiled. It had been a while since she had slapped me for swearing. It brought back good memories. "Sorry, Sister. Damn vampires."

Another slap. "This is not a joke, Paul. Those things are very dangerous. Satan is very powerful, and will use every means he can to harm God's children."

"Have we ever had a conversation that I didn't get abused by you?"

"We've never had a conversation that you acted like a God-fearing adult. You have a quick, forked tongue, and it gets you into as much trouble as your hard head. I will not put up with your profanity or your quick wit. You can joke all you want, but the truth is I love you and I will not stand by and watch you die."

I opened my eyes and saw the fear in hers. She looked away, wiped a tear.

"Paul," another voice called from the doorway.

"Father Garcia."

Father Pablo Manuel Garcia was a small, thin man in his early sixties, bald, and generally soft-spoken. If there was ever a man that hated vampires as much as I did, it was Father Garcia. Sure, he was a priest, a man of God, but he was also a bad-ass when it came to cockroach killing. Without his help and guidance, who knows, maybe I'd be a real cockroach killer or something now.

"It's good to see you're awake. How do you feel, son?"

"I'd tell you, but she'll slap me again."

Sister Mary smiled briefly, then moved toward the door. "Be careful, Paul. May God be with you," she said as she disappeared around the corner.

Father Garcia smiled as he entered the room and sat on the corner of the bed. "Rough night, I gather."

I finished off the water and sat the glass on the floor next to me. "We found another girl last night. Same markings."

"And?"

"I was hunting a cockroach downtown when I was attacked by three human punks. They tried to kill me. I shot one of them. Killed him."

"Dear God," Father Garcia gasped, horror-stricken.

"It was self-defense, Father. They worked for the coffin leeches. It was a set-up. I was attacked and kidnapped by Quinn's men."

"Why would Quinn kidnap you?"

"Seems Maximilian's daughter's gotten involved with a shifter named Piel."

"Never heard of him."

"From what I hear, he's the new flavor of the week. I don't know much about him, but the fang brigade are scared of him." I tried to find a way to make myself come to terms with what I was about to say. "They poisoned me. If I don't find this girl in three days, I become one of them." I was more angry than scared. "I'm asking you to do me a favor and stake me if my time runs out."

"A poison that will turn you? Absurd. They're bluffing you in order to get you to do their bidding." He avoided my request.

"I don't think so. I don't know. Seems there is a growing feud between them and the fur balls."

"Then we kill him, now. Call Detective Price and get a court order. It's attempted murder."

"No, the poison can't be traced, and it's my word against Quinn Rubio's. Not to mention that they are blackmailing me with the punk's death. I'm screwed either way. It's best I do this on my own. Without the police involved, I can play by my own rules."

"But you don't know the first thing about this shifter," Father Garcia bluntly pointed out. "The lycanthropes are no better than the vampires. They could be setting you up just as well. Either way, you die."

"With any luck, it won't come down to that. But if it does, I know silver can ruin their day. I'd feel much better knowing if I was dying, I was lining up dead cockroaches and fur balls alongside me."

"Let me go with you."

It was a great offer, but I couldn't involve the Father. This was my battle, and I was not going to allow anyone to take a punch on my account. "Quinn has made this personal, Father." I looked around the room for any signs that my bag of tools were returned to me from last night, but saw nothing. "Did they leave any of my things with me when they dumped me here?"

"No, but I have a bag of belongings for you in my office. I'll retrieve it when you are strong enough to leave." Bag of belongings is a euphemism for stake, Magnum, crucifix, and other implements of vampire destruction.

"I have to leave now, Father. I didn't finish the staking of the girl the police found last night, and I need to find this Piel as soon as I can. Then there's the thing about a cockroach killing human freaks. My plate's a little full. Staying in bed feeling sorry for myself isn't an option."

"What did you learned about the body last night?"

That's what was great about Father Garcia. He didn't argue with me.

"All the girls had a tattoo with the letters TS and a rose with a barbed-wire stem. Just before I shot Vinnie, he told me about seeing the last girl in the club where this Piel hangs out. It's a fetish club. The girl was a stripper and a freak. I have a feeling there's more going on down there than kinky fantasies. The cockroaches I got to know last night knew more about the killings than what they're letting on."

I lifted myself off the bed as the Tylenol began to control the headache. It was down to a pounding throb. I had my hand on the doorknob before I realized I had nothing on. I turned to face Father Garcia. "Please tell me the sisters didn't find me like this."

He smiled at first. It turned into a chuckle. "I'll get your things." He walked to me, took a deep breath and swallowed hard. "Please be careful, and remember you will always have God on your side. He'd like to see you here every once in a while."

"I spent most of my childhood here. I think I've done my time in church. I don't blame God for what happened, but let's face it: He didn't do anything to stop it either."

He squinted. "Have you started talking to that psychiatrist yet?"

I felt queasy. "I know I should. I've made the appointment twice now, but never followed through. You're right. I need someone to talk to other than you. But I have issues that I don't think any shrink can ever help with. I had the desire to follow through, just not the guts."

"So you didn't see him?"

"No."

"Go see the doctor, Paul. Being bitter all the time is a lonely way to die. You need to learn to open yourself to others. You need to find love and kindness, not just revenge and anger. If not for you, then for your mother and father."

He was right. I'd never really been in love, had a best friend, or even a dog. "I see things differently, Father. I'm not running from love and happiness. I'm protecting those that will have to fill the void if I die one night. I know what that void feels like, and I wouldn't wish it on anyone."

"Paul, I feel as though I have done your parents a great injustice."

"What do you mean?"

"I swore to protect you and watch over you. I made a mistake encouraging you to take up this profession. It isn't what your parents would've wanted. They were lovely people. I felt as though if you had your fill of revenge, you would simply grow out of the anger. Instead it fed it. Everything that happened last night is my fault. I should have made sure you went to college and became a doctor or lawyer or something...human."

"Lawyer? You've got to be kidding me. Those guys chase ambulances, have cheesy commercials, cheat good people out of their money, and ride around in expensive sports cars to compensate for their shortcomings. The brochure sounds good, but it's not for me. I chose this life, and I wouldn't have it any other way."

"Just see the doctor, Paul. Talk to him."

Father Garcia left the room, and I began to plan my day. I had to get downtown to get the 'Cuda, then get in touch with Detective Kansas about the unfinished business of staking the girl. Usually a representative of the vampire council needed to be there, but since Dieter already confirmed the attack last night, I was hoping to go to the morgue and take care of it as quickly as I could. Without doing my duty, the family couldn't move on. What a bitch of a phone call that must be to make

Father Garcia returned and blessed me. I could tell he had plenty
he wanted to say, but knew I was too hardheaded to listen to any
sort of reason. "To answer your question, yes. I will stake you. I
would be left with no choice."

He was right.

CHAPTER SIX

I came to the door I had seen a million times, the infamous word painted in gold on frosted glass. Morgue. It was the last call for all of us. Knowing that I would be lying here one day was an uneasy feeling. With my newfound situation, it might be sooner than later, a thought that sent shivers down my spine. This place freaked me out. Just knowing that no matter how well we treat our bodies or how bad we abuse them, we all end up here. It is just a game of how long we can avoid death.

I tapped on the door, three quick raps. The automatic lock clicked open, and I entered with little fanfare. There were a thousand different smells in the room, none pleasant. I didn't want to know what any of them were. Some things are best unsolved.

"Paul," Dr. Montgomery smiled. She was working on an elderly male body, his chest cavity opened, pieces and parts in pans alongside of the gurney. Like the smells, I didn't want to know what they were. She was in maroon scrubs, brown hair pulled up in a net, neither beautiful nor ugly. Unlike yours truly, she was always pleasant and in a good mood. "I was wondering when you were going to get here."

"How's it hangin', doc?" I said as I walked toward her.

"With pick-up lines like that, it's a wonder you're still single," she said, a smile warming her gravelly voice.

I looked over her shoulder at the body on the gurney. "Is this your date?" I smiled back. "A little old for you, isn't he?" Twisted as it sounds, I actually liked Dr. Montgomery. Maybe it was because we were both into death.

"He had lung cancer. Damn cigarettes got another. You better stop smoking, or you'll end up here one day."

"And I'll just bet you're looking forward to it. I'll be all naked and helpless. No doubt you'll take a peek under the sheets."

"Good thing I have a microscope." Her focus never strayed from the dead man.

"There's something about dead bodies that seems to turn you on. I often wonder what you do in here alone." She rolled her eyes. "I take that back, I don't want to know."

"Death doesn't scare me. You, on the other hand..." Her words trailed off. "You had better watch your step, or like I said, you'll end up here before you know it. It's just a question of whether it will be from smoking or vampires."

"We all end up here one day."

She looked up. "It's not a race to get here, though." A strand of hair was falling in her face. It aggravated me to no end. I wanted to go up to her and just pull it from her head. I followed her stare to the tattoos on my arms. "I'm thinking of getting one."

"A tat?"

"Yeah, right here." She pointed to the small of her back. "What do you think?"

"I think you'd be just another soccer mom trying to prove to herself that her life is a lot more exciting than it really is and that youth hasn't passed her by." Part truth, part joke.

Thank God, she only got the joke part. "I'm serious. What should I get?"

"Spank Me."

"Is that a suggestion or a proposition?"

"I guess you know why I'm here," I said, before we started doing that thing...oh what's it called? Talking.

"It's not to spend time with me? I'm crushed." She put her hands over her heart and gave a fake pout.

"I'm not stiff enough to get your attention."

She looked at my crotch.

"I didn't mean it that way." Blood rushing to my face. "I meant I'm not dead enough."

She stopped what she was doing on Grandpa and shook her head. She wiped her forehead with the back of her latex-clad hand, and walked over to a holding area. In the case of vampires, the bodies are kept in a special area of the morgue under lock and key, with various crucifixes around the room.

"She's a beautiful girl," Dr. Montgomery added as she fumbled through her keys.

"Yeah. Was."

She looked at me with a puzzled stare.

"Come on, what am I supposed to say beyond that? She was a beautiful girl, but she played in the devil's den and ended up some-one's meal. That's how it happens. There are enough dangers and perverts out there without adding sex acts with monsters to the list."

"That's a bit insensitive, isn't it?" She unlocked the door.

"Sorry, doc, but I'm here to cut the head off of a victim who fits the pattern of a serial-killing cockroach. She's a young runaway, lured into the world of vampire sleaze, tortured, mutilated, and killed. I'm sorry if I seem a little intense, but I didn't think bringing balloons or doing face-painting really fit the bill."

Dr. Montgomery dropped her head and unlocked the vault where the girl lay under a white sheet.

The room was cold and sterile. It creeped me out, I could almost sense an evil presence. I looked at the silver gurney and draped white sheet. It was what was under the sheet that I dreaded to see again. It only solidified my hatred for the monsters responsible for this. I remembered seeing her lying there in the field with the missing foot. Revisiting something like that isn't what I called entertainment.

I felt like a demented Santa Claus as I sat my bag of tools on the floor. I would kill her by driving a stake through her heart, followed by cutting her head off.

I pulled the large stake from the bag along with a mallet. These are the tools of a vampire executioner. See, I told you there was no glamour in the job. Trust me, if your guidance counselor suggests this job, walk out of the office and never look back.

"Do you know if the police are any closer to finding the creep that did this?" Dr. Montgomery asked as she circled the body. She lightly touched the girl's arm as she moved past it. Fingers traced the dead girl's face. Gentle. Caring.

"Not that I'm aware." I watched as she continued to run her hand along the body.

"She was so pretty."

"Yeah, you mentioned that."

The dead girl's hand reached up and grabbed Dr. Montgomery by the throat, nails digging into the doctor's skin. As the corpse lifted from the table, Dr. Montgomery screamed in both pain and horror, terrified eyes locked on me. The newly risen beast let out a low growl as it moved from the gurney to the floor, dancing and bouncing. The loss of the foot kept it off balance. Dr. Montgomery's hands reached up to grab the vampire's hands.

"Stay calm," I shouted, moving around the room. Do as I say, not as I do. I kept myself between the cockroach and the doorway. I knew if the monster gained strength, it would kill Dr. Montgomery, get out of the room, and be on the loose inside the hospital.

The vampire's eyes were deep red, filled with evil. It hissed at me as I flanked its move toward the door. I steadied the stake's point right at its throat, but I couldn't get a clear stab with Dr. Montgomery in the way.

"Let me out of here or she dies," the bloodsucker shouted, its eyes darting to the throat of its captive, then back to me.

"Whether you kill her or not, you're not getting out of here alive."

The monster tried to rush me. The loss of the foot was hindering it from getting enough momentum to overpower me. In time, the missing foot would regenerate, but for now it was an advantage for the good guys.

"Please, let me go!" Dr. Montgomery shouted again. She was almost as pale as Fangzilla. Her eyes were wide with fear. She looked to me for help.

I had to make a move, and I hoped it would work. If I waited any longer, the cockroach might gain enough strength to overpower me. I couldn't let Dr. Montgomery make me lose my focus. Chances were she would probably die either way.

I jabbed the stake into the vampire's throat, sending it downward, pushing Dr. Montgomery to the floor. The doctor screamed as she hit and slid from the vampire's grasp.

Call me a heartless bastard if you want, but I couldn't waste my time trying to save the doctor. I had to kill the monster. I would do whatever I could to keep the doctor alive, but there was more at risk here than her.

I brought the Magnum up from my shoulder holster as Dr. Montgomery stood and ran toward me. Her destination was simple. Get out of the room, away from the beast. Problem was, I was in her way. The Magnum and her shoulder met in a violent crash. Shit. I lost my footing and fell. My shoulder slammed into the tile flooring. I felt it dislocate with a distinct pop. Stupid bitch.

Above me, I could see the vampire moving out of the room. It was no longer interested in attacking but instead escaping, bouncing toward the door like someone whose foot had fallen asleep. Like me, it knew where the food supply was.

I came to my feet. I felt like I was running through molasses. My dislocated shoulder throbbed with pain. I had to suck it up. I still had an advantage. The vampire was weak, and I had two feet.

I pulled the Magnum up again. I had a fresh supply of ultraviolet-filled bullets, and this night-crawling hooker was about to burn.

I aimed for its back just as the door opened and two interns entered.

"Shit!"

My shot would be compromised at best.

The fang fritter had a female intern by the throat before I had time to react. Blurring speed. Invisible to human eyes. A snap. The female intern hit the floor, lifeless. This cockroach was not feeding. It was killing.

The young male intern collapsed to the floor. His breathing was quick, but at least up to this point he remained calm, aside from the wet spot between his legs.

The monster was growing stronger as it moved further away from the influence of the crucifixes. A human is no match for stake bait firing on all eight cylinders, but I wasn't above cheating.

The beast kept its eyes on me without saying a word. It would be a duel of quick wits. The intern was going to be the deciding factor in how it got out. The intern hit an alarm on the wall and shouted "Security!"

I heard other voices coming down the hall. They had heard the screams. I could see shadows coming into grotesque view through the frosted window.

"Security!" I heard from the other side.

"Stay out!" I shouted to the shadows. If they came in here, there would be a blood bath.

Dr. Montgomery ran to the door and tried to block it with

Grandpa's gurney. It kept the rent-a-cops outside and the monster inside.

"Tell them to back away from the door or I'll kill him," the cockroach said. It grabbed the man by the hair. I had seen its handiwork. It wasn't bluffing.

"I'll kill you before he hits the floor." There was a dark side of me that wanted to take the chance and fire the Magnum. If I missed, I killed either the man or one of the security officers on the other side of the door. I ran the odds in my head. They were still in my favor. One, maybe two at most would die. Beats the hell out of an entire floor.

"Oh, but you'd be missing out on so much. I have so many wonderful secrets I can share with you. Things right under your nose that you've missed."

If I could get the vampire under control, I could torture it to find out who the killer was. I could use the morgue as my personal interrogation playground. Again, I wasn't afraid to bend a rule or two if it saved other lives in the long run. "It's over. End it now."

"Not without killing him," the blood-licker said, looking back at the intern. "If I die, he dies. Let me go and he lives."

"Not an option." I moved as slow and easy as possible. I had one shot at saving this man's life, and I didn't want to screw it up.

Fighting the pain in my shoulder, I grabbed the intern by the arm and jerked him across the floor. The monster came with him, fangs only an inch from me. Hot, rancid breath filled my nostrils. I held my breath as long as I could.

The monster was now eye to eye with me. The intern was free. With a sacrifice like this, he sure as shit better get away from here. I wouldn't save his ass a second time.

I pulled the Magnum up and stuck it in the vampire's mouth. It bit down. The eyes told the story as it tried to back off the gun. I pushed it deep down the cockroach's throat, not allowing the barrel of the Magnum to come out.

"Who killed you?"

The monster gagged on the barrel of the gun. No response. I didn't want one yet, pleasure before business.

I felt for the silver-bladed knife in a sheath around my belt. Like with Vinnie, I planned to let it burn inside it. I didn't want it to die just yet. Not while I still had an advantage.

The knife went under its rib cage and flirted with its heart. No, not yet. I wanted pain, not death. It screamed in demonic tones.

"Who the fuck killed you?"

"Security! We're coming in!" There were more of them now. Time was running out.

"Who's in there?" A different voice from the other side of the door. Shoulders crashed the door. Keys opening the locked door.

"Vampire! Stay where you are!" I shouted, still holding the captive cockroach at bay with gun and knife.

"We're coming in!"

"Stay the fuck where you are!"

I pulled the trigger. Felt the force of the bullet leave the chamber. An explosion shattered the head of the monster. Ashes and flames shot out of its mouth like a medieval dragon. Heat burned my skin. My goatee caught fire for a second, the smell of burnt hair filling the room. Flurries of ashes fell to the floor like a haunted snowstorm.

I emptied the Magnum into the pile of ashes in a series of explosions and echoed power. Using far more bullets than I really needed. My rage had taken over like an out-of-body experience.

The door crashed open and security officers moved inside. Gurney and Grandpa's guts spilled across the floor. Men flanked to both sides of the doorway, spray bottles of holy water drawn. God, it was pathetic. They were brave only because nothing with fangs was moving. I wanted to yell "Boo!", but resisted.

"Everything's clear," I said as I wiped the ash from my face, chest, spat ash from my mouth. Talk about something that will gross you out. I felt like an ashtray for the occult.

"Where is it?" one of the officers asked, his eyes unsettled. "We heard shots."

"It's dead. I shot it." I spat more ash.

Another security officer entered the room. He looked at the dead female intern with a grimace. Then to Grandpa's display of bloody anatomy. "What the fuck happened?"

He gagged.

Puked.

I swallowed hard. When someone pukes near me, I usually do the same, something about the sound. It's like seeing someone yawn.

I never answered him. Didn't need to.

Taking the phone from my pocket, I called Detective Kansas as the room filled with other rent-a-cops and doctors. The male intern and Dr. Montgomery were rushed from the room. I deliberately didn't make eye contact with them. My guilt forced me not to. I was willing to let the cockroach kill them in order to save the others in the hospital. Did that make me a hero, or a cold-hearted bastard? I was willing to put everyone in the hospital at risk, just to get answers on the killing of a prostitute who had probably caused her own death. Did that make me better than her? Was I truly losing it?

Fuck. I didn't know.

CHAPTER SEVEN

For the second time in as many nights, I found myself in handcuffs. I was in the passenger seat of Detective Kansas' Ford Explorer heading down I-4, destination unknown. The smell of leather was almost intoxicating. It's one of my favorite smells. It was being mixed with another of my favorite smells, coffee.

"God, a cup of coffee right now would really hit the spot," I hinted.

No response. I was sure he heard me.

"I guess that means no to the coffee."

"What the fuck happened back there at the hospital? They say you went psycho on that woman," he finally said.

"Don't talk about it like it was a human. It was a vampire that was killing innocent people. I kept it from feeding off of the others in the hospital, but I'm the one in handcuffs. You're treating me like a damned criminal. A simple thank-you might be in order."

"The intern had a broken neck."

"I know. I saw it happen. The cockroach just killed her. It didn't even try to feed."

"I also have reports that you tortured her before you killed her."

"I don't have to justify my actions. I had paperwork that says it was to be executed. I was only trying to find our killer. More than I can say about the police."

"You see, that's just it. You do have to justify your actions. You're not above the law."

"Just like you to take the cockroach's side."

"Whatever, Paul."

"Whatever, shit. Why am I in handcuffs?"

"I'm trying to save you from the Vampire Council. I'm giving them the illusion you're under arrest."

"So you're saying I'm not really under arrest."

"Technically, no. Not yet, anyway. If the Vampire Council insists on it, then your ass is grass."

"Then can you take these things off me?"

Silence.

"Great. False imprisonment," I said under my breath.

"Anger management. It's starting to affect your judgment. Last night, your running through the city like Dirty Harry caused a young woman to be killed tonight. You used an entire clip on that one at the hospital. I told them you needed therapy. Personally, I think you're a lost cause, but I still think you're better than the vampires." He smiled. "I'm taking you to see a shrink."

"Oh, come on."

I turned and looked out the window as the city passed by. "It's one o'clock in the morning. And the last place I needed to be is in therapy. You know as well as I do what happened back there wasn't my fault. I was interrogating a witness."

"You killed the witness."

"She was already dead. I went there to stake her, remember?"

"So you did."

The night sky seemed a little blacker than I had ever seen it before. Butterflies filled my stomach. I had to get free from this. After last night, I didn't like being in handcuffs. "I need to go. This is illegal and you know it."

"If you don't comply, I'll have to file charges on you. Fuck the vampires; I'll make an example out of you for every vampire executioner and dip-shit for miles. If you had taken care of the corpse last night, we wouldn't have had to take her to the morgue in that state. She'd be dead, and this whole thing would've never happened. And what about Dieter?"

"What about Dieter?" Hearing that name was never a good thing.

"Claims you beat the shit out of some vampire activist last night when he tried to stop you from killing the vampire you were after."

Here it comes. Murder in the first degree.

"And you believe him?"

Kansas opened a manila folder next to him with his right hand, while keeping his eyes on the road. He hit the blinker and exited the freeway at Lee Road. "Here." He pushed a photograph next to my leg.

I'd have picked up the photo if I hadn't been handcuffed, but that wasn't an option. I looked at the Polaroid best I could and felt my stomach churn. I noticed it wasn't a corpse. It was a living and breathing body. The boy in the picture was black and blue and swollen, but alive all the same. I recognized him. He was one of the two that had gotten away.

"Tell me you didn't do that." Kansas sipped on the coffee.

"You think I did?"

"Claims you did."

"Please," I said sarcastically. "You know I didn't do this."

"The Vampire Council is up to here with your violence. They want to press charges on this."

"Why would they press charges? This is a human. What are they going to press charges on me about? Tenderizing their meat? I killed Vinnie. It was my job. This, I didn't do."

The night ran through my head again like a horror movie. The three punks attacked me. There were punches thrown, but not like the ones in the photo. Either the photo was doctored or someone else got to him after I went black.

"Was Dieter there when you killed Vinnie?"

"No."

"I have witnesses that say otherwise."

"Witnesses?" I had a sinking feeling.

"I have statements from other vamps on the street that you threatened to kill Dieter and this guy for being a vampire sympathizer." Kansas took another swig of coffee, studiously not looking at me. "Look, I think I can work something out with the Council if you just do what I tell you. Something like this can get you locked up for a very long time."

"I was the one attacked last night." I knew I had to play this one cool to have any chance of getting Kansas to believe me.

"Who attacked you?"

We moved down a side street, past several office buildings. I tried to keep up with the streets we were traveling on, but the conversation was a bit of a distraction.

"After I killed Vinnie, these punks jumped me. We fought a little. They ran off. Nothing like this ever happened. Dieter is just trying to ruin my credibility. Cockroaches will go to any length for their cause." No need to mention the dead punk unless it was brought up.

"Paul, your anger is really starting to be a problem. I'm not going to baby-sit you any more. If it weren't for me, at best, you'd be in jail right now. I don't give a shit that vampires killed your parents. It doesn't give you a free pass to kill them. The laws protect them now."

"Why would I lie about this? I'm being set up here. I met with

Quinn Rubio last night. He wants me to do some things for him. I guess this is part of his plan to get me to be at his beck and call."

"So you're telling me that you met with the master vampire of Orlando and lived to tell about it? To say you are unpopular down there is an understatement. Quinn would've killed you without thinking about it. He doesn't negotiate, or say please."

"Ever hear of a shifter named Piel?"

"No. Why? Was he in on this too?"

"Possibly. That's why Quinn wants my help. Seems Piel is trying to take over Bat Town."

"What about Oswald?"

"What?"

"Lee Harvey Oswald. Since we're talking conspiracy, I thought you might want to add him to the list. Maybe Elvis."

"Just give me back my Magnum and stakes, and I'll be on my way. Dieter, Quinn Rubio, and the whole lot won't be any the wiser."

"Can't do, my friend. The only way the Council wouldn't press charges was if you agreed to go to see the shrink. It's this or jail. Besides, if you have any information on the killings, you need to let me know. You know, the one who really is a police officer."

I thought for a moment. "I'll take jail." And I was being honest. "Besides, where are you going to find a shrink at this hour?"

"I'm taking you to a doctor with your kind of hours. She only works nights. Treats vampires." He smirked as he pulled into the near-empty parking lot and turned off the engine.

"You've got to be kidding me. You're really going to make me go see a shrink that gets in the heads of blood-sucking cockroaches?"

"She treats whoever needs the help. Not all her patients are vampires."

"Is that supposed to make me feel better somehow?"

"Nope, but that's the tall and short of it. It's your last chance.

Maybe she can help you with whatever has made you such a son of a bitch." He looked over at me and smiled. "Besides, if she gives you a clean bill of health, you don't have to come back."

"You know as well as I she won't do that." My tone grew darker as I looked out the window.

"If you are as stable as you say you are, I don't see the problem."

"Tree-huggers don't give lumberjacks a clean bill of health, vegans don't give meat-eaters a clean bill of health. A cockroach activist ain't gonna give me a clean bill of health. It's political! You know it as much as I do."

"What are you babbling about?"

"I'm the only deterrent left for them. Without me, they would attack and kill everyone in this city. They live for two things: blood and power. And we happen to have both of them. I take that back. We only have the blood. You people gave them the power already. You just haven't realized it yet."

"You know, maybe they aren't the monsters you think they are. I've met some of them that actually seem very normal and likable."

"A lot of people said the same thing about Jim Jones until they drank the Kool-Aid."

"Ever think you might be the Jim Jones around here?"

I thought for a minute. "No, I'm more like the Kool-Aid."

He gave a quick laugh. "Just go talk to her."

"Can I take my Magnum?"

"No."

"My stakes?"

"No."

"Crucifix?"

"No."

"It's suicide for me to go in there without something."

"You'll be safe. They're law-abiding citizens. You can't go up there with weapons."

There was poison in my veins. There was a killer cockroach in the city. And where would I be? On a couch, talking about feelings.

Kansas took the handcuffs off and pointed to the entrance. "What if I make a run for it?" I asked as I stepped out of the Explorer.

"I'll shoot your ass myself."

CHAPTER EIGHT

"Hi, I'm Dr. Lydia Petty. And you must be Paul Isaac." She said my name as though it tasted bad in her mouth. Great.

"So I am."

She was small, maybe five-three, a hundred-thirty pounds. I would guess she was in her late thirties or so. Her long, black hair was pulled back in a ponytail, nice make-up over pale skin. "I hope I didn't keep you waiting too long. It's been a crazy night."

I sat facing her desk in a large overstuffed black leather chair that seemed to almost squeeze you when you tried to breathe. I felt small in it as it hulked around me. "Seems to have been a crazy night for all of us. A few hours ago I was..."

"I know what you did, Mr. Isaac. I meant crazy as in busy, not as in destroying a hospital."

I watched as she skimmed papers from what I was guessing to be my file. I could only imagine all the things that were in it. She moved her finger along the lines, looking up at me from time to time, smiling nervously.

I was really getting a bad feeling about this. "The incident at the hospital was not my fault."

She held a few papers in her left hand, raising them next to her head, elbow leaning on the desk. She never looked up at me as she spoke. "You're a very interesting man, Mr. Isaac." I wasn't sure whether I was supposed to answer or not. I chose not.

She leaned forward and, with a deep breath, spoke again. "Actually, I've heard of you." There was something ominous behind the smile. Sugarcoated hatred, that's what it was. "I know what you are and what you stand for. Most of my patients have had some sort of run-in with you. I'm not here to coddle you or tell you everything is going to be okay. You're the monster here, not those out there in the waiting room."

"I'm not looking to be coddled, Dr. Feelgood. I'm here because I have no other choice in the matter. As for your patients, therapy will be the least of their worries if I find them outside the boundaries of the law."

"That's the problem. You're the one outside the boundaries, not the vampires. That's what got you here."

"No, what got me here is the fact that I was trying to kill a newly turned blood-sucking cockroach that was hell-bent on eating the people in a hospital."

"We don't use the term 'cockroach' here, Mr. Isaac."

"And I don't live by the slogan 'live and let live,' Dr. Feelgood."

"My name is Dr. Petty, Mr. Isaac. When you are here, you will respect me. Do you understand that?"

"Are you this hostile with all your patients, or do I get special treatment because of what I do?"

"I think you are beyond treatment, Mr. Isaac. I plan to make sure that you never walk the streets again. The Vampire Council is fed up with your killing and torturing innocent vampires. Even Detective Kansas won't be able to help you out of this one."

"And if I go to the authorities with everything you just said, then what?"

"Your word against mine. Who do you think anyone of authority will believe? I'm a respected psychiatrist helping both vampire and human alike, while you continue to kill and burn bridges. The first step toward recovery is admitting the problem."

"I don't mean to be blunt, Doctor, but I'm not here seeking your help. I like my life just the way it is. Whatever you read in that report in front of you means nothing to me. Most of it is a pack of lies, or at least exaggerated. The parts that are true, I can justify very easily. We will never come to any agreement on what I do. I kill your meal tickets, and I won't lie, I enjoy it." Kansas had brought me to see a vampire shrink. This was wasting precious time. Time I didn't have.

"So you do, Mr. Isaac, but that doesn't give you a license to become a vigilante. There are laws in place to protect all of society, humans and non-humans. Hating someone is one thing, harming or killing them is another altogether."

"As long as the check clears, right?"

A puzzled look crossed her face. "Excuse me?"

"Willing to sell out for the daisy-pushers as long as the money keeps paying for that new Porsche or the condo on the beach. That's why you're here, doing what you do. If you knew what kind of monsters they really were, if you saw the final results of what they do, you would never do this kind of work. Throats torn out, blood thick on the walls, families grieving. One day you'll end up just like them. You don't beat the odds forever."

"I guess I could tell you the same thing." A cynical smile sprouted. "They're considered monsters because that's what we've been taught from childhood. In reality they're no more monsters than we are. Look at Ted Bundy, John Wayne Gacy, and Jeffrey Dahmer. Those are the real monsters." She got up from behind the desk and walked around the room. "I'll admit there are some vampires out there that kill for the thrill of it. And they give all vampires a bad name. Most of my patients are here looking for help in the same types of problems as anyone else. Not all vampires are happy being vampires."

"Then we should put them out of their misery, don't you think?"

"No. That's what a coward like you would do. You have to remember that most vampires are vampires because they, too, were victims of an attack. They didn't want the afterlife they received. Imagine living forever, watching your loved ones and family grow old and die. Imagine never seeing another sunrise, or feeling its warmth on your face. Depression is rampant among vampires. Of all the vampires in this city, only a handful has ever killed a human. There are plenty of donors out there willing to feed them."

"You're talking about the human freaks that come down to Bat Town to let the fanged cockroaches suck their blood for cash."

She cleared her throat at the mention of cockroaches, but let it slide. "A bit politically incorrect, but overall, yes. I have patients that sit in that chair and cry because they give in to the need to feed on humans. It's a hunger they can't restrain, yes, but they only feed. They don't kill. They don't create new vampires."

"This is all overwhelmingly interesting, but the fact remains the same. The hunger you talk about leads to an increasing addiction to human blood, just like a junkie. Sooner or later, the monster takes a life."

"That's your prejudice talking. It's like drinking alcohol, Mr. Isaac. It must be done in moderation. Humans have killed more humans in this city alone than vampires have done in the entire United States."

"How can you help things that are natural predators of your kind? At any moment one of your patients could rip your neck open, and you know what happens then? Someone calls me, and I have to drive a stake through your heart and cut your head off with an ax. Call it emotional management issues, but you don't get used to things like that, you just get angry. In fact, you should have been with me tonight and seen what one of them did. An intern is dead because of cockroach rights."

The good doctor grimaced again at the mention of cockroaches, but chose not to argue the point. "Let's not talk about them; let's talk about you. Why do you hate them so much?"

"Just lucky, I guess."

"According to your file, you were orphaned at the age of eight. Is that correct?"

"If that's what it says." Give no more info than that.

"I'm asking you if it's correct."

"I guess so, I don't remember."

"Don't remember, or won't?"

"Look, Doc, let's get one thing straight here. I'm not here of my own free will. I don't need my head checked by you, in what I consider to be a hostile environment. The sooner I'm out of here, the better."

"Mr. Isaac, I know more about you than you probably know about yourself. I know about your parents being killed by vampires. I'm very sorry that that happened to you. I even understand your hatred for them. I was hoping to get you to open up about it. I know about the killing of the vampire a few years ago that caused you and Father Garcia a lot of trouble."

"You know nothing."

"I know Father Garcia killed a newly turned vampire in front of the vampire's mother, as she pleaded for his life."

"He had just killed a woman the night before."

"Turned out to be a hoax, didn't it?"

"We didn't know that at the time."

"Who killed the woman, Mr. Isaac?"

"A man."

"Not a vampire?"

"No," I said softly.

"But the vampire was tortured and killed in front of his family because of it. Your vengeance was so great, you didn't think of them, did you? The town nearly lynched the two of you. The tabloids started calling you Saint Avengers. I hear Father Garcia has never recovered from it."

"The vampire would have been killed anyway. He was turned after the laws went into effect."

"Still, you allowed your anger and hatred to overrule your judgment. If you don't address that anger and hatred, you will never be able to step out of your own shadows."

"Are we done?"

"No. It doesn't work that way, Mr. Isaac. You have been brought here for observation for anger issues and battery. This is a police matter. The Vampire Council as well as the vampire community is asking for your neck. They are concerned for their lives and businesses. You have been seen running through crowds with your gun drawn." She slid the same pictures Kansas had, of a man badly beaten toward me. I never touched them. "Now an innocent boy is put in the hospital because you can't keep yourself under control. These are serious charges if the victim chooses to press them against you. You should be counting your blessings that you're here and not in jail."

"I didn't touch that cockroach-loving SOB."

"So he made it all up?"

"Yes, he made it all up."

"And why would he do that?"

"It pays well to work for the cockroaches."

"So the victim got beat up by you for money?"

"No, he didn't get beat up by me for money."

"Then he got beat up for free?"

"You're being blatantly condescending. I'm not the enemy. You're not going to give me a clean bill of health no matter what I say or do. To say I'm innocent or stable would be turning your back on the vamps you serve."

"So I ask you again. Did he allow you to do this for free?"

"No, he didn't get beat up for free. I'm sure he got paid very nicely. I'm just saying I'm not the one that beat him up. I never saw him until tonight when Detective Kansas showed me the picture."

In the office light I could see the face better, and I grew cold and angry at the same time. It was one of the creeps that had attacked me last night, the one with the Ramones' T-shirt. The boy's face was swollen and bruised; purple lakes of violence painted his skin. Dried blood snaked out the left corner of his mouth, one eye swelled shut. The vampires had me set up good. "I never gave them this much credit." I wasn't going to consider the alternative: that I might have been that stupid. I simply underestimated my enemy.

"Are you sure you have never seen this man before?"

"No." I lied. Now I had to wonder about the dead boy. When was he going to come floating to the surface?

"Look again, Mr. Isaac. Are you sure?"

I could tell by the way she was talking to me that she already had a backup plan. I didn't think it was possible to sink any further in the leather chair, but I was wrong. I needed a cigarette and fresh air. Impossible combination, I know, but that's me in a nutshell. Irrational thought keeps me moving, what can I say?

"He attacked me."

"Attacked you? Look at his face, Mr. Isaac. Hardly looks like that to me."

"What about my bruises? Do you think they just appeared out of nowhere?"

"You're going to tell me this young man did that to you?" She pointed to the black spot under my right eye. I would have to agree that it was a minimal wound compared to our poor victim, but it had to amount to something.

"Are you saying it couldn't have happened?"

"He's barely out of puberty, a hundred and twenty pounds wet. I don't think he is a match for you. After all, you kill vampires."

"Alone in a fair fight, probably not, but he was with..." I wanted to minimize the damage. I lied. "He was with another boy. They blindsided me. They had a pipe or something. Look." I turned around to show her the welt at the base of my skull. With my head clean-shaven, it made show-and-tell a lot easier.

"Uh-huh," she murmured, a true skeptic until the end. "So a minute ago, you were telling me that you never saw the boy in the picture, then you say you have met him, but he attacked you. And now he had an accomplice."

"Right."

"There were only two?"

Now my blood went cold. I wasn't sure how to answer this one. Could be that she already knew about the third boy and was trying to catch me in another lie. I could feel my heart pounding in my ears. I was painted in a corner and I had to take chances, but I wanted to leave room for error all the same.

"At least two."

"At least two?"

"Yeah."

"So there could have been more."

"It was dark. They came from behind me. I can't be for sure how many there were. I think I remember hearing three voices. I'm not sure. I was trying to stay alive."

She huffed. "Odd."

"What?"

"At least three of them, maybe more, they had pipes or some other sort of weapon, yet your attacker is the one that has all the bruises. You must be very lucky."

"Like you said, I kill blood-sucking cockroaches. I'm used to the odds being stacked against me."

"Why did they attack you?"

"A difference of opinion, I'd guess."

"You were killing a vampire at the time, according to the report."

"Yeah. Vinnie Gallerani."

"You two had a history."

"You could say that."

"Tell me about it." Her voice grew slightly softer, but I knew better than to fall for the good doc, bad doc routine.

"He escaped from me once before, costing me five stitches." I pointed to the scar above my left eye.

"So you killed him? Well, that evened the score."

"No, he was a confirmed cockroach victim. I had my death warrant for him. You know the rules. Everything was legal."

"Mr. Procnow says you tortured this Vinnie before killing him. Do you find that to be legal? "

"Mr. Procnow is a liar. He would do anything to cause me trouble and tarnish my credibility."

"So you didn't torture Vinnie?"

"No. I was simply persuading him to communicate on things."

"What things?"

"Seems he might know a little about the prostitute that we found. I wanted to see how much he really knew."

"So you tortured him."

"I was going to kill him either way. If it got us closer to the serial killer, I didn't see where the harm was."

"So much violence, Mr. Isaac."

"I do what I do. Violence is part of the game. I'm not above bending the rules if it saves an innocent life."

"You don't think you take the violence a little too far sometimes?"

"No." I leaned back in the chair and crossed my left leg over my right. I looked at my watch. Time was running out.

Dr. Feelgood looked back at the report in the folder on her desk again. Her finger continued to trace the words as though she were reading Braille.

"Twelve," she simply said as she continued to read.

"Twelve what?"

"Complaints against you by the Vampire Council, not counting your latest episode."

"There was no episode last night."

"Richard Willows?" she asked slowly, looking at me with judgmental eyes.

"It was a misunderstanding. I'm not sure how the crucifix got stuck down his throat. He should be more careful what he eats."

"Regina Ray?"

"Self-defense. She was trying to bite me when I pulled her fangs out," I replied. "Surely we're not going to go through all twelve complaints against me in the last year. I had a job to do. All the kills I made were quick and painless as long as they cooperated with me. That includes information I needed to hunt down the predator that caused their demise. I did what I had to do to discourage any attacks against humans. Some called what I did torture or violent, but I think if the victims could speak for themselves, they would want it this way. They would want restitution against the monsters that turned them into a meal. You even said it yourself that most are depressed with what they've become."

"Have you thought about joining a vampire victim's group to discuss the loss of your parents with other victims?" she replied, leaning over the desk as though she would slither into my lap.

"Sorry, not the touchy-feely type and sure as hell not a team player." I gave a half smile.

"I think it would help." Her eyes were full of revulsion. We were on different sides of a very emotional issue, and neither of us was going to give in an inch.

"And what do you say to the group? Sorry for your loss, but throat- ripping cockroaches have rights, too?"

"I try to help them with the denial, anger, acceptance. Help them move past the loss. Help them see that not all vampires are violent, like not all humans are violent. It's the one percent that kills."

"They're a lucky group to have you."

"Not me. They have each other."

"How do you live with yourself, look them in the eyes?" I asked.

"What do you mean?"

"You treat vampires with issues all night, then walk across the hall and tell the victims that it will be all right. Sounds to me like you are trying to play both sides to the middle here. Does either side really find you credible?"

"This session is not about my credibility, Mr. Isaac, it's about you. I'm not the one that's violently going down a road that will land me in prison one day. You're not the law. In fact, the law protects against the likes of you. You are outdated, a dying breed."

"And I protect the humans against the likes of you and your waiting room. If there were more like me, maybe there would be less need for orphanages and funeral homes, but you're no different than the rest of them. Ignore the fact of what they really are out there on the streets. To you, they're nothing more than credit card numbers." I was done. I lifted myself out of the bear-hug chair and headed for the door. I really didn't care what Kansas, Dr. Feelgood, or anyone else did with me. Or what they thought, for that matter. They could all kiss my cockroach-hating ass.

"Have you ever acknowledged your parents' deaths? Visited their graves? Forgiven the vampires responsible?"

This time I said it out loud. "Kiss my cockroach-hating ass!"

CHAPTER NINE

Behind me, bomb-like sounds radiated through the small office. Screaming. Glass breaking. Something moved at violent speed. Low, deep growls bellowed in harmony above the shredding of the unknown on the other side of the door.

Dr. Feelgood's eyes were open wide. The terror and fear on my face were reflected in hers. She stood quickly, then froze, paralyzed by fear like a little white mouse placed in an aquarium with a viper.

I reached for the Magnum that was usually on a shoulder holster, cursed under my breath. All my weapons were still in the Explorer.

Claws scratched along the walls, floor, and ceiling outside. Sounds that, in all my years of vampire stalking, I had never heard. My blood ran cold as I listened to the violence. Under the crack of the door, distorted shadows moved with lighting speed.

"Do you have anything we can use as a weapon?" I looked over the room, finding nothing more menacing than a book.

"What kind of weapon?" Her paralysis gone, she seemed to run in place.

I ran to the door and locked it, in a comical attempt to keep the things at bay. Whatever they were, they would easily pound the door down. But it made me feel better, gave me a false sense of hope.

"At this point anything that I can swing, shoot, or stab with will do. When there are vicious monsters attacking on the other side of a wall, just start grabbing things. A stake, an ax, holy water, anything."

"I don't keep anything like that. I don't want to offend my patients. Trust is a cornerstone."

"I'm going to get mauled by whatever is out there because of trust?"

I was counting on the fact that Kansas had seen the thing or things coming into the building, or at least could hear the chaos and was on his way. I needed backup, backup with firepower.

"Call 911!" I shouted. "I'm willing to go out on a limb here and say I don't think I'll be able to reason with them."

For us, it would be too late, but maybe the cavalry could arrive in time to catch the mystery monsters before they made it back out into society.

"Do you have a gun?" I yelled to Dr. Feelgood as she moved to the corner of the room.

She was already handing me a pistol as I turned from the door. Her hands shook with spasms of terror. Tears rolled down her face.

The screams lessened with each passing second as patients fell victim to the nightmare.

"Heaven forbid you carry a stake or a crucifix to kill the things that might suck you dry during one of your sessions, but I see you have a gun to kill the human kind. Maybe I should be offended. After all, trust is a cornerstone."

She quickly back-pedaled to the far wall of the room. "It has silver nitrate."

I was about to ask her why silver nitrate when the screaming stopped in the lobby. There was no doubt in either of our minds that it wasn't because the danger had moved on.

"They're all dead. We're next," I said, breathing hard. "Sounds like your three o'clock appointment's here, and he's a little upset about something."

"They're shifters."

"Have those a lot, do you?" Sweat beaded on my forehead, and a trickle of it found its way to my eyes, stinging them. I steadied my feet, taking in a deep breath. A new patch of sweat formed on my shirt. My shoulder pounded with pain, in sync with my rapid heartbeat.

We were going to be statistics of a monster attack, violent, grue-some, and bloody. We both deserved it. We both made our living in the company of monsters. The good doc would die for treating them, and I would die for hunting them. In the end, it wouldn't make a difference to anyone reading the obituaries. The readers would simply say we got what we deserved."

"He's found me. Somehow, he's found me."

"Who?" I asked.

"It doesn't matter. He'll kill us both."

I looked at the gun and back to her. "This thing does work, doesn't it?"

"Never used it."

"Are you kidding me? You treat cockroaches with kid gloves, and you don't carry as much as a crucifix. You're an idiot." So much for therapy and here I thought things were going so well, up until we were attacked by creatures of the night. "Wait 'til I fill out the 'How are we doing?' card. I have plenty of feedback."

I took a quick survey of the room, searching for another way out. I looked at the window and began to back toward it. I kept my new weapon pointed at the door, staying on the defensive.

Below, I could see a small strip of grass next to the building, maybe six feet wide, flanked by shrubs. Lights flooded the parking lot in sprays, fading into darkness until the reach of the next lamp. I saw Kansas' Explorer. The darkness had swallowed all the rest.

"Bust out this window," I yelled.

She looked at me like a puppy that has heard a strange sound.

"Do it! Or I'm gonna use you to bust it out." To her benefit, she didn't argue. Good girl!

She picked up a fire extinguisher from the back wall. I watched in disbelief as she carried it in both hands as though it weighed a thousand pounds.

Ahead of me, the monsters were clawing at the door. The walls literally started to move with each violent thrust. The door was no match for whatever was out there. I gripped the gun in my hands so tight it hurt. All the circulation had been stopped by my anticipation. I wasn't sure how many bullets I had, so I wanted to see my target. Shooting randomly at the door wouldn't gain us anything. But anticipation is a bitch.

The first real smash into the door broke the upper hinge. Light from the waiting room flooded into the doctor's office. Bright streaks of red painted the once-off-white walls. Handprints in crimson, embossed in violence, lined the upper edges. I already found my stomach tightening. I could only imagine what the lower half of the room held. After this scene, if I survived, I would need therapy.

Behind me, I heard the extinguisher hit the glass with a flat thud, followed by a hollow thump. The glass hadn't given way. Time was running out. Whatever was out there would be in here in a matter of seconds.

It would be just my luck that when I pulled the trigger I would simply hear a melodramatic click. I didn't have time to check it now. Whether the gun was empty or not really made very little difference at this point.

I could see Dr. Feelgood's movement out of the corner of my eye. She was picking up the extinguisher for round two. Moving as fast as could be expected, but when you have things breaking through a door that will eat you, no one moves fast enough.

"Come on, doc, break the window." I shouted as the creatures ripped the door from its hinges. It flew forward, spinning end over end, crashing to the floor.

Now the nightmare began. I could see the monsters in front of me. Werewolves. There were five of them, hair wet and sticky with blood, shining in the candlelight. Yellow eyes looked into my soul as we made eye contact. Once white teeth now shone pink with blood and ripped flesh.

In the lobby, I could see the carnage. It was as if the patients had been puréed. Heads severed from bodies. Arms and legs were hanging on overturned chairs.

"Move!"

Dr. Feelgood ducked as I fired a shot at the window. Glass shattered across the floor, raining down on both of us as the smell of gunpowder filled my nostrils. Smoke engulfed us. I could hear Dr. Feelgood cough to the point of gagging.

"Jump." I commanded.

"What?" She looked out the open window, as if she had a choice.

"Jump!" I repeated.

"I don't think I can do it."

"Do it, or I'll push your ass out!"

The fur balls were now moving toward us, only feet away as I fired the first shot. It caught the lead dog in the heart. It yelped in pain and crashed to the floor, sliding wildly to my feet. I had to jump to keep from being knocked off balance.

Feelgood stood on the edge of the window. I backed up next to her and gave her enough of a push that she jumped on her own. She screamed as she gave way to gravity and met the ground. Her legs quickly buckled under her.

I fired a second shot at the approaching fur balls, taking out a second one. Its head snapped back as silver nitrate punched its skull. Yellow eyes, once focused on yours truly, were nothing more than orbs staring into space.

Butterflies in my stomach started to stir. The ones you get when you look over the edge of a tall building, or jump from a high diving board.

I was about to jump when a hand reached out and grabbed me. I nearly wet my pants. When you are two stories in the air, a hand reaching out to grab you doesn't come to mind.

I turned to meet the owner of the hand and felt the butterflies turn into buzz saws. Dead eyes looked back at me. White skin wrapped around a morbid smile. Fangs of pearl glistened in the fluorescent light. The vampire was actually levitating outside the window, Virgil. You know, the one that punched the snot out of me when I was handcuffed to the chair.

It wasn't going to be my night.

CHAPTER TEN

The vampire held tight to the wrist of my gun hand, threatening to break bones, but I was determined to keep hold of the gun. I had an arsenal of tools in Kansas' Explorer, but I didn't think asking my captor to allow me to get them would be an option.

Fang Boy moved away from the outer wall. Rather, floated away leaving the werewolves at the window. Their yellow eyes reflected in the light, teeth showing through furry lips. They darted in and out of the window several times, testing their nerve to jump. It looked like a demented game of Whac-a-Wolf. I could tell by their body language that it would only be a matter of time before they were out the window.

I looked in the parking lot and was relieved to see red taillights from Feelgood's car. She had escaped. She was the lucky one, so much for helping the underworld. It gave her a first-hand look at the dark side of the things that go bump in the night. She would live. Most became corpses, or worse.

The blood leech and I quickly floated to the ground, landing rather softly compared to the crash landing the doctor had. I somehow felt guilty for pushing Feelgood out the window now. Floating to the ground was a strange experience. The downside of it was the fact that, unlike the vampire, I didn't float. I was literally hanging as an extension of the night creature's arm, causing me a great deal of pain, particularly in my dislocated shoulder.

I tried to pull away from the monster as I gained my footing. I was no safer now than I was on the second floor. I had simply changed monsters to die by. I had taken a punch from this one, several in fact, and knew that it was quite effective.

"Calm down, Avenger. I am not going to kill you. Yet." Yet. Now there's a loaded word. He smiled as he walked at a pace that could be mistaken for a light run.

"I may not return the favor."

Virgil looked at the gun in my hand and smiled. "Silver nitrate. You cannot possibly think you can kill me with that. Besides, we have not the time to debate who will kill whom."

"How do you know it's not ultraviolet bullets?"

"I can smell silver, Avenger. Putrid smell, but not deadly. Put your toy away. And before there are any more hollow threats, I know you are not carrying any other devices known to kill a vampire. You are as helpless as a baby."

I was dragged to a nearby pearl-white Cadillac STS. I pulled at the grip the cockroach had on me, trying to get free. The tension tightened with each tug.

"You are making this much more difficult than it should be."

"Good."

"You will not think so if those things get to you first."

"What makes you think that? At least they haven't poisoned me."

"No, but they will kill you all the same."

He looked back, keeping an eye on the wolves. He fumbled for his keys. I heard the beep-beep of the car alarm being disengaged.

The double flash of taillights and the pop of the door lock giving way.

"Get in." Virgil commanded.

"I'll take my chances with the werewolves, thank you." I tried to keep from being pushed into the car.

"It was not a request." He plucked the gun from my hand, shoved me into the passenger's seat. His strength was easily that of ten men. "If you want to see the sunrise again, Avenger, you will do as I say. Try and run, and I will put a bullet in your brain. It will make no difference to me."

"If that's true, then let me go or kill me now."

He ignored the request.

The blood-sucking cockroach opened his door and practically fell in the driver's seat. The door slammed shut. Engine ignited. Lights on the dashboard came to life in a spectacle of gauges, dials, and electronics. The black leather seats still smelled new, but with a hint of blood. I know; it's all in my head.

We moved with complete disregard for red lights and stop signs. Tires cried out in pain, trying to grip the pavement. Sirens sounded in the distance. I saw the red and blue flashing lights in the distance and said a little prayer for the officers. No way would they be prepared for the freak show they were about to see.

"Mind telling me why I'm being kidnapped for a second night in a row? Lyric spreading her legs for someone else now?"

He ignored the question.

I tried to keep from screaming as we intersected an eighteen-wheeler. Headlights illuminated the inside of the Caddy. We narrowly missed the grill, the diesel horn shouting at us at heavy metal decibels. The near miss with the semi didn't even make the vampire flinch. I guess when you're one of the undead, things like that just don't bother you.

"I asked you a question, you miserable piece..."

"Keeping you alive."

"Since when do blood-lapping cockroaches do search and rescue? Maybe you should be the one rescuing Maximilian's daughter."

"You are of no use to us dead, Avenger. Trust me, the Vampire Council would have loved nothing more than to see you perish at the mouths of heathen dogs."

"You just happened to be in the neighborhood?"

"If they killed you, you would not be able to complete your task for Maximilian and Mr. Rubio. You completely underestimated the severity of the situation. By killing everyone, Piel creates a diversion from his real plan." His voice so monotone and dry, he could have passed as a robot. He glanced in the rear-view mirror every few seconds. "That is, to kill you before you have a chance to kill him." His hands were tight on the steering wheel, his body bolt upright in the seat like a crash-test dummy. Headlights danced behind us like an illuminated kite tail.

I turned around and saw the headlights of the car in hot pursuit. The fur balls were back. Gotta give them that, they were persistent.

"That's what I love about you guys: you always think of others. How did you know where to find me?"

"We simply followed the dead bodies. Death seems to be your bedmate."

"Is that why you set me up with the false battery charge?"

A deep laugh came from his lungs. "Nice touch, no? Truth is, destroying your credibility is imperative. Too bad we did not count on you getting carried away at the hospital tonight. You could have saved us a great deal of planning. We had to make sure things were in place in the event that you did something stupid, such as notify the police about your predicament. Things had to be taken care of. The young man you refer to, as you Americans say, took one for the team. Not to mention the dead body tied to your gun. Call it planting a seed. Piel wishes for you to help him overtake the city from the vampires. It is my job to make sure you stay safe from his vengeance and to keep you from any alliance with him. Piel knows well of your hatred for us."

The car continued to move faster down the interstate. Fur balls still in hot pursuit. I glanced at the speedometer. It read 106 mph.

I reached for the gun and quickly put it to Virgil's head. "Stop this car, now. I have no problem with blowing a hole in your dead cranium. Stop it now, or you'll find out firsthand who my next dead body will be. I want the antidote to the poison, and I want it now."

He glanced over at the gun, but his hands never left the steering wheel. "Trust me, if it were an option, I'd feed you to the lycans myself."

A shot rang out. The back window of the STS shattered into pieces. A bullet hit in the dash, missing my arm by less than an inch. The vampire swerved. Tires squalled. Thrown off balance, I hit the dashboard. In a motion too quick for human eyes, Virgil grabbed the gun from my hands.

The gun was pointed back at me. "Putting a bullet in your head would have a much better effect. You and I have a lot to settle when this is all said and done. We can discuss this further at that point."

"Do it," I said.

He looked at me, puzzled. "You confuse me, Avenger."

"Pull the trigger. Put the bullet in my head. Let's settle this right here and now."

He laughed. "A way of cheating your predicament."

"No, a way of cheating the Council."

"Killing you is such a wonderful and intriguing thought, but keeping you alive might be better sport for all of us."

A second shot rang out, hitting the quarter panel. An explosion of sound hurt my ears. I had grown stiff, anticipating the next shot. Expecting it to find its target.

The fur ball's car was now beside us, the passenger window even with the blood-sucker. Like good shifters, they were now in human form. I guess it's hard to hold the steering wheel with paws.

"Hold on!" Virgil yelled as he swerved into the black car. Metal hit metal, friction and aggression mixing with sound and force.

I braced myself for a series of swerves and bangs. Neither car gave any ground. Both were out of control. The fur ball with the gun wasn't able to get another shot off. The cars continued to slam each other.

Virgil pulled the gun up and pointed it at the fur ball. Suddenly, a car entering the interstate pulled in front of us. The STS swerved in a violent ballet. Tire smoke filling the car. I braced myself for the inevitable crash. We seemed to actually be gaining speed.

The car came to an abrupt stop as it hit a concrete wall. Well, the spinning stopped. Instead, we were rolling end over end. Twisted metal ground into the pavement. A series of vicious views: sky, pavement, sky, pavement, sky, pavement. Shattered glass rained inside the car, cutting my face like a jigsaw. The momentum shook me like a rag doll.

When the rolling stopped, we were upside down. Gasoline and burnt rubber fumes mixed in the air.

For a few seconds, there was nothing but deafening silence. I took a deep breath, trying to regain air that had been knocked out of me. I fumbled with the seatbelt, bracing myself so when I released the catch, I wouldn't just plummet to the floor...uh, roof.

I wasn't sure how badly I was hurt. My adrenaline had kicked into hyper drive. My will to live pushed me on. I survived the crash, but I was far from being out of trouble.

What was left of the windshield was cracked into shards of spider webs. Green glass bowed in the middle, hanging on in places. Virgil had been thrown into the glass and was now lodged half in and half out of the car. He was facing the sky, steering wheel piercing his side. If he had been a human, the crash would have brought death instantly. He had fed tonight. Blood leaked from his wounds, turning his white dress shirt red. The windshield was a crimson prism. His face was hidden behind the splintered glass and red fluid.

My plan was simple: get out of the car as quickly as possible. I gave a final tug at the belt and it gave way, sending me tumbling back to earth. My head took most of the fall, despite the bracing. I landed on pellets of glass. I looked quickly for the gun as I exited the car.

Bat Boy moaned as he began to move. The windshield had him pretty well in place. He wasn't going anywhere for a while, and was thus no threat to me. Things were looking up.

My shirt was wet with sweat and stained with blood. I was relieved to find the new blood stains were minimal. I considered myself very lucky to be in as good of shape as I was in after that stunt show. I tried to stand, but my muscles were still far too weak. This took effort.

The vampire screamed. The sound was like an eagle's cry, high and sharp. It wasn't the first time I had heard a daisy-pusher writhing in pain. It gave me wonderfully awful ideas. "Killing you will be a pleasure unlike anything else." I told him. "I'll do it as slowly as I can. After all, you are one of the ones that poisoned me. An eye for an eye. I guess I won't be the first to die after all."

"They will kill you. You will not live long enough to bask in your glory. The werewolves are bloodthirsty savages."

Through the glare of the headlights, I saw three shadows approaching me. I didn't have to guess who they were and what they planned to do. They were all tall, over six and a half feet. Their long, flowing hair made them look more like members of a heavy-metal band than fur balls. The middle one had something in his hand that looked a lot like an ax. To say this made me a little uncomfortable would be the understatement of the century.

I had come to terms with the fact that one-day, a vampire or some other monster down here might kill me, but to be axed was something altogether different. If what the blood-sucker had told me was true, I was in serious trouble.

"Where's the gun, Virgil?"

"It will not do you any good, Avenger."

"Where's the gun?" I grabbed his throat and squeezed with everything I had.

They were now close enough that I could see their faces, the blank stares in their eyes. But that was not the disturbing part. Apparently, the fur balls had not counted on this chase and needing a new set of clothes. All three were completely naked, and extremely muscular. More like athletes than monsters. I refused to look lower. I had self-esteem issues as it was. I began to pray to God that I wouldn't be killed by three naked men.

"Tell me now, you miserable creep! Where's the gun?" My hands still clamped around his neck.

"You have become so accustomed to violence you forget that I cannot choke, Avenger."

"I know you don't breathe, you freaking moron. Now where's the gun!"

"Here. Take it and bless the world with your bloodshed." He handed me the gun.

I pulled the gun up to face the three fur balls. "Back off or you're dead, flea bags," I said to no one in particular.

They actually stopped. The one with the ax turned his head to look at me. He smiled and then began to walk again.

"I'm not joking. I'll blow your goddamn head off." My hands shook with fear.

The vampire continued to howl in pain across from me. He was now trying to get out of the windshield prison, looking like a demented reptile coming out of an egg. "Help me. They will kill us both."

The shifters were now only twenty feet from me. My decision

was made. I held my breath and squeezed the trigger, only to hear a hollow click. The .22 was empty. Could things get worse?

As the trigger snapped, the middle wolf, the one with the ax, stopped in his tracks. When the gun turned out to be nothing more than a delay, he smiled at me and continued to walk.

Virgil began to laugh. "Should have chosen your allies more wisely, Avenger."

I was out of other options. I had nothing else up my sleeve, and with the thought of my throat being ripped out my motivation to run was at an all-time high. My knees had a different idea. They wouldn't support my weight. The crash left them with no strength. It was as if I had just finished a marathon.

The middle fur ball now stood in front of me, and I could see things on his body that made me a little uncomfortable. I was going to be axed and eaten by a naked man. I hoped the obituary would be kind.

I closed my eyes and waited for the blade to hit skin. With my eyes closed, I could still hear the footsteps on top of me. They moved away. I peeked out of the corner of my eye only to see the fur balls had moved past me and were now standing over the trapped vampire.

He looked up at the three men and hissed. Blood-suckers and fur balls are, by nature, natural enemies, and this wasn't a welcome committee. I knew firsthand that these three streakers were not above spilling a little vampire blood.

"Virgil." The man with the ax said to the bloodsucker as he bent his knees to squat over the monster.

"Go ahead, kill me. It will not change anything. Quinn will have all of your heads."

I wasn't sure if the fur balls were organized or powerful enough to go head-to-head with Quinn and the fanged cockroaches, but one thing was certain: lines were being drawn. Piel was a lycanthrope with cojones the size of cannonballs.

The middle naked man laughed and stroked Virgil's face. "Now, now, Virgil. The vampires have brought this upon themselves, and you and Quinn both know it."

"Go to hell." Vigil spat blood on the naked man in a series of crimson dots.

The naked man stood and lifted the ax. In one quick move, he brought the ax down on Virgil's throat. The fang-head was dead. Virgil's head rolled next to me. His eyes were already beginning to sink back into his skull.

"He had it coming to him," Ax Man said.

"I wanted to be the one to kill him," I replied.

The three naked men looked back to me, their faces expressionless. I couldn't get a good feel on what they were going to do, but my imagination had enough ideas to leave me cringing.

Ax Man moved to me first, his ax still dripping with vampire gore, a bloody combo of blood, meat, and whatever other hellish stuff made them up.

"I'm not going to beg for my life. Crying like a little girl isn't my thing." Not yet, anyway.

"Paul Isaac, come with us," Ax Man commanded. His mouth nearly growling.

"And if I don't?"

"It wasn't a suggestion." Blond hair, long and curly, his yellow glowing orbs stared at me. Until I had a name, I'd call him Blondie.

"Where am I going?"

"Piel has called on you. It's not wise to make him wait."

"What does he want with me?"

Apparently, I was asking too many questions. The third, a fur ball with auburn hair, grabbed me by the shirt and lifted me off my feet, towing me toward the black car. I might not live to tell about it, but I was about to be face to face with the new alpha male shifter- who was quite possibly a very demented serial killer.

Joy.

CHAPTER ELEVEN

We moved down Hughey Street, past the police headquarters to Church Street. Bat Town was divided into two parts, split in half by the interstate. It was full of glitz and neon, mobs of pedestrians, and a gridlock of cars moving at a snail's pace. The vampire district hid the sins and death that was only inches under the surface.

Headlights glowed as a single light, dancing among the shadows, making their way to the shops, shows, and bars that made the place irresistible to the masses. Sounds polluted the air: the distant thump, thump, thump of the bass from the clubs, murmured conversations of pedestrians, the sounds of the interstate above.

The district was framed nicely among the backdrop of skyscrapers, looking like giant bodyguards, hovering and watching. The stars were drowned out by the flashing lights, dancing across the sky like acrobatic ghosts.

The Jag turned right onto Church Street. After what happened tonight at Dr. Feelgood's and the execution of Virgil, I would think the three naked men might be pressing their luck just a little by entering the vampire district. Word travels fast down here. Not to mention that being naked in Bat Town might draw a little attention.

To my left was Jackson Street, where the last body had been found. It was still very fresh in my mind. I could still see her, smell the death. Yes, death has a smell. Not the foul odor of decomposition, but something altogether different. It was a pure smell, neither pleasant nor pungent.

We pulled in front of the Lunatic Moon. Glowing blue lights outlined the six-foot letters over the entrance. A neon wolf with a seductive smile looked you in the eyes. The building was white, two stories high, with a large bay window on each side of the royal blue French doors that served as the entrance. The door was flanked by royal blue rope and white stanchions, zigzagging from the sidewalk to the front door. The hopeful filled the roped-off area, trying to talk their way into the club. Most were women, but not all. Things that happen here are pleasing to both sexes, but tonight was Ladies Night, featuring a display of Bat Town's best male strippers and sex acts.

A bloodsucker stood in front of the doors. He was working the crowd, making decisions on who got in and who was left out. He was dressed in an electric blue silk shirt, buttoned only half way. Black pants and shiny black dress shoes reflected the lights from the blue overhead sign. The bloodsucker looked over the crowd like meat, picking out the prime cuts for inside.

The two lycans in the front seat quickly got out. Blondie moved around the front of the car, while Auburn moved back to my door and opened it.

"I feel a little overdressed," I said to Auburn.

Ax Man got out of the car as well, moving around the back, joining the two that now towered over me like gargoyles.

"Let's go!" Auburn shouted out to me. "Make a scene, and you die." His eyes added that arguing the point would result in a lot of unnecessary pain.

"I'm sure there will be plenty of that later," I said under my breath.

I got out of the Jaguar and joined the three men, feeling the heat hit me once again. In Orlando, the heat doesn't take a night off all summer. I could hear the music coming from the club a lot more clearly now.

I took my habitual inventory of weapons, which left me with a sinking feeling. I had a .22 that was empty.

As we walked through the thick crowd toward the front door, I glanced at the sign typical of all the clubs down here. "Attention: No religious artifacts, wooden objects, ultraviolet, or silver of any kind."

"Check him," Ax Man said to the doorman.

I took a deep breath. He had a hand-held device that he ran over club dwellers, searching for contraband. I stood at attention as the doorman ran the device down the front of my body from my head to my feet.

"Ahh, what do we have here?" he smirked. "The great Saint Avenger is here for the dinner and show?"

"I'm all show, roach," I said.

"We'll see about that," the vampire replied. "By the end of the night, you just might be more dinner."

"I could kill all of you, and I honestly think I could casually walk past them unnoticed," I said, looking at the crowd.

"I could do the very same thing. In fact, one night very soon, I will. That's a promise."

Now that I had a closer look at him, I could see his black eyes, so typical in vampires. I made sure not to get caught in his gaze. His power wasn't anything terrible, but I wasn't willing to take a chance. He had a tattoo on his left arm of a mermaid with over-exaggerated breasts. On the underneath side of his right wrist, however, was a tattoo that made me jump as though I had seen a ghost: the letters TS, a rose with a barbed-wire stem. Everything melted away except for that tattoo. Since the murders, I had become obsessed with the tattoo, and now I had a warm body sporting one.

I did my best not to react to it. If I made it out of here alive, I wanted the element of surprise when I interrogated him. How violent the interrogation was would be up to him.

"Empty your pockets, or I'll kill you right here," Auburn said.

A gun shoved into my stomach. "Now, we don't want any drama tonight," Blondie whispered, breaking my stare from the doorman.

I almost laughed, but knew it would be a fatal mistake. "After all that happened tonight, you have the audacity to say you don't want drama?" I turned to face him. "I have nothing on me that's religious or silver."

"I know you got to be packing something. Now, where is it?" the stake donor said, boiling with anger. "Give me the crucifix. Slowly." The last word slithered from his lips.

"Get it yourself," I said.

"Don't be a smart ass. Take it out. Now." This from Auburn.

"Or what?"

"Or I'll eat your heart out right here."

"I don't have anything on me. You can check."

"Run the scanner on him again," Ax Man commanded.

The vampire ran the scanner over me one more time. No alarms went off.

"He's clean," the cockroach said. His thick British accent made him stick out like a sore thumb. He began to laugh.

"What?" I asked, a little defensive.

"Funny how you get mad when you think you are the butt of the joke and the only one that doesn't get it," the vampire said.

"We'll see who's the butt of the joke by morning."

"You're awfully cocky for someone without anything to defend himself with. You don't even have a toothpick to run through my heart. You must either be extremely confident or very stupid. I'm betting on stupid."

"Are you sure you checked everywhere for weapons?"

The smile evaporated. He was noticeably nervous, fidgeting with the scanner and the tickets in his hands, which were shaking.

"Yeah, I'm sure."

"Then why are you shaking?"

"I ain't shaking."

"Scared?"

"Not of you. I cut up and kill things like you. Just like the hookers you've been finding lately."

A chill hit me. It wasn't far-fetched to believe that this blood-licker might be the killer. The last body we found was only a block from here. From what Kansas and I had uncovered, the doorman at the Lunatic Moon fit our profile.

He looked at the three fur balls. "Don't keep your boss waiting."

They picked me up by my shirt and shoved me through the door. My heart raced, anger and anxiety battling inside me. I had just been face to face with something far more evil than just a walking blood bank; this one was a possible serial killer. Hopefully, I wouldn't end up in a body bag before I was able to tell anyone about it.

"Enjoy the show, Avenger," I heard from behind.

CHAPTER TWELVE

The main floor of the Lunatic Moon was a large banquet room filled with about a hundred round tables. Shiny blue tablecloths glowed in the light of the large candle on each surface. Six chairs circled each table, blue ribbon flowing down their sides.

People packed the room, dressed to the nines. They were eating, drinking, and laughing. Couples sat close together and exchanged soft kisses that urged more. Ant-like waiters delivered food, took dishes, and seated those just entering.

There was a sea of conversation. The music had disappeared into background noise, as soft as the wet kisses. The loud music was saved for the shows.

Yes, the shows.

A stage ran down the middle of the room, bright lights glaring on it like a runway. A dressing area ran behind it. I know; I had been here once before; no, not for the shows, freak. I had found one of my clients hiding in here once before. He was a stripper. Sorry, ladies, I was only doing my job.

The narrow end of the T-shaped stage cut through the banquet room, with tables lined up along both sides. A mirrored ball rotated above it. Points of light danced on the faces in the crowd.

"Cigarettes, Mr. Kasey?" a young woman said to Ax Man. She was about twenty years old, tan skin, sapphire eyes, perfect white teeth. She wore a French maid costume-ruffles, fishnet stockings, low-cut top. She had a tray of cigarettes across her stomach. With her looks, she would be able to sell ice to an Eskimo.

Kasey brushed her away with his hand, as though she was a fly. He moved by her with animal-like grace, slithering through the crowd, Blondie and Auburn trailing behind.

We worked our way down the left side of the room. A staircase ran up the wall to a balcony level. Lush carpet cascaded down the staircase, leading to a destination still unknown.

At the top of the stairs I could see one banquet table set up, a royal blue tablecloth draped over it like a casket. Eight chairs faced the runway below, polished cherry with royal blue cushions. The two chairs in the middle had higher backs than the others, reserved for someone more honorable than yours truly. Before each chair was a place setting consisting of a royal blue plate, silverware wrapped in a royal blue cloth napkin, and a crystal wine glass.

Three figures, two men and a woman, sat at the table, patiently waiting for the next show to begin. Two of them looked at us and smiled, friendly, shallow smiles, ones of mysterious endearment. This made me nervous. When monsters smile at you, you usually look tasty.

The first man nodded. His red hair stood out like a firestorm, pulled back into a ponytail. He had high cheekbones, deep eyes that seemed to project from the back of his head. Muscles bulged from the sleeveless black leather vest he wore. A thin goatee framed his equally thin lips. Even in human form, he took on animal-like qualities.

Next to him was the most luscious woman I had ever seen. She was Hispanic, about five and a half feet tall. Curls of long brown hair hugged her face in flowing mazes of sexuality. She possessed smooth caramel skin, and full lips, painted pastel pink that sparkled magically in the candlelight. Her breasts strained the fabric of her black silk blouse, which caught the light and practically filled the air with lethal intoxication. Her face smiled before her lips curved. Aquamarine eyes glowed like diamonds, threatening to light the dim room all on their own. She looked through my soul, almost begging me to smile back. Hunger was moving from my stomach to lower places.

The one that didn't smile sat all the way to the right and seemed to be very bored. His black hair was shoulder length and wavy. His skin was pale, closer to white than flesh color. His dark eyes gave him away. He was a daisy-pusher, not a fur ball. No attempt to look human. Tonight he was all blood-sucking cockroach. His long narrow face was nearly obscured by the waves of hair, leaving him with a mysterious look that was hard to read.

I could smell the aroma of meat cooking somewhere close by, making my mouth water like a common dog. It was more of a natural reflex than pure hunger. In my position, appetite seemed to be pushing things a little. A cigar would hit the spot a little better right now.

"Sit next to Angie," Kasey said, pointing to the high-backed chair next to the woman.

I looked at the naked man and then back to the chair. I didn't have a good feeling about this. I was falling deeper into a world that was hard to get back out of alive, and now I was being asked to break bread with them.

"Go on. You're the guest of honor tonight." Kasey said, smiling out of the side of his mouth. "Excuse us while we go change into something a little less comfortable." This time they all howled into a full laugh. He began to walk toward a door to the right of the table. He stopped to look at me again. Nothing threatening. Just observing.

"I'm not hungry." I said dryly. "I'm a little too nervous to enjoy eating with the Addams Family."

"Now, don't be rude, Avenger," the vampire said. He never smiled. In fact, he seemed a little pissed about something. Maybe it was just me. Shame.

"I think I'll just walk. I've seen enough of the freak show tonight." I began to move toward the stairs.

"Come join me, Paul. I don't bite," the woman called Angie said. Her voice was almost sweet enough to put on my tongue and taste, smooth and hypnotic tones, sprinkled with a devious purr.

"And if I don't?"

"Then I shoot you," Kasey replied, now showing a .45.

"Where the hell did you get that from? Never mind, I don't think I want to know."

"Sit down, now. Unlike Piel, I have no need to keep you alive."

"But if you kill me, he will have no need to keep you alive."

"Now."

I did as he commanded. No sense fighting the little battles. Bigger ones were on the horizon.

Angie giggled like a schoolgirl as I sat next to her. Her enthusiasm showed in her face, but again, that is usually a bad thing. Monsters have a different perspective on humor. I had a feeling I was the punch line.

"Thank you, Paul."

She had called me Paul. Things were at least looking up. If I had to fight my way out of here and kill them all, at least I would make hers quick and painless.

"Don't tell me the greatest vampire slayer in the city is shy." She placed a hand on my knee. Nothing sexual, just touchy-feely. She bent forward to look into my eyes, which were facing forward out toward the empty stage. Conversation was never my strong point, add awkward to the mix, and I was definitely out of my element.

"Who says he's the greatest?" the blood-sucker chimed in. His melodic voice slithered.

I turned to face him, keeping my eyes low until I could sense his power.

"He's got a gift, Jonathan. A way with your kind. Rumor has it, he can look into the eyes of vampires and not get drawn in." She talked about me as though I was her prom date.

"Is that true, Avenger?" His voice sent chills up and down my spine. "Can you really look into my eyes and live to tell the tale?"

Shit, this is going to get ugly. Note to self: Never eat with the enemy, no matter how hot the monster next to you is. "Doesn't your life suck enough, Jonathan? Looks like you're already the furries' pet of the week."

Angie giggled again. Her hand traced along my spine, nails scratching playfully. I held my breath. I knew she was far more dangerous than she looked. In a quick move she could easily shove her hand into my back and pull out my heart before I knew I was dead. That's the fatal thing with female monsters. Just because it has tits doesn't mean it can't kill.

"Pet," she said playfully. "Paul called you a pet."

Jonathan leaned in our direction. He looked like a fool, and he knew it. A vampire dominated by a shifter was on the lowest of all social ladders. To not be able to dominate me, a human, was icing on his humiliation cake.

"I'm no one's pet, Avenger, I assure you. You talk a good game, but I think that is all you can do."

"You're not powerful enough to beat me. I can sense your power, and without a doubt you're a newly turned piece of stake bait. Your vocabulary gives you away. The fur balls found you before you rose, and kept you to do their bidding. I'd bet on it."

"Remember this face, Avenger. It'll be the one that kills you tonight."

"I'm remembering your face. When I leave here tonight, I'll be back to stake your pet ass."

"This is going to be so hot," Angie said, now practically on my lap. Her perfume was like raw sugar. "Show him, Paul. Show him what you can do. Do it, and I'll be your personal pet." The last word was liquid coming out of her mouth. It took on a life of its own, possessing.

"I don't need a pet. And if you don't mind, I'd really like for you to sit in your own chair."

She gave me a pretty pout, filled with mischievousness. She placed her hands across her chest like a spoiled brat and slammed back in her chair. Her lower lip stuck out until it melted into a smile, then a pucker. Her eyes swallowed me whole. Her mounds of flesh bounced with the movement like jelly.

Four servers moved around the table, filling glasses and serving hot bread. They were dressed in royal blue tuxes, like the waiters downstairs.

"Don't you just love this place, baby?" Angie squealed.

"If I ever get out of here, I'll throw out everything blue I own. I feel like I'm under the damn sea." To Jonathan, "Care for some bread, Jonathan?" I buttered my own bread and handed the basket to him.

He slapped the basket out of my hand. He was breathing hard and deep, trying to control his temper.

"Shit, we have more in common than I'd like to admit. You have anger issues, too. I know this great doctor..."

"Look in my eyes. Prove you can do it."

"Jonathan, save what little dignity you have left." Angie was back on me again, trembling with excitement. Her hand was around my shoulder, fingers touching my throat.

"Now!" He shouted, slamming his fist on the table, his empty wine glass bouncing off the table and hitting the carpet with a soft thump.

I watched it roll back and forth on the floor, then looked at him. "You can't even break a wine glass, Jonathan. How do you expect to challenge me?" I took a sip of my wine.

"Try me."

Without a word, I locked eyes with him, calling on all the anger and vengeance within me.

Jonathan began to twitch as he tried to gain power. It was now a wrestling match of wills and mental strength. Very few humans can do it and live to tell about it.

I began to force the vampire to fall in my control.

Pick up your fork, I commanded.

"No," he groaned, all the time reaching for the fork.

Pick it up.

"No." The fork was in his hand now. His long, thin white fingers were wrapped tight around it, streams of blood pooled between his fingers.

Point it toward you.

"Stop!" He screamed in my mind. His hands shook as the fork moved toward his face.

Put it in your eye.

The fork moved closer to the eye, almost touching the eyelashes.

"Please!" He screamed.

"Fuckin' A!" Angie exclaimed. "He can do it!"

The fork now touched the white of the eye, causing the lids to flutter violently as the fork prongs began to compromise the pupil.

"Please, no," he begged. Prongs now dipping into the white flesh of the eyeball. Water began to pour down his cheek, slowly turning pink with blood.

"Do it, baby," Angie urged. "God, I'm so hot right now."

"Stop it!"

This time it was Kasey. He was fully dressed, finally, in a black silk shirt with royal blue accents and tight leather pants. The other two men joined him, dressed in a similar fashion.

"Ah, the three amigos!" I said.

"As gracious as Piel has been to you so far, you want to harm his guests," Kasey said reproachfully as he sat between the blood-sucker and me. The other two men took their seats to my right.

"Maybe he should keep his pet on a shorter leash." I broke the hold on the cockroach, allowing the fork to fall back to the table. Jonathan gasped for air, then collapsed against the table, his elbows catching him before he hit head on. His hands immediately went to the injured eye. "Besides, he's a blood-sucking cockroach. The wound will heal before the main course is served. All that was really harmed was his ego."

"Perhaps," Kasey said, looking at me as he slowly unrolled his napkin, placed it in his lap, and took a piece of bread from the basket.

Angie leaned in as close as skin and whispered, "Give me your hand."

I turned to face her. Her smile was ravenous, full of life, excitement, and possibly lust. She grabbed my hand quicker than I could react. It was the monster in her. In one quick motion, she placed my hand in her crotch, rubbing it across smooth leather pants that felt more like slick skin than clothes.

"Feel that?"

She shifted so that I could see her eyes again and embrace her energy. "That's because of you." Her voice returned to the soft kitten-like purr that she used. A low, soft laugh, almost evil, escaped her.

The lights dimmed to total darkness, and cheers rose to an absurd level, much like a rock concert. Whistling pierced my ears as I tried to find any source of light. Being in the dark with these things was not a comfortable feeling.

Hot breath hit my neck, and it wasn't Angie. I pulled my arm free from her and started up to swing at the intruder, when I was blocked by another hand. Shit!

I struggled to free my arm and tried to stand as the body above me forced me back into the seat.

"Take this," the voice said. I felt a dark power around me. Then again, you imagine a lot of things when you are in the company of monsters in the dark.

I felt something heavy fall in my lap. I touched it, and felt the shock run from my hand to my spine. It was a gun. It felt like a Glock, but I couldn't be sure in the blackness. The cold steel felt good in my hands, smooth and deadly. Its weight excited me like an aphrodisiac.

"Who's there?" I whispered, but the pressure released my arm, the hot breath disappeared. I was left in the dark with the monsters...and a gun.

CHAPTER THIRTEEN

Lights hit the stage, music poured over our ears like a waterfall. Bass rattled my teeth. I could see the people at the tables on the first floor standing and cheering. An uncontrollable frenzy was taking over. Everyone in the balcony began to beat their feet against the floor. Shock waves of sound thundered across the room, as if Trojan horses were about to enter.

The men at my table seemed to be far more reserved, leaning back in their chairs as if they were either not interested or so jaded that they no longer cared. They sipped wine and pulled at the bread.

Angie was screaming and jumping. I hadn't expected anything less. She began to clap and whistle as the spotlights searched the crowd.

I put the gun in my jacket and looked around the table at all the fur balls, hoping no one had seen it. I began to sweat, anticipating things to come. I was now a little less compromised, or at least I hoped. For all I knew, it was part of the show and everyone was waiting for me to make my move.

I scanned the room, looking for anyone that might be my potential savior, and saw no one. The four waiters were standing along the back wall behind us, looking forward toward the stage.

I looked for Piel. I had assumed the empty chair was for him, but then again, I know what assume stands for. I thought about Lyric, realized that she could be close enough to touch and I wouldn't know it.

"You're gonna love this shit," Angie shouted and hugged me tightly. She planted a wet kiss on my cheek.

"Who's supposed to be sitting here?"

"Piel." She continued to watch the empty runway, clapping and whistling louder.

"You didn't say that with much love."

"What's love got to do with anything?" Binoculars went to her eyes.

A waiter came by to fill the glasses with more wine. Other waiters now leaned over us, picking up the bread plates and replacing them with royal blue bowls of salad filled with rich green lettuce, purple onions, tomatoes, and croutons.

"I didn't know shifters ate vegetables."

"Piel wants us to be more mainstream. More human. Thinks we will be accepted better that way."

"Is he coming any time soon?"

Her attention finally drawn to me, the binoculars came down, her eyes lit up, and she smiled wide as she leaned in placing her arm around my neck, drawing me close to her face. Close enough that my eyes blurred. "In more ways than one."

"I'm sure I don't want to know what you meant by that comment."

"Tell me when, baby." She poured the dressing over my salad.

"When."

"I wasn't talking about the dressing, love." She licked her fork seductively.

I ignored the act, but knew it showed on my face anyway. Her devilish smile gave it away. "Is Jonathan the only cockroach Piel has?"

"He's got plenty." She took a bite of the salad.

"Really?"

"Oh, yeah. When you're an alpha male, you fuck who you want."

"Does that mean our boy Jonathan is a date? Where are the others?"

"Why? Do you want one?"

"No. Just trying to see why I'm here."

"Here." She put the fork of lettuce and tomato in my mouth.

"Are they all vampires?" I tried to swallow.

"Not all. Some are human freaks. Some are vampires. Some are all the above. Depends on what he likes to have for dinner."

"To eat with or simply to eat?"

"Whichever he desires. He loves to meet people that have the same hatred as he does for the vampires."

"And why am I here?"

"To enjoy yourself. Piel is a big fan of yours."

"Of me?" I took another bite of salad from her fork. It was clear I wasn't going to get to feed myself.

"Yeah. He likes your style. He likes anyone that the vampires hate. He's been watching you for a long time."

"I'm looking for a girl that might be one of his pets. In the vampire circles, there's a rumor going around that he's hooked up with the Master of the City's daughter."

She giggled. "You have beautiful eyes."

The curtains opened up and a figure appeared in the shadows. The crowd began to scream even louder.

On the stage, a nude man began to move out on the runway, dancing to the music, muscles coated thick with oil, tanned from head to toe. So much for a strip tease. He had skipped all the mystery and gave away the big surprise right off the bat. No pun intended. His black hair poured over his shoulders and down his back. I had hoped Kasey and his two thugs were going to be the last nude men I would see tonight, but I was wrong.

Women were now leaving their tables and rushing to the edges of the runway, holding their hands out to the naked man. Cameras flashed like strobe lights.

He continued to slither along the runway, the colored lights painting him in a rainbow of hues. He stopped dancing and looked over the crowd, cupping a hand over his eyes. I could tell he was a shifter. The lights were probably not a problem for him. Simply an act to stir the estrogen in the room a little more.

"Whoooo wants a faaaannnntaaasy!" an invisible announcer shouted over the P.A. system. His words shook the room, volleyed by the screams that followed.

"I love this part!" Angie shouted.

On the stage, there was a stream of women, mostly undressed at this time, stretching their hands toward the man on the stage. All hoping to be picked for something. But what?

The stripper chose a woman from the hundred or so that were gathered around the stage. Cheering could be heard all they way on the second floor. I sat back in my chair, allowing my stomach a chance to settle. It wasn't like I was going anywhere anyway. My mind was far too distracted to do anything else.

"Here we go, baby," Angie screamed in my ear.

"Somehow, I don't think we will be excited about the same thing."

Another track began to play, and the large crowd below began to clap to the beat. The woman began to kiss the man, tongue running deep in his mouth. She was nude except for a pink lace thong. She was small compared to the stripper, with perky tits and short brown hair that barely touched her shoulders.

The stripper's hands began to explore her body, running them gently down her back, up across her shoulders, down her back again, over her rear end. The crowd went crazy as he began to take control of her body. The woman grew limp in his hands, allowing him to bend her into any shape he pleased.

Two other men came out from behind the curtains, hoods over their heads, leather shorts their only clothes. They pushed a large wooden structure, a wall, out to the middle of the stage next to the stripper and his conquest.

After the structure was in place, the two men walked back off the stage with little fanfare. The woman was deep into another kiss, tongue threatening to go all the way down his throat. Her hands were moving along his chest. Fingers exploring. Her body now glistened with the oil from the stripper. It gave her an artificial glow in the lights.

The stripper allowed her to move her hands further south, touching his manhood for a quick second, before he pushed her away. He stalked around her several times, like a panther. She moved in smaller circles, following his gaze, lost in his stare.

The man now looked to the mobile wall next to them. I could now see the hand and foot restraints on it. He gestured like a magician, calling the crowd's attention to the wall.

The woman glanced at her friends, at the base of the stage, and placed her hands over her eyes as if she were embarrassed.

The stripper led her gently to the wall, moving with a showman's flair. He snapped her right hand in the cuff, then kissed her gently on the mouth, exploring her wanting lips. She did not fight against the bondage, but instead seemed to grow more aroused with the restraint. The stripper cuffed her left hand to the wall, sucked on her erect breast. The woman arched forward, inviting him to take in more of her. He obliged.

He worked his way down her body to her belly button, lapping like a large cat with a bowl of warm milk, taking in her tastes. She squirmed under the exploratory act. Her friends on the floor began to take pictures and cheer with wild excitement.

"Nothing's more erotic than a man who binds me," Angie whispered in my ear, followed by a long, soft kiss to my cheek. A purr roared from her stomach into her throat.

"And they say I need therapy."

The stripper now had the woman in complete bondage, hands and feet cuffed to the wall. The thong panties the woman had been wearing were now missing, exposing her to the room. If she minded, it didn't show. In fact, she seemed to be more turned on by the extra exposure than embarrassed by it.

He took a black scarf from a woman in the crowd and sniffed its entire length. He bent down, pulled her face up to his and kissed her as deep as he had the woman on the stage. She fell backwards in a puddle of desire, allowing those behind her to catch her fall.

He whirled to face his victim. Her eyes locked on his, allowing him to devour her desire, feeding off the tension.

He placed the scarf around her head, covering her eyes tightly. She nodded slightly and smiled as he stepped back to admire what he had done. She licked her lips as she waited for the next move.

As the music continued to play, he began to change before our eyes into a giant serpent. His human flesh yielded to scales of gold, yellow, and black. Fifty, maybe even sixty feet in length. He dwarfed the cuffed woman on the stage.

I watched in horror. I had never known a shifter to change into a giant serpent before. Wolf, rat, panther, yes, but never a serpent.

My body grew numb as I watched the snake continue to move around his prey, slithering in circles of death. Scales moving in slow motion. I tried to gauge the reaction of my tablemates. Surely I wasn't the only one that found this a bit disturbing.

Jonathan and Kasey sat with bored eyes. Kasey finished his salad, looked at me, and smiled.

"Enjoying the show, Avenger?"

"I'm not amused with it."

"Blood makes him squeamish," Jonathan added, showing his fangs. "This is no different than when you feed a mouse to a pet snake. It's natural order,"

Kasey leaned forward. "It's kind of exciting when you indulge in the act."

"It's not against the law to feed a pet snake a mouse. This is sick." I felt my ears ringing as the blood began to flow faster in my veins. "He's not going to eat her, is he?"

"Is that a rhetorical question?" Kasey asked.

"No, it's not."

"What did you think he was going to do? Fuck her?"

"I've got to stop this." I began to stand from my chair in protest.

With animal speed, Kasey pinned my arm to the table. "Sit down. Enjoy." His yellow eyes burned into my sight.

"How am I supposed to sit here and watch this happen? I'm not going to let this take place, in front of all these people, and not do anything about it. You can kill me if you want."

My hand was in my inside pocket, wrapped around the gun, when the serpent on the stage caught my attention. I wondered if I was hallucinating. The serpent was growing legs, front and back. It was turning into a dragon.

I didn't remember standing. Paralyzed, I looked at the stage with an all-new horror. I had tracked, battled, and killed vampires. I killed werewolves and ghouls. But never in my life had I battled a dragon. I felt my legs growing weak as I sat back down. My brow was wet with sweat, my heart racing at an alarming rate.

The dragon was nearly as long as the runway. The woman on the stage was now screaming. For the first time, I was glad that she was blindfolded. She pulled against the cuffs, twisting and arching, but the cuffs held firm. The more she screamed and fought, the louder the crowd cheered.

"You look a little pale," the fur ball next to Angie said to me. He laughed and took a drink of wine, his yellow eyes never leaving me.

"Stop this," I answered back.

"Relax and enjoy the show," the fur ball answered back.

The dragon ran its pink, wet tongue over the skin of the cuffed woman. She screamed with fear as the tongue moved across her. There was no longer the rush of heat. Her friends on the floor continued to scream excitedly, which just pissed me off more.

"How can they let this happen? What is she, some sacrificial lamb? She had no idea what was really going to happen, did she?"

"Relax, my friend," Kasey said.

"Screw you all."

I tried to stand again, finding my legs still very rubbery. I was no match for the monster on the stage, true, but I couldn't just sit and watch this thing eat the woman.

A hand grabbed me and pushed me back to the chair, buckling my knees with force. It was Angie.

"It's okay, Paul. It's what she wants to happen. She'll be all right." Her eyes sparkled baby blue. I had never seen a fur ball with such eyes.

I pushed the gun into her ribs. "I'm more than willing to put the first bullet in you, beautiful or not. Let me go, you twisted bitch," I whispered, trying to keep the gun as much a secret as I could. I was showing my hand, but I hoped only to one monster.

Her smile melted away in confusion, but she kept her eyes on me. She tried to smile three separate times, only to find the action wouldn't form. "Just watch, Paul. You'll see." Her eyes led me back to the runway, where the dragon now was on its hind legs, standing in front of the woman as cheers from the crowd began to escalate again.

The dragon began to hunch the woman with incredible force, its tail swishing back and forth. The crowd began to clap with each thrust, wanting more, growing with lust.

"She came here to fuck, baby. It's all about the pleasure," Angie said in a series of purrs, moving closer, running her tongue across my lips, small licks forming pools of exotic saliva.

I wanted to pull away. I couldn't. I wanted her to continue. I wanted more. Even in all the horror of what I was seeing and feeling, I wanted more. Her power rode me, wild and unforgiving.

I closed my eyes and tried to break the connection. I could feel my head spinning, but I wasn't willing to fall under her control. I clutched the gun, trying to make sure she didn't slip it from my hand.

"Tell me you won't kill me, baby. I trust you." I heard her say from a distance. It was like falling. I couldn't stop the sinking.

"I won't," I answered back. I realized I was falling in a trance, but my mind was no longer my own. My God, she was the strongest one of them. That's why Piel had her sitting by me. He knew I would let my guard down with her.

I pulled my mind back with everything I had. I dug my nails into my arm, trying to shock my body into the pain I needed to regain my thoughts.

Her grip loosened as I pulled. In a few seconds, I was free and looking into her eyes again. Human-like eyes. Innocent to those that didn't know better.

My thoughts and actions flooded back, melting away the hypnotic trance that Angie had lulled me into. I was somewhere between anger and confusion.

"Don't you ever do that again," I said, ashamed of my desire and weakness.

"I didn't do it to hurt you or embarrass you. Simply to show you she felt no pain or fear."

"I guess the screams are part of the act?"

She smiled, but this time it was forced. "Sometimes. Sometimes a girl wants a little pain with her pleasure. They aren't that different, you know."

The remaining cobwebs in my head cleared as a waiter leaned over my left shoulder and placed a plate in front of me. I looked at the pleasantly displayed dish. It was a work of art. Prime rib, cooked rare, a baked potato smothered with butter, and peas and carrots, all framed with parsley frills. The smells were intoxicating; my hunger began to override the macabre show before me.

I looked toward the stage and realized I had been under Angie's spell longer than I had thought. It hadn't been just a few seconds, but much longer. How much longer was the big question? Looking out over the stage, I saw neither the woman that had been cuffed to the movable wall nor the shape-shifting stripper. It was as if they had vanished into thin air. The stage was now empty except for a disturbing splash of color that I hadn't noticed during the act, as though someone had spilled red Kool-Aid.

I immediately felt for the gun, finding its cold metal still waiting for me like an old friend. I began to relax.

She caught me searching and smiled. "See, it's all about trust. I trust that you won't kill me, and you trust in me for everything else."

"Who gave it to me?" I asked, ignoring her comment.

"The security here leaves a lot to be desired. Sometimes the enemy of your enemy is your friend."

"What's that supposed to mean?"

"It means if you're going to kill someone, make sure it's someone that plans to kill you."

"What did they do to her?" I asked Angie.

"You need to relax. Another outburst like that, and William will kill you."

William. Well, at least I had a name for the fur ball next to her. He smiled at me as he chewed his prime rib, and then gave me a quick salute with his first finger.

"Eat up, my friend," William added as he wiped his mouth and took a sip of the red wine.

I looked back to Angie, who was still smiling at me. "Why didn't you mention the gun to your pack?"

"Because I know you won't kill me. And if they take it away, you won't be able to kill anyone else."

"Seem kind of sure of yourself. Who says I won't kill you?"

"Who says I'd care?"

I left the elusive answers alone. "What happened to the woman and shape-shifter on the stage?"

She scooped up a bite of baked potato with her fork and brought it up to my mouth. "Hungry?"

"No. What happened to the woman? And I'm quite capable of feeding myself, thank you."

"She got what she came here for," Angie answered as she turned the fork from me and ate the bite herself.

"Which was?" I asked.

"Are you always this tense?"

"You know it's murder."

"You can't save the whole world, Paul. Everyone makes their own choices. Your ideals don't apply to all. It's just like with you. Your laws say you can't torture and kill vampires, but you do. To you, it's justified in the end. The rules are the same here. It was her choice to live or to die."

"It didn't appear that way to me. I saw the look on her face. She didn't want what was happening to her. It wasn't her choice. You saw that."

She leaned her head on her hand, and her big curls flowed to the table like angel's wings. Her eyes were tender, yet dangerous. She was grace under pressure. "Ever ride a roller coaster?"

"What?"

"Answer the question. Have you ever ridden a roller coaster?"

"Yeah. What's that got to do with anything?"

"Right before you went over the first big dip, did you get scared?"

"Maybe."

"Did you scream? Want to get off? Wish you never got on the thing?"

"Get to the point."

"Same thing happens here. They get scared of the unknown. Wish they hadn't gone up on stage. But in the end, the rush is worth the second-guessing. The thrill of being out of control."

"It's not the same, and you know it. We're talking murder, not some thrill ride."

"It is all in how you look at things. Not everyone finds life exhilarating in the same ways. Some only float through life, experiencing nothing, only watching. Voyeurs to the outside world. They disconnect and wait for death to end the ride. Lonely and depressed. Tonight, she wasn't a voyeur, she was a participant. She was not invisible in the crowd, but the center of attention. She was cheered, loved, cherished. What happened to her was a gift, not a punishment. Don't presume to think you know what is best for everyone. In most cases, we are wrong."

"You think killing her was a gift. You really are that twisted, aren't you?"

"She came here of her own free will."

"Laws are in place to protect against things like this. Whether she wanted it or not isn't the question. Sometimes laws protect us from ourselves."

"Many say the same about you. It's addictive."

"What's addictive?"

"Fetishes, Paul. People next door to you have them. People walking down the street beside you have them. We are told from infancy to suppress them. Hide in shame because of them. It's a lie. Desires are what make us who we are. Not everyone wants the same ol' same ol'. To some, tortured skin is a release of the desires, not the barrier or the forbidden. Some people get tattoos for the pain, not the artwork. Pleasure and pain are wonderful together."

"You're all murderers."

She smiled and leaned in for a kiss on the cheek. I let her. "Be a Boy Scout all you want. It's one of your best qualities." She lifted a cut of the prime rib to my mouth. I refused again with a raise of my hand.

"Is Piel showing up any time soon?"

"Sorry I'm late, Mr. Isaac," a voice behind me said.

CHAPTER FOURTEEN

Piel stood behind me like a statue, as if waiting for me to tell
him that it was okay to sit down. At least he was clothed;
he wore a white silk shirt, black pants, and black leather
belt with a silver buckle in the shape of a howling wolf. His long
hair was in loose waves that flowed around his Latin face like a
black ocean. His cologne was strong enough to make my eyes
water. I could feel power and strength radiating from him.

"Hope I didn't keep you waiting." He sat in the chair next to me,
and the waiters immediately brought his plate of prime rib,
steaming hot with all the sides. "Ahh, this smells wonderful, don't
you think?"

"I didn't think you'd have an appetite after the show."

As a second waiter filled his wine glass, Piel cut into the meal
and began to eat at lightning speed. Knife and fork danced around
each other.

"I simply gave the crowd what they came to see." Piel looked
over at my plate, which still sat untouched and growing colder by

the second. He stared up at me, those eyes now more human than beast. "You don't like it?"

"I'm just not hungry right now."

"I'm starving. These shows take everything out of me. Builds up one hell of an appetite."

"I'm sure killing does," is what I wanted to say, but chose to change the word "killing" to "it."

"So, did you like the show?" He chewed on the meat, his fork already shoveling baked potato on the prongs, swirling it around in the blood on the plate.

"Probably more than the woman did." I chose my words carefully; I didn't feel like going into full pandering mode.

He laughed, looking at me again like a mischievous child. "I doubt that."

"Why am I here? I'm done with small talk."

"I'm a big fan of yours, Mr. Isaac. I've done my research on you. I know you inside and out." He took another drink of wine and leaned back in his chair. A breath escaped his lungs in a loud huff, his hands folded across his stomach in artful fashion.

"I'm sure I'm not here because you want an autograph."

He pushed the plate away and laughed. Then the smile evaporated and he looked at my face, studying it, almost as if he were memorizing it. "Have you met our other guests?"

"Some."

He looked past me, toward the end of the table on my right. "Down on the end is Christopher, next to him is William, and the lovely lady next to you is Angie."

"We've met," Angie said playfully.

The smile on Piel's face returned. "I bet you have, sweetheart."

He turned to his left and began again. "This is Glenn, Kasey, and on the end is Jonathan."

"A cockroach," I added.

"Excuse me?" Piel asked. A puzzled look crossed his face.

"Sorry. Vampire."

Piel laughed again. "Yeah, he's a..." he paused. "A cockroach." His laughter ended instantly as he turned to Jonathan. "Found him."

"You make him sound like a stray dog. It's illegal to keep those things after an attack. You know that, don't you?"

Piel took a drink of the wine. "Since when did you fight for vampire rights?"

"That's just it. He doesn't have any rights. He is legally dead. Allowing a victim to rise as a vamp is illegal. Somehow, I don't think I'm telling you anything you didn't already know."

"Helps keep the numbers in check, huh." He watched a waiter pour a second glass of wine. "Too many vampires, the humans become extinct."

"To an extent. It is also a law to keep the humans from stealing the bodies. Before the law went into effect, families of the victim would sometimes keep the bodies with them, knowing in three days the body would rise again. They hoped that by keeping the bodies, they would somehow get to keep their loved one with them. Having them as undead cockroaches was better than losing them altogether. Problem was, many times the victim would rise, hear the calling of the master, need to feed, and kill the entire family. It got to be very messy. Things I'm sure you already know."

"Mine has risen, and no one has been killed. Unlike the missing men I sent to see Dr. Lydia Petty." There was a darkness rising in his voice. "Two, to be exact."

"I left you three. Seems fair to me." I looked at the blood-licker. "Whether he has killed or not doesn't make a difference. There will still be a warrant for his death, and you'll be charged in harboring him. Of course, after what I saw tonight, I think that will be the least of your worries."

"I don't believe this. The great Paul Isaac, mad at me for keeping a subservient vampire. I would have thought better of you."

His face lit with laughter again. "So, should we kill him now, or wait 'til after dessert?"

"We can't kill him until I get a death warrant. A representative of the vampire community must be present, as well."

"Whatever happened to the good ol' days when you could just kill the damned things? Now there's all this paperwork and court orders. I never pictured you as one that cared much for the rules when it came to these things."

"You all became legal. That's what happened."

Piel shook his head. "Ironic. I save your life, bring you here to see the shows, feed you well, make you my guest of honor, and all you want to do is kill my pet. Not very civil."

The first part was all I heard. "Saved my life?"

"Yeah. The vampire would have killed you. Surely you remember what happened tonight?"

"I remember a lot of killing."

"Virgil was getting a little impatient with the works of the Vampire Council. He wanted you dead. My men killed everyone there because otherwise they wouldn't have gotten to you in time. We didn't know who the killer was at first, so we had to exterminate them all. Besides, they were just, as you say, cockroaches.

"As for being here against your will, leave if you want, but know there will be more attempts on your life. They want you dead. I'm offering you an alternative. Let's not point our daggers at each other. I think you would agree that my men could have killed you if they wanted to. You live because I say you live."

"That's the second time in as many days I've heard that line."

Dessert arrived as we talked. Chocolate French silk pie topped with whipped cream and chocolate shavings. Piping hot coffee, its rich aroma filling my lungs, was poured into our cups. The plate of prime rib that had sat in front of me was gone.

"You don't think it's true?"

"You just seem a little too confident that I won't kill you as easily as I kill the vampires."

"Save your threats for the vampires. You do not threaten me in my house. I decide who lives and who dies, and that includes my pets." Anger in his voice again.

"So I'm only here because you felt the need to save my life? Let's be honest. You need me for something. If you didn't, I wouldn't be here. You don't really think I'm buying all this, do you?"

"No." He filled his mouth with pie. I guessed it was so he could think about his answer if he chose to elaborate. He swallowed, then continued. "I brought you here to tell you something about the killings."

"Okay, you have my attention. Go ahead."

"They all have something in common."

"I'm listening."

"They were all patients of Dr. Lydia Petty."

"The shrink that serves the blood-suckers?"

"Yes." He hissed as he reached for the coffee. "Now you know why they want you dead. Flushing out a serial-killing vampire could hurt business. They thought you knew more than you did. You just happened to step on a landmine. Virgil wanted you dead before you could say anything."

"And how do you know this?"

"Let's just say I've heard a rumor and leave it at that." He smacked his lips and returned the cup to the table.

"And why would you tell me this? What's in it for you?"

"Mr. Isaac, should I be offended?"

"Maybe. I know better than to believe you would go to all this trouble unless there was something in it for you."

Piel laughed again. "See, that's what I like about you. You don't pull any punches."

"I'm still waiting." I looked him in the eyes and stood my ground. "I'm not in the mood for mind games."

He took a breath, seemed to wait for the right words to come to his lips. He tried a couple of times before he finally spoke in a hushed voice. "How well do you know the doctor that you saw tonight?"

"It was our first meeting, but somehow I have a feeling you already knew that."

"Why were you seeing a shrink, anyway? You don't strike me as the emotive type."

"It was ordered by the Council, more or less."

"They sent you to see Petty?"

"Actually, I was taken there by Detective Kansas, not the cockroaches."

"Ahh."

"What?"

"If you hadn't been so good at what you do, you would've been looking for someone else to get inside your head." His words were coated with controlled anger. "Virgil apparently thought you were there because you found out about the patients of Dr. Petty."

"Your point is?"

Piel smiled, his eyes showing the beast (or would that be beasts?) in his eyes. "We have a deep history, Dr. Petty and I." The smile disappeared. "Ten years ago, I was in prison. A lost boy, so to speak. Someone that could have faded into the walls and no one would have missed me. I had no family, no friends. If I disappeared, it would have been easy to cover up."

He took a drink of the coffee in front of him, allowing the taste to fill his senses. "Columbian, like me."

I looked around at the other dinner guests. They listened, but never spoke.

"Our own government began running a series of experiments on the lycan virus. A series of military experiments to see if they could somehow alter the virus and make it more controllable in a hostile environment. I was chosen to be one of their guinea pigs and injected with the lycan-mutated virus. At the time, none of us were allowed to live among humanity, but if it somehow benefited society, it was okay. I became the United States military's freak project."

"That's why you can change into all those creatures."

Piel shook his head. "At first, the virus didn't seem to work. I didn't turn into anything; I had a growing torture in my muscles when the moon was full, but did not shape-shift. As time went on, the torture got worse, and I began to change into things that I didn't remember. I would completely black out and wake in a pool of blood, not knowing whose or what kind." He played with the pie in front of him for a second, but never really tasted it. "My shape-shifting became more and more violent, but my memory became clearer and clearer. I was scared shitless. I didn't know anything about lycanthropy at the time. I didn't know what was happening to me, and there was no one around that would help me. I was expendable. I knew that I had to escape and tell someone about what was happening in those labs. It wasn't just me, hundreds of people were experimented on. Some died. Some were killed. Some of us had a worse fate: we lived."

His breathing quickened as he recounted the story. "One night when I changed, I became desperate. I had learned to control my animal side months earlier, yet didn't show them everything I could do or the strength I had. Their underestimation of me was their downfall. I killed them all, slowly and with great suffering. I wanted them to see me when they died.

"I escaped from the laboratory and ran. Just ran and ran, as far away from that hellish place as I could. I lived in the swamps of the Everglades for a week. In time, I began to work my way back out of the Glades and looked for help. I didn't know much English, didn't understand anything that was happening to me, and knew that humankind was not going to be on my side. I was easily worth more dead than alive. I was an escaped experiment and common prisoner. Still, I held on to the hope that someone would know what was going on with me and how to help.

"Late one night, I met up with a doctor leaving the hospital and took her hostage. I wasn't going to hurt her; I needed her help. I knew that walking into a hospital and telling the emergency room doctors what had happened wouldn't work. The military had men staked out there and throughout the city. I had to do something drastic. I honestly thought I was going to die from the virus. You know, like AIDS or something. Sometimes I wished it would kill me."

"Dr. Petty was the doctor?"

"Yeah." He paused. "I told her everything that had happened, and guaranteed her safety if she helped me. I begged her to help me. We drove around all night and into the next day. She finally drove us to her office in Miami, where she planned to hide me until she could get help. I really thought she was on my side. Instead, she called the military. I was cuffed, dragged off to God knows where. I was again forced to kill to escape. Even now, after all these years, after the laws have been passed, I have remained a wanted man, hunted for the murders of seventeen military personnel. I live my life looking over my shoulder, moving and changing my appearance to stay one step ahead."

"So you blame Dr. Petty."

"Wouldn't you?"

"I guess to an extent, but what does that have to do with me?"

"She's feeding your killer the victims."

I could feel the chills run up my arms. "How do you know that?"

"They were being treated for issues by the good doctor. Demons that they could no longer hide from."

"Doesn't mean she had anything to do with the killings. Just a coincidence."

"She feeds the girls to the vampires. She looks after the vampires like a guardian angel."

He pulled out a picture of a young girl. She was young; I'd say early twenties.

"I'm worried she might be your next body."

"And?" I said as I studied the picture.

"And she was supposed to be here tonight. Didn't show up. No answer on her cell phone. Just disappeared into thin air."

"Who is she?"

"Her name is Lyric. She's the one you are looking for."

He had to see my body convulse.

"What's wrong, baby?" Angie asked. Her energy pricked my skin. Before, her hands felt erotic on my body, but now they were nothing more than an irritating distraction. I pushed her away.

"Where is she?"

"What do the vampires want with her?" Piel asked.

"You know what. She's Maximilian's daughter."

Piel laughed. "She's not his daughter. She's a human stripper."

"You're telling me this girl is a human?"

"Yeah, why?"

"Why would Rubio and the other vampires lie about her? What did they want with a common stripper?"

"That's what I want to know."

I was standing before I knew it. One minute I was sitting and talking to the alpha male shifter, who was no more a werewolf than I am, and the next moment I was standing over him with my gun drawn.

"Don't fuck with me," I said, checking to make sure my back was to as few of them as possible. I retreated, keeping the Glock pointed at Piel's heart.

Piel's expression was comical, as if he couldn't believe what I was doing. "Have you lost your mind, my friend?" His GQ smile still there.

"You knew I was coming for her, didn't you? You son of a bitch."

"You don't need a gun to have her. Find her and you can get your jollies off on her."

"No, she's more and you know it. I know who she really is, and I'll kill anyone that stands in my way of getting her back alive."

Piel began to stand, looking at me with animal eyes. He was still trying to play things cool, but I knew there was more danger to him than I wanted to deal with. I wasn't equipped to take on all these monsters tonight, but I knew I would have to kill them all to get out alive. "Why do you need her so bad? I'm beginning to believe you love the vampires more than you'd like to admit."

"They poisoned me. If I don't get her to them in three days, I die."

Kasey moved around to my side, and I swung the gun in his direction. "Take another step and I'll put a bullet in your heart."

He stopped and looked back to Piel. Piel waved him off.

"Smart move," I said. I wasn't sure who was going to die tonight, but Kasey was nearly the first.

"Lyric is Maximilian's daughter, and you know it."

Piel laughed loudly. "Maximilian's daughter? Are you really that mad?"

"No." I steadied the gun again. "I was sent here to get her back. And I'll do whatever it takes to make that happen."

Piel showed me the palms of his hands. "I mean you no harm."

"I'm not buying it. The element of surprise is what keeps you alive or gets you killed."

He kept smiling. It made me feel like a fool. Here I was with the gun, and he was laughing at me.

"How fucking ironic. You work for the bloodsuckers now, huh? They're messing with your mind. They're hoping you'll kill me."

"I just need the girl. I don't work for any of you freaks." I answered back, glancing at the others. They were moving around in a circle, trying to get behind me, except for Angie. She was watching everything, taking it in. Her face was blank when she looked at me. I continued to walk backwards, flanking them.

"You sold out," Piel said as he watched the others around him. "The world's greatest vampire executioner is now in their pocket. It's all head games."

"What do you mean, head games?"

"He's fucking with you. Lyric isn't Maximilian's daughter any more than she's yours. She's nothing more than a vampire freak. Goes clubbing at all the monster sex bars. Now she's missing. They want her for something, I'm sure, but it isn't because she's family. Chances are, you don't have anything running through your veins that will kill you either. They know you. They know you'd try to kill me to save yourself. After you did, they'd all deny everything and walk away."

"If Lyric isn't Maximilian's daughter, why do they want her?"

"Don't get yourself killed over one of his lies," Piel cautioned.

The two lycans to my right shifted to the werewolf form and began to move toward me. Fast. I moved the gun around to meet them. Pulled the trigger. Felt the gun kick me back against the wall. The bullet struck the one called Christopher in the jaw, sent him to the ground. I turned the gun on William and dropped him with a bullet to the chest. It was close range; blood splattered my face, oozing warm down my cheek. I rubbed it off as quickly as I could, a reflex. There have been cases of humans catching the lycan virus through bodily fluids other than saliva.

Piel and the others began to change to monster forms, Piel to a large scorpion, Kasey and Glenn to wolves. And then there was Jonathan, the fang boy, smiling wide at the attacking creatures.

The inside of the Lunatic Moon went black. Pitch black. Never a good sign. I pointed the Glock in the direction I'd last seen Glenn and Jonathan and pulled the trigger a couple of times. I was scared, and not afraid to admit it.

I felt Jonathan grab me and throw me across the room. He might have been a recently turned vampire, but he was still very strong. I reached for the crucifix I kept in my pocket, only to be reminded that it was still in Kansas' Explorer.

I pointed the gun at the chest of the ultraviolet challenged. It wouldn't kill him unless I got a good shot to the heart. The trigger went off, exploding in the side of the monster.

"Nice try, Avenger, but your bullets won't keep you from dying tonight," he said as he bit down on my shoulder. I did everything I could to keep standing.

Teeth sank deep in my skin and flesh. He didn't so much draw blood as tear chunks of my shoulder out. My muscles ached as I pushed against the monster binding my arms. The pain in my shoulder forced a shout from me. I couldn't move, but I couldn't stay still either.

The vampire screamed in pain as it was pulled off of me. With the weight gone, I greedily sucked in a breath, allowing the air to fill my lungs again.

I heard a thud above me, followed by a falling body. I guessed it was Jonathan. The mystery man had somehow gotten to him.

"You are going be all right. They're gone," the voice said, panting.

"Who are you?" I asked. I sensed power, strong and old. There was a vampire nearby, one that wasn't Jonathan, or so I thought. Then again, my senses were evaporating with the loss of blood.

I could hear light steps moving away from me.

"Hey, who are you?" I asked again, but the voice did not reply.

I stumbled in the darkness trying to find the stairs. I had lost a lot of blood, but refused to pass out in here. The bad guys were still close by, and I was still in their house. My ears rang, my muscles shook, my head spun.

CHAPTER FIFTEEN

I woke in my own bed, sunlight hitting in my face. Gold cotton sheets wrapped around me, the comforter kicked to the floor. I don't remember how I got home. I was simply happy to be in familiar surroundings. I remembered leaving the Lunatic Moon around four in the morning, but blacked out after that. The large red numbers I looked over at the digital clock read 5:33 p.m.

I sat and swung my legs over the edge of the bed, then noticed the vampire bite had been bandaged. Odd. I wasn't sure I would've gone to all that trouble. I wore a pair of gray underwear briefs and nothing else. Still, I had on more than most of the people I had met the night before. I felt good about that.

The bite was tender, swollen, and bruised. The pain zapped in synch with my pulse. I was kicking myself for letting a bloodsucker get that close to me. Until last night, I had a perfect record against them. But I'd been focusing on the fur balls, leaving Jonathan an opening to kill me. And he would have, had it not been for the mystery man.

Folklore says being bitten by a vampire will turn you into one, but that is hogwash. You have to be drained by one or bitten by the same one three times. So don't worry about that.

I skimmed a hand across my hairless scalp and ran everything through my mind, coming to the only conclusion I could. I had to find Dr. Feelgood, and quickly. If everything Piel had told me was true, she was the key to not only the killings, but also to possibly getting Lyric back. Feelgood had the gun with the silver bullets in her office because she knew the fur balls would be coming for her sooner or later. My only concern now was that she'd run. After the freak show I saw last night, I can't say I'd blame her if she did.

Automatically, I grabbed a Winston and my lighter from the nightstand. It was the start of my morning routine, which included pouring a cup of the coffee that, thanks to the automatic timer, would be freshly brewed. I didn't remember getting home last night, or anything that had happened when I got here, so the chances of me having filled the coffeemaker with fresh grounds and water before turning in were slim to none. Such is life.

My unforgiving legs threatened to send me to the floor. I stood for what seemed to be an eternity before moving to the bathroom. Every muscle ached, every joint in my body cried out in protest. My balance was less than reliable.

After peeing and washing my hands, I slowly turned off the water and listened carefully. I lived alone and knew all the sounds in my house. They were my sounds, my creaks and noises, and I knew all of them like old friends. But now there was something else here. Something new. Foreign.

I grew rigid as I listened to more sounds, downstairs, movement.

Slowly, I reached under the sink and pulled out a 9mm filled with ultraviolet bullets. They may be overkill since it was daylight, but I chose to err on the side of caution. A lot of people in town would rather see me dead than alive. And fur balls can move around in the daylight same as you and me, so it wasn't that far-fetched to think the intruders could be Piel and his happy little circus.

I opened the bathroom door and stepped out as slowly and quietly as I could, searching for any signs of the intruder.

Still I heard nothing. I stopped every few feet and listened for the phantom sounds, hoping I was just being paranoid. The pain in my shoulder caused me to wince. My hand instinctively touched it softly, as if that would ease the pain. It didn't.

The rustling sounds came from below once more. It wasn't a bird outside, it wasn't the wind, and it wasn't my imagination. Someone or something was in the house.

I sat the 9mm on the chest of drawers and pulled on a pair of jeans from the bottom drawer. The jeans weren't going to help me in any way, but if I had to chase the bad guys down the street, I'd rather do it in pants. The last thing I wanted was to be running with things dangling everywhere. The events of last night were still fresh in my mind, and I knew what it was like to be on the receiving end of the show.

I opened the top drawer to the chest and pulled out two hunting knives, which had been blessed by priests. They were heavy and solid, with silver blades and ivory handles striped with rubber for better grip. If I was about to party with fur balls, a little silver never hurt. I thought about the sawed-off shotgun under the bed, but decided against it. I was able to maneuver better with the smaller weapons. I picked the 9mm back up and worked my way to the bedroom door, which was open just a crack.

I peeked through the opening. No bodies, no motion, not even a shadow. I pushed the door open just wide enough to slide my body out. The hardwood floors creaked under my weight. The sound seemed to echo through the otherwise silent house.

To the right of my bedroom were stairs leading to the dining room. Moving on the balls of my feet, I peered over the railing. Through the glass of the large grandfather clock, I caught grotesque images of the intruder, but I couldn't tell much about him. Didn't matter. I had the safety off and the two knives neatly tucked away. I was ready to do damage to whatever was down there.

I kept the 9mm in front of me and scanned the hallway, making sure there wasn't a creepy-crawly hiding behind me. Nothing. I wasn't convinced the invader in the dining room was the only one, however. I held my breath as I moved across the short span of hallway, keeping my back against the wall. The open floor plan allowed me to look down into the living area, but also allowed the intruder to look up. If he glanced up here now, I was a sitting duck.

From time to time, I caught more ghostly images of the intruder reflected in the china cabinet. I could see a red shirt and jeans, but the figure passed so quickly that I couldn't make out much more.

My blood ran cold. The intruder could very well be the man that gave me the gun last night and killed Jonathan.

I held my breath as I eased down the steps, hearing the sounds magnified in my head. The only way I would be able to sneak up on the mystery man below was if he was deaf. If he was a fur ball, it didn't matter anyway. They had exceptional hearing, and probably heard me rise up out of the bed.

The intruder had been sitting on the couch, but now he was coming back toward the kitchen, and more importantly, back toward me.

I flattened myself against the wall behind me and waited for a clear shot as the intruder came into the dining room.

Dr. Montgomery screamed, dropping her book. Then her eyes rolled back in her head as she collapsed to the floor. I moved the 9mm to my other hand and tried to grab her with my good arm all in one swoop. Instead of breaking her fall, I fell with her.

"Dr. Montgomery, are you all right?" She was lying on her back like a corpse; her eyes open wide and unblinking. She looked as though invisible hands were choking her.

"Dr. Montgomery, can you hear me?"

Slowly, she turned toward me, her hands finding my arm-the hurt one, of course. I swallowed the pain.

"I'm sorry, Paul. I was trying to be quiet."

"Can you sit up?" She shook her head and pulled on my injured arm to raise her self up. Sometimes you just can't win for losing.

"Can I get you a drink of water or something?"

"No, I'm fine. You just scared about ten years out of me." She smiled at me as she shook her head. The smile turned into a lunatic laugh, loud and obnoxious, cackling. "You should see your face. I don't think I'm the only one that lost ten years."

"I'm not used to people walking around in my house. You're lucky I didn't put a bullet in you."

"I'm sorry, Paul, I didn't mean to make you angry." Her laughter subsided to a giggle. She wiped away the tears that had formed in her eyes.

"Dr. Montgomery, what are you doing in my house?"

"I wanted to make sure you were okay before I left. I had to stitch you up this morning. You lost a lot of blood, and your vital signs were low. "

"What do you mean, okay?"

"You nearly died today. I was truly scared there for a while."

"A little more information."

"This morning, I got a call from someone saying that you were passed out on the sidewalk down on Church Street. They said it was a vampire attack and that if I didn't come down and get you, you might die." The laughter exited her eyes, replaced with distant fear. "God, there was blood everywhere. You were as white as a sheet when I found you."

"Who told you?"

"I don't know. I had never heard the voice before. He just said it was urgent that I get to you before they did."

"You mean the blood-sucking cockroaches."

"Yeah."

"Why would someone call you to come down to Bat Town and pick me up off the street? Weren't you in the hospital yourself? Shouldn't you still be in the hospital?"

"One question at a time!" She replaced the smile in her eyes. I liked it better. It matched. "They were just making a fuss last night. Observation, they call it. I am one of the gang there, you know. They just wanted to make sure I was okay after what had happened. I don't blame them." She held her hands out to me. "Help me up."

"You should still be there." I pulled her back to her feet with my good arm. She came up easily, with a quick bounce. "I'm not the only one that had a bad night."

"Thank you," she said in a pant. "No, I released myself about an hour after you left. The last thing I wanted to do was relive it over and over again, with doctors and nurses hovering over me. After what I saw, I just wanted to get out of there. There was no way I would've been able to get any rest there."

"Should've let your husband look after you. He works there, right?"

"Usually, yes, but he's in Seattle at a convention until next Saturday. I wasn't going to get pampered by anyone, but greenhorn interns anyway. Those college kids don't know which end of the thermometer to use." Her eyes filled with tears. "Oh, God, I shouldn't have said that."

I put my hands on her shoulders. "No, no. It's okay. You didn't mean anything by it."

"Oh, God, that woman was so young. I can't believe that thing did that to her."

"That's why I keep telling you, you can't be too careful around them. You never know what they'll do."

"I guess we all found that out the hard way."

"So, let me see if I can fill in some gaps here. You get a call from someone that says I'm passed out on Church Street. You leave the hospital, pick me up, bring me back here, and take care of my bite."

She wiped the tears from her eyes. "More or less. Whoever your friend is, he saved your life. You owe him."

"I'd thank him if I knew who he was. I'll ask Kansas when I talk to him. He's the only logical answer, although it brings up another series of questions. Like why he didn't take me to the hospital himself, or how he got your number." I glanced at the front door. "How'd you get in?"

"Your keys were in your pocket."

"Told ya you wanted to get in my pants."

She punched me softly. "Stop it."

"What else did the man say? Was he there last night? Someone gave me a gun when the lights went out."

"He said Piel plans to kill you. He thought you'd be safer here than at the hospital, which is why he had me bring you here." A mysterious look filled her eyes as she looked at my shoulder. "Is this from the vampire that killed all those women?"

I shook my head. "I don't think so." I gave her the very abridged version of what had happened. "Now, about the caller, what did he sound like?"

"Deep voice, calm, short."

"You could tell he was short by listening to him?" I asked to make her smile again.

"No, you idiot, he was short with his answers." The smile melted as quick as it came. "You really had a shoot-out with the werewolves?"

To Dr. Montgomery, all shape-shifters were fur balls, no matter what they changed into. Monsters scared her, and that was as far as her interest in them went. I was proud of her for that.

"I guess we're even now, seeing as how I've saved your life," she said, trying desperately to regain the smile, but failing.

"I guess so. Thank you."

"The man said something about you killing Piel or the girl dies. Do you know what he meant?"

"Some of it."

"Are you going to kill Piel?"

"I may not have a choice."

"The man said Dr. Petty has something to do with the girl that attacked us at the hospital. Is that true?"

"Possibly. Seems there are a lot of things that need to be answered. All I know is I have to get to her before the monsters do. You know Dr. Petty?"

"She and my husband work on cases together. She works with them after they leave the hospital."

"All I know right now is that she's got a lot to explain."

She looked at my tattoos, following them up my arm to my chest. "What's this one mean? The angel above your heart."

"It's my guardian angel. She keeps me safe." I smiled at her. "I'm sorry, I'll get a shirt."

"No, no, you're fine. I guess you need to let her know she didn't do so hot last night."

"What do you mean?"

"Well, you nearly died last night."

"But I didn't. See, she did her job. You bailed her out."

"Ever think about giving this lifestyle up and settling down?"

"Why, you available?" I joked.

"No, but I know a lot of single women at the hospital that lose their breath when you walk by."

"Maybe I'll shower next time."

"You're avoiding the question. If I set you up on a date, would you go?"

The smell of coffee reached me, and I turned to follow the scent. "You made coffee."

"Coward."

"Me? Avoiding a question?"

"Yeah. I'll get you a cup. Sit." She pointed to the brown leather couch in my living room behind me as she began to move toward the kitchen.

I felt odd in my own home for the first time. I was grateful for everything the doctor had done for me. She had saved my life and for that I was truly thankful, but I needed to process everything. There were phone calls to make, cigars to be smoked, and monsters to kill. I knew I wouldn't be able to get any of those things accomplished while she was here. I was kicking myself for talking about the coffee. It only gave her an excuse to stay longer. "I can get it myself. The coffee, I mean."

"Absolutely not. You need your rest. Just because you're not dead doesn't mean you don't need to take it easy. That's a nasty bite. It's either me or one of those cute little nurses that has her eyes on you." She gave me a stern look and pointed to the couch.

I held up my hands in defeat and went to the living room.

"You take cream and sugar?" She yelled from the kitchen. I couldn't see her, but I could hear her rummaging through the silverware.

"Just black."

"I have to have mine doctored up before I drink it. No pun intended. The caffeine makes me too jumpy."

"Which means you must've already had about three cups."

Her laughter floated from the kitchen.

I walked over to the bay window in the front of the living room and pulled the white curtain back and looked in the driveway. There she sat. The 'Cuda. Life was back in order for now. I quietly picked up the phone that sat on an end table to my left. I don't know why. Guess it was the thought of being caught by Dr. Montgomery and being yelled at for exuding any energy at all. I needed to call Kansas and tell him what I knew. If he could track down Dr. Feelgood, we might be able to find this Lyric, whoever she really was. It didn't matter to me if she was human or vampire; I just needed to find her before Quinn and his goons did. Lyric was a bigger piece to the puzzle than I was led to believe. The thought had crossed my mind that I was in a no-win situation, set up for defeat by Quinn. He wanted my last few days to be lived in terror. Still, before I succumbed to the poison, he would go down in flames. I wanted to talk to the doorman at the Lunatic Moon again, too. There was something about him that made my skin crawl.

Piel and Dr. Petty might know a lot more than they were willing to tell, but the glaring truth remained, a bloodsucker had killed the women.

I dialed Kansas' cell phone, then called out to Dr. Montgomery while it rang. "You drove the 'Cuda back here?"

"No, it was already here. I'm not sure how it got here."

The phone rang three times before Kansas picked it up. "Detective Kansas."

"Kansas, it's me."

"God, man, I thought you were dead. I've had men sweeping through Bat Town all day. Where in the hell are you?"

"So I take it you're happy I'm alive?"

"Cut the Kumbaya crap. Where are you? I have men out there wasting time looking for you."

"Home. Look, I need to talk to you about last night."

"No shit. I've got another body down here. Same guy."

I felt my world crushing down on me, hitting me in the gut. "What does she look like?" I still had the picture of Lyric in my jacket, wherever that was now.

"Missing her left arm from the elbow down."

"That's not the kind of description I meant." I could tell Kansas was preoccupied; pushing my luck wouldn't get me any closer to the answer I hoped for.

There was silence for a second. "I'm sorry. I guess I should ask if you're okay. I was afraid I got you killed last night."

"Nothing I can't handle."

I told him about the meeting with Piel and all the aftermath.

"Didn't you see the bloodbath at the Lunatic Moon?" I asked.

"No. We had a report that someone saw you down there, but came up empty." He let out a deep sigh. "God, he put her in a dumpster. She can't be more than twenty."

I had lost Lyric, but revenge for her death was running through my mind. The killings had become personal to me now. "I'll meet you downtown. We need to find Dr. Petty, and probably Quinn Rubio. I'll rattle the vamp's cage at the Lunatic Moon and see if anything falls out."

"The hell you will. This is my case, not yours. If there's any interrogation, I'll be the one doing it, got me?" His voice was now stern and agitated. "I'll put as many men on this as I have. I'll talk to the doorman and let you know what I find out, but you will not be anywhere near me, you got that? I need you down here on the double so we can get this cleaned up. You are not to get killed on my watch. If the Council finds out you've been talking to anyone with fangs, they'll put us both under the jail."

I was silent. "Paul, you there?"

I shook my head. Little help it was for Kansas.

"Paul, answer me, damn it. You there?"

"Yeah, I'm here." I reluctantly answered.

"Do you understand? You do anything other than what I'm telling you and I swear to God, I'll kill you myself."

"I got it, but you'll be too late to save her your way."

"Who?"

"Dr. Petty. Either Piel or Quinn Rubio will kill her. Piel, because he has a score to settle with her. The vamps want her dead before she talks."

Dr. Montgomery returned to the room with a steaming cup of coffee in one of my large Indian Motorcycle mugs. It smelled wonderful.

"Paul, you fuck this up and I swear I'll see to it that you spend the rest of your life in prison. We do this my way. We will get in touch with Dr. Petty and see what she has to say. I'm sending someone over to put her into protective custody as we speak. Just keep in mind, your informant is nothing more than a killer himself according to you. Don't put too much stock into his words. And you better not be making all this up because I made you go see her last night. It's not gonna get you out of therapy."

"I'm gonna go." Dr. Montgomery said in a whisper as she put her purse on her arm.

I shook my head and tried to smile as I was being cussed out. I took a drink of the coffee. It burned my upper lip and tongue, but I needed my fix now. I couldn't wait for it to cool down.

I sat the cup of coffee on the end table and hugged the doctor tightly across the shoulders. "Thank you," I whispered back.

She sat a bottle of pain pills on the table and gave me whispered directions of how to take them.

"They're samples, it's okay," she assured me as she walked to the door.

I motioned her to stop until I was finished with Kansas.

"Kansas, did you call Dr. Montgomery last night?"

"Why the hell would I call her, Isaac? The woman's been through hell and back."

Need I go further? I already had my answer.

She looked at me for the answer. I shook my head, and her face dropped. The mystery continued for both of us.

"Look, Paul, I gotta go. Get down here when you can." The phone went dead.

"I can drive you back to the hospital," I said.

"I don't think so. You'll be hopped up on painkillers in a minute and I'm not going to be in a car with the likes of that. Sorry for eavesdropping, but I heard what was said. Stay home. You need your rest. Let someone else chase the monsters tonight."

"I wish I could tell you I would, but it'd be a lie." I walked her to her car.

She hugged me again. "Please take care of yourself, Paul. This was more serious than you seem to believe." She said looking at the bandage on my shoulder.

"Oh, I believe it. But monsters don't take the night off. Neither can I."

CHAPTER SIXTEEN

I called Kansas back and got directions. She had been found by two sanitation workers in a dumpster behind a row of industrial warehouses on the corner of Division and Grove Park, just down from Church. Grove Park was more of a service road than an actual street, with little or no traffic after business hours, making disposal of the body easy. A large chain-link fence lined the right-hand side of the street. It was the part of town that made you feel uneasy. Go any further down, and things got dangerous quickly.

I had changed into a black UCF T-shirt, black jeans, biker boots, and a studded belt. I wore my 9mm in a shoulder holster; Kansas still had my Magnum and other supplies in the Explorer. In the backseat of the 'Cuda, I had an extra set of clothes that I could change into later if the skies opened up. Well, that's what I told myself, anyway. It sounded better than the truth. Truth was, I usually brought extra clothes because I had a knack for getting blood on the original ones, sometimes my blood, sometimes somebody else's. Fringe benefits, gotta love 'em.

I parked next to the other familiar sets of wheels, now taped off as a crime scene parking area. Several police cars surrounded the scene, along with the private ones I knew like the back of my hand. Price smiled and waved as he began to move toward my car.

He appeared to be more of a huggable bear than a grizzly one. His gray eyes looked at me through the top of his glasses, perched as always on the edge of his nose. Sweat beads glistened on the bare skin atop his head, which was framed by a horseshoe of graying hair. His light blue button-up shirt was damp with sweat under each arm and down the back to the waist of his dark blue pants. Summer in Florida and Detective Price didn't make good bedfellows. He breathed hard as he walked to my window. He was smiling even in the middle of death. Maybe he was jaded. Maybe it simply helped keep the demons away at night. In either case, I smiled back. It took no effort to do so. I liked Price.

"Paul!" His big voice echoed. "You cost me twenty bucks, you loser." He leaned against the door of the 'Cuda.

"How did I lose you money this time?" I sat there, hoping he would see I was trapped in the car as long as he leaned against the door.

"I bet Kansas twenty that you'd show up on the Indian."

"Have you seen the sky lately, Price?" The heat inside the car baked me like a potato. Even with the threat of rain, it was hot. "Not to mention the fact that my shoulder hurts so bad, holding up a vintage motorcycle would be hell."

"I know, but I still didn't think you could resist. My dad had one just like the one you put together. Wrecked it. Shame."

He pushed his glasses back up his nose. Sweat trickled down the side of his face. "Thought you couldn't wait to get on it. You know, wind in your hair. I thought that was what you were all about." He grinned. "You play a good game, Paul, dressing all in black, tattoos all over your arms and everything, but secretly you're nothing but a wimp sitting around listening to Judy Garland records."

"Truth is, Price, I knew if I brought it, you'd crash it and I'd have to kick your butt. You wouldn't want Orlando's finest seeing you get your butt kicked by a man that listens to Judy Garland records, would you?"

He laughed. "Tell me you don't really listen to her records."

"No, I'm a jazz man myself. Jaco Pastorious is a god."

Price laughed and leaned away from the door. I seized the opportunity and opened the door enough that it made him automatically step back.

"My anniversary is next week. Can I borrow it to take the lady out on the town?"

"She won't ride in a car with you. How do you think you'll get her on a motorcycle?"

I got out of the car and we automatically began walking toward the mass of officers, detectives, and investigators.

"Heard you had a bad night."

"Apparently not as bad a night as our victim. My stomach is already threatening to spill the hamburger I ate on the way."

"You ate before this?"

"My fault. I know better. I don't care how many times I see this stuff I always run the risk of tossing my cookies. Just when you say you've seen it all, something a little more twisted and cruel slaps your face."

"Seriously, you okay?"

"I will be. I'm better than the cockroach that bit me."

Price chuckled nervously. "This guy's real sick, Paul. I mean real sick."

"What can you tell me about this before I have to see it myself?" I lit a cigar and allowed my lungs to fill with aromatic smoke.

"Oh, you don't even want to know. She has been whipped, cut a thousand times, and her arm..." he trailed off.

"I see the death squad's waiting for me to examine the body and put on the show."

I ducked under the yellow tape and shook my head at the officers standing on the other side. Guard dogs, I call them-they were there to keep out the press and onlookers, while we tried to make heads or tails of the mess inside the tape.

I could see the familiar people ahead of me looking over the body, collecting evidence and taking pictures. I was late getting to the scene; most were done with their work and were simply waiting on me to cut off the head. They didn't have to hang around, but they wanted to see it. They found it entertaining, I guess.

I stopped as I glimpsed the body through the jungle of legs in front of me. Her short purple dress was torn and dirty, as though she had been there longer than she truly had. I still wasn't close enough to tell much about her, but my heart wasn't in it. I already knew this one, which made it a little more personal.

Kansas was down on one knee, looking at something on the body, moving her clothing with his pen. He saw me and rose. "Sorry to bring you down here like this. I know you must be hurting pretty bad, but I wanted you to see. I wanted to know if it was your girl."

I pulled photograph I had of Lyric from my pocket. I had to be sure. "It's okay. I need to see this." I took a last drag from the cigar, and then sat it on the sidewalk away from the crime scene. I didn't want to take a chance of blowing ashes across the body. Seemed disrespectful. My mouth felt like cotton. My heart raced. What I was about to see could seal my fate.

The police officers surrounding the body gave me plenty of room. I got the full effect of the damage that had been done. Her skin was milky white, lips purple, her makeup mixed with grime and debris from the dumpster which had been her final resting place. I know I talk a tough game, but I almost cried as I looked at her. She still looked as though I could shake her hard enough to wake her. But she was gone. I understood how families could steal the corpse and let it rise in their homes.

I looked at her face, then at the picture. I tried to keep my hands from shaking.

"Is it her?" Kansas asked, walking toward me. I could tell he expected the answer to be yes. We both did.

"No."

"You don't look very happy about it." Price said.

"I'm relieved it's not Lyric. But now I'm worried as well. I wanted to find her at first simply to save myself. But now... She's still out there, possibly chained, being tortured. If what Piel told me is true, I'm no longer trying to save a daisy-pusher's life. I think that's what makes the difference. Knowing she's human makes it more personal for me. No matter how twisted a person becomes down here, they're still human. I know that shouldn't make a difference, but it does. Forget my own life. I want the monster that's doing this no matter what. I want to see this blood-sucking cockroach executed before my time runs out."

"Paul, I need you to look at the wound and tell me what I don't already know," Kansas said as he bent down over the body.

"This one put up a fight," I said.

"Why do you say that?" Price asked as he squatted next to me.

"Found a lot of skin under her fingernails-the ones that are left. This one didn't go as quietly as the others."

"Now all we need to do is find a vampire with scratches on his face and neck." This from Price.

"Doesn't work that way with cockroaches," I added. Price was old school, thought all monsters were like humans in terms of gathering evidence. He'd never quite adapted to the underworld forensics.

"What do you mean?"

"Cockroaches have a quick regenerative attribute. They are able to heal almost instantly from something as superficial as a scratch. He probably has no signs of the struggle by now."

Kansas pushed her head to the side, though I could have seen the wound whether Kansas turned the body over or not. The entire side of her throat had been ripped out.

"He made it personal. Anger more than feeding," I said as I examined the wound. "He did this for the thrill. Muscles ripped apart, jutting out of the wound. Her neck bone's broken in half. Only the flesh is keeping the head from rolling away. The monster that did this has a real talent for torturing."

"What else can you tell me?" Kansas asked.

"Our cockroach couldn't put this one under his spell like the others. She wasn't in a trance when she died. That's why this one seems more violent than the others." I looked at the wound closer now, hoping to put more clues together. "There's a lot a body can tell me about my vampire, I just have to find the things it has to say."

"In other words, he wasn't able to get her to look into his eyes," Kansas said.

"Right. I don't know how she did it, but unfortunately it caused her more pain in the long run. Normally a blood-sucker will put you in a trance to keep you docile while he feeds on you. It keeps the victim from fighting and thrashing. That didn't happen here."

"She doesn't have the TS tattoo like Sheri and the others," Kansas added.

"So that was the name of the girl we found the other night?"

"Yeah, Sheri Charlesworth."

"He's branching out, possibly. Maybe mistaken identity. Perhaps it was on the missing arm. Doesn't mean we aren't looking for the same guy." We stood again.

"One of the guys that found her, found a phone number in her purse. It's her roommate's. She's over there being questioned," Price said.

"So she had a purse?" I asked. "Usually a woman's purse is a treasure chest of information."

"Well, that's just it. The purse is there, but there's no wallet or general information. Nothin' in it but lipstick, Certs, and a hairbrush."

"Are you sure the men that found her didn't take the wallet or discard it somewhere?"

"We're looking into all that," Price chimed in.

"We got lucky, though. Seems her roommate got a new cell phone number yesterday. It was the number the guys found on the piece of paper. Her ex-boyfriend wasn't taking the breakup so well." Kansas said, as he looked back at a young woman in the back of one of the Orange County Sheriff's cruisers, talking with Jane Rook, another officer on the scene.

"You called the boyfriend, right?"

"Yeah, we have an officer tracking him down," Kansas replied.

Detective Price and I nodded. There was a moment of awkward silence.

"See if we are making any progress on this," Kansas said to one of the officers nearby nodding to Jane and the girl in the cruiser. The officer moved toward the car.

"So, safe to say this was a vampire attack?" Price asked slowly, his glasses moving back down his nose.

"Yeah," I huffed. "Any luck in finding our good doctor?" I said to Kansas, looking at the girl.

"We have her in custody at the station around the corner. She's giving a statement as we speak. You need to be there, too, since you were a witness as well. I'll see what she can tell us about the girls. If they were her patients, we should be able to build a case. But don't get your hopes up. Still doesn't make her guilty even if they all were her patients. It doesn't prove anything," Kansas warned. His face hardened, and a large index finger poked me in the chest. "We need to finish up here first. I don't want a repeat of last night. We do this, and we do this now, no matter what."

"Where's our good buddy Dieter? I swear he runs late some-times just to keep us from getting on with the inevitable."

"We left a message with the Vampire Council that we needed a representative down here as soon as the sun was gone. Should see his ugly ass any time now." Kansas remarked.

"I want to get this over with. Stake the girl, cut her head off, take out the heart and get out of here. I don't have time to play the waiting game."

"I don't think any of us are here because we want to be," Kansas snapped back.

"What about the ticket-taker at the Lunatic Moon? You got someone going down there, don't you? Even though they are probably gone by now, he had scratches on his face last night. We can still get some DNA to prove one way or the other."

"Workin' on it. We'll be talking to everyone down there, believe me. If what you tell me is true, we may be closing that little shop of horrors for good," Kansas said

The officer returned from the cruiser, and Price met him halfway.

"You're gonna need my help with backup down there. Don't send just anyone. They'll come back in a body bag. Piel is far more powerful and dangerous than anything I have ever seen around here." I stepped back from the body. I had seen enough. Other examiners were moving past me to do their dirty deeds.

"Has anyone seen Dieter?" Kansas asked, impatience in his voice. It was good to see Dieter was aggravating more than just me tonight.

Price began to walk back to us, patting the officer on the back and smiling. Not a "Hey, I have a great joke" kind of smile, but a "I got something" smile. I hoped I was right, anyway.

He pushed the glasses back up his nose again. The sweat stains were growing by the minute. "If we don't get this man to air conditioning soon, he will drown in his own fluids," I said quietly to Kansas.

"Gentlemen, got a name," Price said as he slapped a piece of paper against his hand. "Anna Martinez."

"Great." I was already thinking about the connection with Feelgood and started to open my mouth.

"I know, Paul. We'll check," Kansas said before I could ask.

"Talked to the roommate. Seems she made a missing person report on our Anna this morning." Price looked at me. "And there's more."

I didn't have to ask my question again. I was on a roll.

"I know why the vampire couldn't put her under."

I wasn't even going to try this time.

"She was blind."

"Blind?" I blurted out. "That opens up another set of questions."

"Yeah, seems she was on, and I hate to use this term, a blind date with a vampire she met on some online dating service for women that want to meet and date vampires," Price added.

"So when she didn't show up at the apartment the next morning, the roommate contacted the police."

"Yeah." Price shook his head, his hands on his hips.

"Did the roommate get a description of the dream date?" Kansas asked, the last two words sprinkled with darkness.

"Better than that. Seems the two girls talked about the man before the date took place. Our vic told the roommate some things we might be able to use."

"Can we talk to her?" I asked.

"Yeah, come on. We got her statement. You can go over it with her." Price said. He turned and walked back to the cruiser.

Officer Rook saw us coming and began escorting the young woman to us. The girl's face was red from crying, tears still streaming. She held her arms close to her body, as if trying to make herself thin enough to disappear. She was Goth to the max. Bright pink hair. Dark eyes, thickly rimmed with mascara that coursed down her cheeks. Black lipstick. Enough facial jewelry to start her own shop. A dog collar with silver spikes encircled her neck. She wore black and white horizontal-striped shirt under a leather vest with purple embroidered roses, black jeans, and a black leather belt with silver studs. Knee-high black suede boots with stiletto heels, fringed at the top, finished off the look.

"This should be interesting," I said under my breath.

"Ms. Tina Howard, this is Detective Price, Detective Kansas, and Mr. Paul Isaac. They need to ask you a few questions," Officer Rook said, pointing us out to Goth girl.

She nodded. Her eyes showed pain, and fear. She was shivering, but I don't think it was because she was cold; it was nearly eighty degrees. She looked at the ground in front of her feet, not making eye contact.

"Ms. Howard, thank you for your time. On behalf of all of us, we are deeply sorry about all this," Kansas said to her. It was odd to hear Kansas being polite and caring. Then again, maybe it was just me, he was nasty too. I doubted it though.

Kansas took all the usual information again. Things like address, phone numbers.

"You and Anna were roommates, is that correct?" I asked her.

"Yeah."

"How long have you been roommates?"

"I just moved down here from New Jersey about two months ago. Anna had placed an ad. I answered it." She fidgeted nervously.

"So about two months," I repeated back to her.

"I guess so."

"You told Officer Rook that Ms. Martinez was out on a date last night and never came back this morning."

"Yeah. He was from an online dating service."

"And what was the website called?"

"Undeadinbed.com."

"Undead in Bed?" Price chimed in. "Jesus, gotta love technology."

"And how do you know this?" Kansas continued.

"I told her about it. Being blind, she was having trouble meeting guys. The site has different fetishes. I helped her upload her picture and profile. She had a computer that was made for a blind person. Voice command or something like that. I just showed her how to get her information on the site." For the first time she looked up, meeting Kansas' eyes.

"You mentioned they cater to fetishes. What do you mean?" Kansas continued.

"It's a website for women who want to meet and date vampires. Some of them are into strange things, like girls that are deaf or blind. Things like that."

"Have you used the site yourself?" I asked her.

"Yeah. I mean like, not looking for someone that was, like, weird. Just mainstream vampires and stuff. Some of them are really hot," she said with a nervous laugh that melted away as quick as it had come.

"Is that how you met the boyfriend that is giving you trouble?" Price asked.

"No."

"Are all the men on the site vampires?" Kansas asked.

"Yeah, I think so."

"So she met someone on the site."

"Yeah. She was, like, really excited about it. They talked on the phone for hours, laughing. It all seemed so harmless. She was happy, met a hot guy and all. I was, like, happy for her."

"How could you go to those sites? They are dangerous, sweetheart," Price said, the father in him coming out. "You could end up like this, too."

She stared at Price, looking even more like a scared little girl.

"So you and Anna were good friends?" Kansas asked.

"I guess so. I mean, we hung out from time to time. Mostly I felt sorry for her, though."

"But you two got along."

"Yeah. I thought she was sweet."

"And your boyfriend, did he like her?"

"Like, was he hot for her or something?"

I heard Price snicker under his breath. I punched him lightly with my elbow and tried to keep from smiling myself.

"No, did Ms. Martinez and your boyfriend get along. Did he have a reason to get violent with her, do this kind of thing?"

"Anna didn't like him. Said he tried to control me too much. But, like, never said anything to his face. She was scared of him, didn't want him around. She told her boyfriend about it, and he told Anna he would talk to him, help him come to an understanding."

"You mean beat him up?" I asked.

"Maybe. I don't know. I was hoping so, in a way, sort of." Another nervous smile emerged and faded, like a flash of lightning.

"What was Ms. Martinez's boyfriend's name?" It was a voice I recognized, and it wasn't Kansas. "Dieter Procnow is on the scene. Let me count the ways I'm overjoyed. So good of you to show up." He had arrived out of thin air. One minute, empty space, and the next, instant sunshine crispy, just add water.

"Please, do not be petty at a time like this, Paul. Allow the young woman to answer the question. Your insults will get us nowhere."

"Nigel is all I know."

"Ahh. See there, gentlemen? All you needed to do was be polite and patient."

"You know him?" Price asked.

"Just because he's a vampire doesn't mean I know him, Detective." Dieter said in a low, rough voice. He slowly turned his gaze away from Tina to me. "I would have guessed you would be behind bars by now, if not dead."

"I think Price meant to say you might know him because he was a sleaze ball." I couldn't help myself. "And after our little get-together the other night, trust me-someone's gonna die."

"Things are going well, I hope." To Tina, "What else can you tell us about Ms. Martinez's date?"

"He works at the Lunatic Moon part-time." Tina added. "He's got, like, some kind of accent or something. Anna thought it was hot."

"What did you say?" It just came out before I could stop it.

"Anna thought he talked hot. Said she was going to let him fuck her that night."

I forgot I was talking to a girl barely twenty years old. "If I hear the words 'like' or 'hot' one more time, I think my head is going to explode," I muttered to Price. I shook my head, trying to not look like she had given me a wrong answer. "No, I mean where he worked. You say he works at the Lunatic Moon?" I looked over to Kansas, who nodded slightly.

"Yeah, he wanted to be a stripper there one day. He was trying to get his foot in the door."

"Was Anna seeing a doctor for anything?" I asked.

"Not that I know of," she answered.

"Are you sure? No shrink or nothin'?"

"You mean was she, like, crazy or something? No, she was fine. Can I go now?"

"I'll take care of this. You and Dieter go do what you have to do," Kansas said to me. "Your bag is still in the Explorer if you need something." He stopped me again. "Wait till she's gone, though. I don't want her to see it."

I shook my head to let Kansas know I heard him. "One more thing. Did you see the guy Anna was dating, Ms. Howard?"

"Just when he came to the door. We didn't invite him in. Our rule when dating vampires. So in case they turn out to be creeps, they can't come in and kill us."

"You didn't invite him in because you thought a vampire couldn't come inside unless invited?" Kansas asked.

"Yeah."

"You know that's just a myth, don't you?" I asked.

She grew quiet. "No."

"Yeah, it is. They can come in anytime they want. Anyway, back to Anna's date. Did he have any tattoos that you could see?"

"He had a couple. I don't know." Confusion crept into her voice.

"Can you describe any of them?" Price asked.

Her eyes lit up. "Yeah, there was one that was cool as hell. It was on his wrist. It was of two letters, T and S, something like that, and a rose," She pointed to its location on her own arm. "The rose had, like, this barbed-wire thing where the stick should be." It was the most animated she'd been all night.

"Not the greatest of descriptions, but it's good enough for what we need. Our friend Nigel has a tattoo in the same place as the man at the Lunatic Moon. Coincidence? I don't think so," I whispered to Kansas.

"Of a stick?" Kansas joked.

"I don't find it funny."

"Something I am missing?" Dieter added.

"Your head, if I get the chance." I answered.

Kansas, Price, and Rook finished up with Tina and hurried her away. The last thing any of us wanted to do was cut off her room-mate's head while she was close by. It was the law, anyway. No one can witness a staking without credentials. Dieter and I went back to the body, and he reluctantly agreed it was a vampire attack.

"Tell Maximilian I know about Lyric," I told Dieter. "Tell him I'm coming to kill him."

He looked at me with puzzled, dead eyes. "Whatever do you mean?" He tried to remain calm, but I could tell he was nervous. I wasn't sure if even he knew why at this point.

"Lyric isn't Maximilian's daughter, is she?"

He smiled. "If you do not find her in time, your fate remains the same. I would not waste time on whose seed she is."

I shoved my 9mm in his chest. "If I die, you'll go with me, don't forget that. I'll take you all with me."

"I am sure you will try. We will see who is still alive and who is dead by the time the sun rises in the morning." His voice had texture to it, sharp and cutting, dangerous and dark. He smiled.

"How's Virgil these days?" I asked, knowing he had to know he was dead by now.

He hesitated for a few seconds. "Watch yourself, Avenger. Some of us are not willing to allow you the limited time you have."

"Is that a threat, Dieter?"

He shrugged. "Your episode with the good doctor last night has many in the district worried. It seems as though the guilty are growing scared enough to take matters into their own hands."

"What's that supposed to mean?"

"Simply put, my friend, whether you find Lyric or not, your life may still come to an end. Some think your visit to Dr. Petty's was for more than your own benefit. Possibly that you're getting too close to a well-kept secret."

"If you know anything about these killings, and you don't say anything, you know we can stake you right beside the killer."

"Rumors. That is all I have heard. Nothing more than street gossip. If I knew a way to stop these killings, I would. They are becoming quite boring and sloppy."

I walked away and got my bags before I did anything I'd regret. I'd stake poor Anna, cut out her heart, cut off her head, but I'd be fantasizing about doing it to Dieter. I only hope fantasies come true.

CHAPTER SEVENTEEN

D r. Lydia Petty was sitting at a desk in the Orlando Police Department. She wore a light blue sundress, her hair neatly pulled back with a large bow in matching blue with white dots. Her glasses magnified her eyes, the eyes of a woman who was tired and just wanted to go home. Her skin absent of makeup, looked pale. The last twenty-four hours had taken a toll on her.

Her eyes locked on me as I approached. I couldn't get a good feel as to whether she was glad to see me or waiting to slap me. Then again, I get that a lot more than I'd like to admit. She was rigid and motionless, like a mannequin.

"Ms. Petty, thank you for waiting. Can I get you a cup of coffee or something?" Kansas asked as we approached.

"It's Dr. Petty, Detective."

"I apologize, Doctor. Can I get you...?"

"Am I under arrest for something?" she interrupted.

Kansas took a deep breath and looked at me. "You remember Mr. Isaac."

"I do, Detective. You aren't prone to forgetting patients who push you out a second-floor window."

"I think it was better than the alternative. You never told me that you had a beef with the fur balls. Maybe you should put that in your little brochure next time."

"Again, am I under arrest?"

"No ma'am, you are not under arrest. I just needed to ask you some questions about some of your patients."

"Such as?"

"We just came from another murder scene. I don't know if you are aware of it or not, but there have been a series of murders along Church Street over the last few weeks. Human prostitutes and strippers have been attacked and killed by a vampire."

"I'm aware. I can read, Detective."

"Well, Dr. Petty, we have reason to believe that the victims have something in common. Something you can help us with," Kansas stated.

"What could that possibly be?"

"Were they all your patients?"

"Doctor-patient confidentiality, Detective. You know better than that." She looked over to me. "Why is he here?"

"He's on the case with me," Kansas said. Another officer brought over cups of coffee for each of us. Kansas and I grabbed ours quickly. Feelgood pushed hers away as if it were something found on the bottom of her shoe.

"Last night, you told me that Mr. Isaac was a disturbance to the case and that I needed to see him right away. Tonight, he's back on the case. I know I'm good at what I do, but I don't think one night of therapy did that much good."

"He's the best at what he does."

"I'm sure he is. I've heard that from a lot of his victims. The ones that are still alive, anyway."

"I think things would've gone a lot better if I didn't have to shoot my way out of therapy in the first place," I added.

"You think I called the wolves there?"

"No, but a simple favor wouldn't hurt. I saved your behind last night. If it wasn't for me, you'd be dog chow right now."

"The girl we just found was an Anna Martinez. Was she one of your patients?" Kansas interrupted.

"I've told you, doctor-patient confidentiality. I can't respond to that even if I wanted to." She added, "I'll wait until my attorney gets here to answer any more questions. "

"I can get a court order if I need to," Kansas shot back.

"Do what you have to do, Detective."

"You mean like this?" Price said, walking up behind her. I hadn't seen him approach; he simply appeared as if by magic. His stout body towered over her, left hand on his hip, right hand holding out a stack of papers.

"What's this?" The smirk evaporated.

"My sister is married to Judge Henley," Price said. "I made a few calls down to the courthouse and got a search warrant for your office and a subpoena to make you talk." He tossed the paperwork on the desk of Detective Kansas. "I'm getting rather tired of pulling young girls out of dumpsters, girls who fell victim to a serial-killing vampire. Sounds like this one should be right down your alley. A real head case."

Dr. Feelgood looked over at me, then to Kansas, and finally at Detective Price. "I think I'll wait for my lawyer before I answer any questions," she repeated.

The smell of honeysuckle filled my nostrils. A sweetness only found in wet dreams. I could feel her presence before I turned around. Feelgood's lawyer had arrived, and she was someone that I knew personally.

"Sorry I'm late, Lydia." She looked to Price and extended her hand. "Detective, I'm Veronica Powers, Dr. Petty's attorney."

Veronica Powers was sophisticated and elegant. The long, flowing blond hair that I had remembered was now in a tight bun in the back of her head. She was all business tonight. Her makeup was polished, but understated. The entire office stopped to watch her pass, breathing in her beauty, watching her cat-like walk, the rhythmic sway of her hips. It was still hard to picture someone this beautiful feeding off of a human body. It was all I could do not to stake her where she was. She was one of the blood-sucking cockroaches that had poisoned me.

"Detective?" she said to Kansas as she held out her hand. It was as if I was invisible.

Kansas stood and shook her hand like a schoolboy. A chair appeared from nowhere as the office scrambled to get close to her. She sank gracefully into the chair, looked over at Feelgood and smiled. Someone else brought her a soda, which she waved off. It was at this point I realized most of the officers had no idea she was a vampire. Powers, on the other hand, was enjoying the attention.

"Ms. Powers, I'm Detective Kansas."

"I almost expected you to kiss her hand. Thank God you saved what little dignity you had," I whispered to him.

"This is Paul Isaac, vampire expert," Kansas concluded.

"Vampire expert?" She snorted. "All right, I'll go along with it for now."

She looked over to me. Her eyes were as cold as they were the first time I saw her, a true ice princess. Being as beautiful as she was, I guess you could get away with a little attitude. Where Angie had been just flat-out screaming with heat and lust, Veronica Powers was a well-educated, formal, and timeless beauty.

"I will be representing Dr. Petty this evening. Any questions you have will go through me. Is this understood?"

"Fine," Kansas said.

"Is my client being charged with any crime?"

"No. We need to ask her a few questions about an unrelated matter," Kansas answered.

"An unrelated matter?" Her voice was soft yet firm, like a cobra, ready to strike at any given moment. "I think she's been through enough tonight."

"I'm sure she has, and we apologize for the inconvenience." Price added.

"Do you have the paperwork in place for Dr. Petty to answer your questions?"

Price pointed to the paperwork on the desk.

"What do you want to know, Detective?" Powers asked.

Kansas sipped his coffee. "I'm sure you know about the murders that have occurred in the vampire district over the past few weeks."

"I'm aware."

"All the victims have something in common. We hope Dr. Petty can help us with it."

"They are all patients of my client."

"Yes. We were hoping to ask her a few questions about the girls in hopes that we can get closer to finding the killer. I assure you, your client isn't under suspicion in any way. But we can't ignore the fact that there is a common link. It is quite possible that the killer is also a patient of hers, or had direct contact with them somehow. We just need to know if she could shed any light as to why they were patients."

"You can ask." She looked at the papers on the table, but never touched them.

"Thank you," Kansas said. To Dr. Feelgood, "Doctor, the four girls that we've found over the past few weeks, were they indeed your patients?"

"Yes."

"Why were they seeing you?" Kansas asked.

Feelgood shifted in her seat. "They all had issues with hurting and cutting themselves. They were having thoughts of suicide."

"Any reason why?"

"They had an illness that they couldn't keep under control."

"Which was?"

"Apotemnophilia."

"Come again?" Price asked.

"They desired amputation. They felt it would make them whole. Arms and legs that were otherwise in perfect working order. They actually thought having the limbs removed made them more desirable."

I felt my skin crawl. The images flooded before I could stop them.

"So let me get this straight," Price said, walking around the two women. "You are telling me all our victims suffered from this..."

"Apotemnophilia," Feelgood answered.

"Yeah, that. They wanted to have a leg or an arm cut off, just because?"

"Correct."

"Why?" Kansas asked.

"No one really knows. Some have histories of sexual abuse, drug abuse, or other disorders such as depression, but those were only by-products. In some cases, it was what caused the abuse. A way to escape. Others had this desire since they were very young. Cutting off the tip of a finger or toe, moving to a whole finger or toe. Sometimes escalating to other areas."

"How could they do this?" Price asked.

"It's an imbalance in the brain. They feel as though they are not complete until the amputation. Being whole was the imperfection. One of the patients, Carmella Brown, your first victim, had actually cut her toes off before coming to me. She had been in the hospital several times for amputation. Some people have sexual desires to be with amputees."

"Why didn't you tell us this when you saw the pattern?" I asked.

"You don't have to answer that," Veronica snapped.

"Ms. Powers, there are woman dying out there. Your client is feeding them to a serial killer by not reporting the patterns she was seeing."

"Excuse me?" the maggot magnet shouted.

"She saw the pattern, and she did nothing. I can't stand it anymore. These girls had a sickness that even I can't explain, but that doesn't mean they should have been murdered for it," I said.

"Mr. Isaac, I did everything I could to help them. They came to me with suicidal tendencies. I was trying to help them with the disease. Most of them had overdosed or thought of other ways to end it all before they cut their appendages off. One of the girls had a rubber band around her finger for two days, trying to cut off the circulation. Can you imagine how painful that had to be? I got them the help they needed. Through medication and therapy, they were getting better. I don't appreciate you accusing me of having anything to do with their deaths. They had an illness, true, but I wasn't going to betray their trust." She slammed her fist on the desk as she spoke.

"But you have a history of betraying trust, don't you?" I said coldly.

"What is that supposed to mean?"

"I'm not sure what crock you told the police about the attack at your office, but I know the truth."

"And what would that be, Mr. Isaac?"

"Ever heard of a man named Piel?"

"Can't say that I have."

"Really? He happens to have been behind the massacre at your office. Piel told me about how he was betrayed by you."

"Piel is a liar and a killer. He's the one you should be questioning here, not me. I don't appreciate your accusations. I hope to God you've found him and locked him away."

"Thought you never heard of him."

She shook with anger, her pale skin now mottled red.

"Dr. Petty, please excuse him. He doesn't know when to shut his mouth." Kansas glared at me.

"Well, at least that we can agree on," Feelgood added.

"So it's possible that our killer either didn't mutilate the bodies, or only assisted in it," Kansas said to Feelgood.

"Yes."

Price asked, "And they want this because of sexual gratification?"

"Sometimes. Not always."

"And can I assume that there are partners of these people out there that are turned on by the act? Is that what I understood you to say earlier?"

"Yes, there's a demographic of men that find amputees a real turn-on. They seek them out. Whoever killed those girls probably fits that mold."

"The latest girl we found was an Anna Martinez. Was she one of your patients?" Kansas asked.

"No, I've never heard of her. Now, if you don't mind, I'd like to go home," Feelgood answered.

"We won't keep you here any longer than necessary, I promise," Price said.

"She's answered your questions. Now find the killer," Powers interrupted.

"Not all of them," I answered.

"Thank you, gentlemen, I think that will be all," Powers ignored me as she stood, seeming to lift Feelgood up with her.

Price chimed in again. "Please, I'm a father. These could easily have been my daughters. I don't want this bastard to kill anyone else, Dr. Petty. I'm not accusing you of any wrongdoing, but for the sake of the other women out there, please tell me if there are any other patients of yours with this disorder. Could one of your patients be behind all this? Anyone that you know of that gets their rocks off on amputees?"

She looked over to the bloodsucker for direction. Powers reluctantly agreed. "One more question and that is it. If my client is not under arrest, then you have no reason to hold us here."

"I can think of only one," Feelgood answered.

"Who?" all three of us asked at the same time.

"Evan Falkner. He's been a vampire since the fifties."

"Isn't it a bit odd that there was only one man in the support group?" I asked.

"Not really. It's just the way it worked out among my patients."

"What can you tell us about Evan?" I asked.

"He is obsessed with this type of woman. He likes desires of torture, cutting, binding, all of that. He has a history of violence that we are controlling with medications."

"What kind of history?" Price asked.

"As a child, he used to amputate tails and legs off of animals, dogs and cats mostly. At the age of fifteen, he amputated his sister's pinky finger to see if she could handle the pain. Her pain turned him on. He later raped and killed her. Spent some time in prison. Friends brought him to see me about a year ago. He was trying to pay someone to cut his own legs off."

"Who was the someone that was going to do the amputation?" I asked.

"He wouldn't say. I was trying to find out when all this happened."

"But I thought vampires could rejuvenate body parts or other wounds. Wouldn't the amputated limbs just grow back?" Price asked.

"Normally yes, but if the wound is sealed with excessive heat or bound with silver, it could stop the rejuvenating process," Veronica Powers answered. "Vampires with the condition have cut their appendages off just for the sexual pleasure it gave at the moment, let the appendage grow back, then do repeat the process. An advantage of being a vampire, I guess."

"You call that an advantage? Sorry, I'm appalled at that logic." I said.

"Where can we find Mr. Falkner?" Price asked, looking at me over the top of his glasses.

"I have his information at my office in the records, but he works at the..."

"You'll need paperwork for that." Veronica Powers interrupted.

Price tapped on the paper on the desk. "Got it." He took in a deep breath. "Ms. Powers, we need to talk to this man."

"He just got a job at The Coffin. Seems keeping a job is not his forte. He has a reputation for being a womanizer."

"Were all these people with the condition in a support group, or did you meet with them as individuals?" Kansas asked.

"Just as a group. They met on Thursday nights. They all had been Baker-Acted for suicidal tendencies. All except Evan. I was there for them when they got out of the hospital. I was trying to form a solid support group."

"Dr. Petty, each of our victims, with the exception of the last one, had a tattoo on their body. Do you know about a tattoo they all had in common?" Price asked.

Feelgood looked at the lawyer before answering.

"Yeah, I know what it means." She began to fidget again. "It's part of a nomadic underground club that meets in undisclosed places. It changes each time they meet. It's called Tortured Skin. It's a club that caters to the painful side of sexuality. Each of the women was involved with it. A few were dominatrices. Others were submissive. It was a group that met where no one would judge them for things thought to be taboo or alternative."

"Come again?" Price's eyes showed disgust.

"They mix pleasure with pain, everything from bondage to whatever. They are a select group of individuals that play with sex and death just for the thrill of it. Not long ago, they burned and tortured a girl. She nearly died. But believe it or not, it was her sexual fantasy."

"Does she have this same problem with..." Price began.

"Apotemnophilia?" Dr. Feelgood finished.

"Yeah, that."

"She has her own issues with drugs, sex, and everything else. She's not a patient of mine, but I know she was Baker-Acted herself once. She was treated for an overdose by Dr. Montgomery."

"From the morgue?" I asked.

"No, her husband, George. She overdosed at one of the parties. You see, Tortured Skin is more of a cult. I don't think she overdosed. It's more likely she was poisoned."

"And these are willing participants?" Price asked.

"Yes and no. Seems the humans can't help but go back again and again. The only way out seems to be death. Painful addictions they can't control, even if they know it will kill them eventually."

"Who makes up this group?" I asked Feelgood.

"Humans, vampires, shape-shifters."

"How can we find them?"

"They are extremely secretive. They meet in abandoned warehouses and office buildings throughout the city. They are very elusive."

"Do you know of anyone we can talk to about finding the next party?" I asked.

"Evan is a member."

Kansas stood. "Thank you for your time, Dr. Petty, Ms. Powers. We will bring the search warrant with us to get the address of Mr. Falkner. We are going to need the names and addresses of everyone in that support group."

"Do you really think Evan's a killer?" Feelgood asked.

"I think it might be a good idea that I talk to him and see. Our killer so far matches everything you've described, but we can't say for sure. In the meantime, I want to place you in protective custody."

Feelgood started to speak, but was cut off by Kansas' raised hand. "I know, I know. You might not want it, but let's look at the facts here. Someone wanted you dead last night, and you are a key in the murders. Whoever is doing this might see you as a risk. Especially if they knew you were here talking to us," Kansas said. "Until we have Piel under arrest, and talk to Evan Falkner, I insist."

"Detective..." she started again.

"If for nothing else, Dr. Petty, do it for me."

"I'll be fine, Detective. Piel will not be coming for me. Please respect my request."

"Aren't you worried they will try again?" I asked slowly. "Piel plans to kill you. If I hadn't been in your office last night, he would have succeeded."

"We've answered all the questions we will answer for tonight, Detective," Veronica said to Kansas.

In a moment's time, the two were gone. Every male officer at every desk and in every cube stood and stared as Veronica Powers left.

"So what do you think?" Kansas asked Price.

"I think this man makes deals with the devil," I said, looking at Price.

"Why's that?" Kansas asked.

"He doesn't have a sister. What are these papers?" I asked, picking them up. They sure weren't warrant papers.

"The insurance papers from my glove box. We didn't have time to wait for a real search warrant. We had Dr. Petty here, and time isn't on our side. I don't know about you two, but I'm getting tired of fishing young girls out of dumpsters. I needed to take a chance." He chuckled and patted me on the back.

I smiled. It was genius.

CHAPTER EIGHTEEN

I left police headquarters and headed to The Coffin to talk to Evan Falkner. It wasn't my first choice in assignments, but I wasn't given an option. I was sure the real action would be in arresting Nigel and Piel at the Lunatic Moon, but that task was already taken by Kansas and his team.

A shadow of a man was leaning against the hood of the 'Cuda. I felt my body stiffen and reached for the Magnum-instinct when you hunt things that go bump in the night.

The breath left my lungs in a rush as my eyes adjusted. It wasn't Piel, Quinn, or any of the other monsters that I had grown to love so much, but Father Garcia. He looked up at me as I descended the steps that spilled out onto the sidewalk.

"Should I ask why you are here?" I asked.

"Fulfilling a promise." His voice was shallow, as though he has just left a funeral. I realized he was here for my funeral.

I lit a cigar and let it fill my lungs with pleasure.

"You should quit those evil things." He waved away the smoke.

"I know, but then again, I have a very good chance of being

dead by the time the sun rises." I stopped in front of him. For the first time in the last three days, I was scared of what might happen to me. Father Garcia being here made things a little too real.

We got in the 'Cuda and headed for The Coffin, at the far end of Church Street. It was close enough that we could have walked from the police station, but it was always better to have a quick getaway if things got hairy. And with stake bait, things always get hairy.

"Where are we headed?" Father Garcia asked, keeping his eyes straight ahead. It was almost as if he was afraid to look at me. Afraid of letting things get too personal tonight.

I told him about Evan and all the fringe stories that led up to finding him. Father Garcia took it all in, shaking his head as I brought him up to speed.

"So how did the talk with the psychiatrist go?" Father Garcia asked after a long silence. I found it almost a comical response.

"Here I am telling you about almost being killed by a pack of fur balls, then a vamp, finding another victim, and the mystery man at the Lunatic Moon, and what is your response? How was my talk with the psychiatrist?"

"Yes." He gave me a small smile.

We made the left onto Church Street, under Interstate 4. A large crowd was moving along the street, packed tight. Their silhouettes danced in the glow of the neon.

"I don't think it's going to work out, Father."

"And why not?"

"The shrink is a monster sympathizer, and she doesn't exactly think I'm worth saving."

"So you did go."

"Kansas made me."

He took a deep breath and turned to me for the first time. "You can't keep making excuses for the pain. It only breeds more anger and drives you further into solitude. I know opening up to people is not something you are comfortable with, but you have to stop hating and learn to love. Hate is a lot like a cancer. If you leave it unattended, it will take over and kill you."

"Father Garcia, after tonight, it might not make a difference whether I deal with anything or not. There's something that might kill me first."

"Not if I can do anything about it. But if it comes to that, be right with God. When was the last time you saw me for confession?"

"It's been a long time since I've been preached to, even if it seems appropriate. You have a point." I sighed. "If I live, I need to get my feelings under control. I need to talk to someone, I know. Admitting it is something different all together. Maybe it's macho, but admitting I need help with my head is something that I can't deal with. It almost makes death worth it."

"What do you remember about that night?" he asked. His voice was quiet again. Shadows played along the outline of his face.

"Not much, Father. I was only eight."

"But you remember more than you have told me, don't you?"

"Maybe. I don't know. I mean, I remember coming home from the movies. I still had the box of popcorn with me when we walked in the house. It was pitch black. I remember my dad pushing me back out the door and locking it. He yelled to me to run as fast as I could. I heard my mother scream. It was the worst sound I had ever heard in my life. Screams that haunt me like living nightmares. I heard my father yelling. Shots fired. Demonic sounds. Sinister laughter. Things inside the house breaking. More screaming, then silence."

"But you ran, like your father asked you."

"Yeah." I fought the tears welling in my eyes. "Even to this day, it's so real I can touch it, feel it, hear it."

"And you feel guilty."

"Of course I do. I mean. I survived. I should have helped them. Saved them. Instead all I did was run."

"How, Paul? You were eight years old. What could you have done?"

"I don't know. I mean, I run the night through my mind almost every day and think of ways I could have saved them. There were so many things I did wrong. I was just too scared to do anything."

"You were just a child. You did what they would have wanted. You lived."

"And what good did it do? I became an orphan. They should've been there when I went to Scout meetings and got my badges. They were supposed to be there to teach me to drive. They were supposed to be there taking pictures of me and my prom date. There was graduation, there was Christmas, there was, was...everything. I feel cheated."

"You are angry at them for dying."

"Yes. No. Maybe. I don't know. All I know is that it sucks."

"You have to live and be happy for them. They'd want it that way," Father Garcia said.

"You make it sound as if it's easy, as if you can flip a switch and instantly become happy. Well, you can't. You just can't. My childhood was taken from me. Other than you and the church, I have no one."

"You have no one because that is what you choose. God wants to love you. There are people out there that would love to love you, a good woman, a good friend. You have closed yourself off from the outside world so tightly that no one can get in."

"You're right, I have. I have saved myself from having them taken away from me, or me from them. I don't want my kids growing up without a father."

"Still beats knowing you will die all alone." He twisted in his seat for a second, cleared his throat and spoke words that would change my life. "There is more to your parents' death."

"What are you talking about?"

"You don't really think they were victims of a random vampire attack, do you?"

"Why wouldn't I think that?"

"There's a lot more to the story than you know. You were far too young and fragile at the time, but it's my fault that I've not told you the truth before now. I guess I just wanted to let sleeping dogs lie. But you deserve the truth."

"The truth?"

"Your mother and father were activists for the legalization of the vampires," Father Garcia said.

I nearly ran off the road. "What do you mean, activists?"

"Your father never helped me kill vampires, like I told you. Well, he did for a time, but grew tired of the death. He began to push for their legalization after he met your mother."

"You're lying." It sounded childish as I said it, but it was out of my mouth before I could stop it.

"I'm not saying your father was a bad man. He wasn't. I thought of him as one of the greatest men that I've ever known. But the truth is, he and your mother were working to legalize vampires in our society, not to kill them. He was fighting for what he thought was right."

"Look, just shut up. I've heard all this bullshit I'm going to." I was growing angrier by the second, and I wasn't sure if it was because I'd been lied to, or because of the truth about my father and mother.

"I don't mean to anger you, but I thought you should know the truth."

"Why, because I'll probably die tonight? So it will clear your conscience? Save it for your lost souls at the church, Father."

"I don't want you living with this lie."

"I want to live with the lie. I like it better."

"Not all the vampires wanted the legalization to go through. With

legalization came accountability. They would have the same responsi-
bilities, taxes, and laws as we do. Some found that to be something
they didn't want to deal with. They could be sued, drafted, sentenced
to prison just like the rest of us. Vampire laws would be abolished, and
that was something the old school vamps weren't real keen on. They
saw your mother and father as a threat. Your parents lost their lives
because they were trying to take the monster out of the vampire."

"You're a liar."

"I'm sorry to drop this all on you now, but you'll have to deal
with it one way or another. You're right; you shouldn't have been
handled with such kid gloves."

"You didn't come here to help me, didn't tell me this for my
sake. You're doing it for you."

Father Garcia refused to look me in the eyes. That was a good
thing. I was so mad that I knew I'd say something I'd regret. My
fingers dug into the steering wheel. I kept my gaze straight ahead.

"What about you? Have you dealt with everything that
happened a couple of years ago?"

"We aren't talking about me; we're talking about you."

"Sounds like a cop-out to me. I see the pain in you to this day. It
wasn't your fault, either, yet you have built these walls around yourself as well."

He looked down. "I have put it in God's hands."

"Bullshit."

"Don't use that kind of language with me."

"Don't tell me that God had eased your heart and soul. It's as
much a lie as telling me my parents were bleeding hearts for the
cockroaches with fangs. I'll never buy that."

"No he hasn't, but what he has done is given me forgiveness and
peace to live with myself." He looked at me and half smiled. "But
this isn't about me, it is about you."

"Look, Father, my mom and dad were murdered by these things,
and the killer is still out there, with the ability to live forever. Until a

few minutes ago, I believed they were merely victims. Now I come to find out that they were killed because they wanted them to have rights. Screw forgiveness. I don't need it. And you are right. This is about me. I'm the one that has to go on living with all this. I have a right to be angry. And if what you are telling me has an ounce of truth to it, then I'm way past angry, because that can mean only one thing: They died at the hand of the creatures they were trying to help. I think I'll hang on to the hatred. It keeps me alive."

"I just don't want you to end up like me."

"Like you? No way. You are married to the church. I like getting laid every now and then," I tried to joke.

"You're going to hell, you know that?"

He was right, I probably would.

CHAPTER NINETEEN

I parallel parked the 'Cuda next to The Coffin, which, like every other bar, club, and restaurant down here, there was a large crowd gathered outside, looking in. It was known to be a very posh restaurant and nightclub in the district. It had to be, it was owned by the Master of the City himself.

The doorman spotted us right away. He gave me quick glances from time to time. I continued to watch him from inside the car, readying myself for finding Evan. I went over my arsenal and took a deep breath. When comfortable, I asked, "You ready? We can discuss the other stuff another time. Right now, all I want is to see a cockroach die."

"As ready as I'll ever be," Father Garcia answered. There was a new awkward silence between us. It wouldn't evaporate.

Without another word, we got out of the 'Cuda. Father Garcia put on a suede jacket, filled with an array of weapons. I pulled on my leather trench coat. It was a bit cumbersome, but it had the most pockets. I would sacrifice comfort for necessity. It was a hot night in Orlando, which meant our leather jackets made us stand out like sore thumbs, one of many necessary evils in our line of work. It would be great if we could blend and move about with ease, but such is life. I threw the rest of the cigar down one of the drainage holes and blew the last of the smoke from my lungs.

The doorman was now very distracted with our approach, as well he should be. I had no beef with him, other than what he was, but he didn't know that. Father Garcia and I were like the grim reaper for his kind.

"You ain't comin' in here," GQ snorted as we approached. He moved in front of the entrance, spread his legs and crossed his arms.

"Don't worry, we aren't here to kill you. Unless you do something to change that," I said to him.

"Anytime you come down here, someone dies. I have orders to stop you if you try to come in."

"Who gave you such orders?"

"Mr. Rubio."

"Well, you need to tell Quinn that if we don't get in, he is obstructing justice. We have a court order to talk to one of his employees."

A puzzled look grew on his face. "Who?"

"He's playing dumb, how cute," I said to Father Garcia, then turned back to the doorman. "Evan Falkner."

"And the priest? What's he doing here?"

"To give you your last rights if you don't cooperate." I moved the trench coat away so he could see the Magnum. Often I can just show the weapons and the fang boys will back off a little. They hated me, but they hated dying a little more.

His eyes went to the Magnum. "What? Am I supposed to be afraid of that? Of the two of you? You look like damn S&M flashers." He began to laugh.

"Have you ever been shot with one of these?" Father Garcia asked as he walked toward the monster, showing his weapon of choice, a 9mm.

"No, but I know a couple of parents that could tell me firsthand what it is like to see their innocent son get shot by one. And I know you ain't allowed down here no more."

"And you don't think I'll put this in your stomach? Let me tell you about the pain it'll cause before you die. The bullet will rip through your skin, leaving a hole that I could put my fist through. Tearing and exploding through your organs, bringing about pain that you couldn't even imagine. For a split second, there would be blood, but that would quickly give way to a burning sensation as the ultraviolet catches you on fire. You'll burn from the inside out, until the shell of your body becomes an inferno of heat, exploding all over the nice, clean sidewalk. You'll be a pile of glowing ash. Pity to go through all the pain for such a trivial thing as not letting us talk to one of the employees inside."

I looked over at Father Garcia. "I'm impressed. It's good to hear a man of God tell it like it is." Note to God: Something missing in churches of today.

GQ slowly moved away from the door and waved us through. "I'm still calling Mr. Rubio."

"You sound like a little boy tattling." I moved through the door.

He put his hand on my chest. "You need to leave your weapons at the door."

I pulled off my crucifix and handed it to him. He pointed to the basket he was now holding. "In here."

"No, I want to hand it to you personally."

He motioned for us to go inside.

"Smart cockroach."

The inside of The Coffin was black and white, accented with bright primary and secondary colors. Sorry, I took art classes in school. The floor was a well-polished black-and-white checkerboard pattern. The tables were draped in white tablecloths and surrounded by black chairs pinstriped with the same bright colors. Each table was topped with a white candle in a small glass bowl;

light flickered throughout the room like tiny stars. Art deco lighting fell from the ceiling in soft bars. A small band, consisting of a piano, classical guitar, violin and upright bass, played on a small stage to the left.

The room was packed with people, most innocent humans, which made me nervous. The last thing I wanted was to have a shoot-out in the middle of a crowded room. I kept telling myself it might not come down to that. Chances were, Nigel over at the Lunatic Moon was our killer, and Evan was nothing more than a psycho vampire. Redundant, I know.

I looked around as the shadows turned into people. Waiters moving around in white tuxes with black buttons, neon-colored bow ties, and matching cummerbunds of red, blue, yellow, purple, or green.

A woman in a black form-fitting skirt and white blouse stepped in my path. "May I help you gentlemen?" Human. She was nice to look at, with long black hair, high cheekbones, and pale lips. According to her gold rectangular nametag, her name was Gillian.

"We need to talk with one of your employees," I replied.

"And who would that be?"

"Evan Falkner."

"Ahh, Mr. Falkner." A dark smile rose on her face. "I'm sorry, gentlemen, but he doesn't work here anymore."

"We would still like to look around. See for ourselves," Father Garcia answered from behind me.

"Look, we don't want any trouble from you. We are a law-abiding establishment. I don't wish for you to turn this place into a shooting gallery. You two have quite a reputation," Gillian said, looking at Father Garcia.

"We just want to look around. We have reason to believe he might be in danger," I added.

"But I told you, he doesn't work here anymore."

"Then you won't mind us looking around." I pulled out the court order. It was real this time, not just Price's insurance papers. "I promise. We won't be a nuisance to you or your guests." It was a promise I wasn't sure I could keep, but I didn't care.

Gillian looked at the papers from my hand as if it were a dead animal. "You have fifteen minutes, then I'm calling the police. And Mr. Rubio."

"You do that. We've got a lot of catching up to do."

"Not so fast," Gillian said as she moved back in front of me.

"What is it now?"

"I'll escort you, to make sure the search goes smoothly."

"Smoothly?" I asked.

"Yes. Your presence makes the vampires very nervous. You have a reputation for senseless killing. If I'm with you, there's a chance they might not panic."

"Lead the way, then," I said, ushering her forward.

She looked at me for a few seconds before moving. "You can leave your weapons at the front. I've already told you he's not here. No one is allowed in here with those things. Orders from Mr. Rubio, personally."

"I don't think so, sweetheart. I have a license to carry them, and have no intention of handing them over."

"At least keep them hidden as we walk. I don't want any of the patrons to feel endangered."

"Then you should warn them that the restaurant is full of coffin maggots. And I'm not talking about the little bugs."

She turned and started to walk. We snaked along the side of the restaurant. She was moving along at a fast pace, trying to get to the kitchen of the restaurant as quick as possible. I slowed my pace just to piss her off just a little. Petty, I know. Too bad.

We entered the kitchen: blinding white light, drab white walls, and a circus of activity. Waiters and cooks in a lunatic ballet, dodging one another, lifting trays, yelling orders, stirring pots.

As they saw us, silence enveloped the kitchen like a blanket.

Every set of undead eyes was on us. Only the boiling water ignored our entrance.

"Good evening," I said in my best Dracula voice.

"What's he doing here?" one of them said.

"I know why he's here!" a male bloodsucker said, snaking a large knife around Gillian's throat and pulling her to him. The blade slid into the top layers of skin, and a crimson line of liquid formed around it. A dangerous fear gleamed in his eyes, the kind that's willing to kill as many as he could before we got to him.

Gillian screamed, "Help me!"

"Ironic. A few minutes ago you were disgusted by what I do. Now I'm sure you wouldn't mind me killing a cockroach. Decisions, decisions." The kitchen emptied in a matter of seconds, leaving just the four of us in the room.

"Back off, or I'll kill her!" the blood-licker shouted.

"Easy, big guy, you don't want to hurt her." I kept my body very still. The last thing I wanted to do right now was cause him to overreact.

"I ain't gonna die tonight."

"What makes you so sure you are gonna die tonight?" I was willing to play Dr. Phil if it saved the woman's life.

"Don't play with me, Avenger. I know why you're here." He moved with Gillian, flanking any move I might make. The knife still set against her skin, trails of red madness trickling from her throat. She swung in his arms like a rag doll. Tears formed in her eyes, eyes that were begging me to do something.

"I'm not playing with you. I'm simply confused as to why you think I'm here to kill you."

"You kill the ones like me."

I could feel Father Garcia behind me, trying to move around to the other side of the vampire. "What are you talking about?"

Father Garcia stopped in his tracks, held up his hands and spoke. "We're not here to cause you any trouble. Let the woman go, and let's talk this through. I'm a man of God. I'm not lying when I tell you that you are not who we are here to talk to. Key word: talk."

He always was the rational one. He wanted to talk things through, while I was waiting on a clear shot. Different strokes, I guess.

"I didn't want this to happen to me. I didn't ask for it," the vampire added.

"Ask for what? I'm getting tired of the twenty questions."

"Becoming what I am."

"And you are...?"

"A vampire."

"Ahh. Now it makes sense. You've been turned since the new laws came about," I finished.

"That's right. I have an automatic death sentence. It's not fair. I haven't done anything wrong. I'm not going to die tonight." He now had his back to the back door. It wasn't difficult to see what his plan was.

"Let her go, and we'll let you go." Father Garcia said from behind me.

His words, not mine. My thoughts were more along the lines of "two for the price of one."

"We aren't here to kill you. I don't even know who you are," I told him.

"You're lying. I missed being grand fathered in by twelve days. It's not fair."

I looked into his eyes and began to sink into his thoughts. It was a dangerous move. Sometimes vampires can surprise me with their strength and put me in a very dangerous position, but in my situation, I had very little to lose.

I could feel him trying to pull away, but I held on with everything I had. It was a process that I was learning slowly, since I had very few willing cockroaches that would allow me to practice. Such is life.

He screamed as I began to fill his mind with my own thoughts. "I'll kill her! I'll do it, man."

Gillian shrieked as he became more and more violent with the knife. It worked against her neck in bouncing slices, leaving small red marks, but so far they were all superficial wounds. I kept the pressure on. I was committed now. If I let up, Gillian would die.

I began to attack the arm holding the knife, tried to lift it off her neck, feeling the resistance of the coffin critter. He began to foam at the mouth, sweat pouring from his forehead, but the arm moved away from Gillian's neck.

"I'll kill her, I swear it!" he screamed again.

With the knife about five inches away from Gillian's throat, Father Garcia moved in and grabbed her in one swift move. She crashed into his arms, gasping for breath, tears flowing down her face as she sank into his chest.

I released the cockroach and watched him fall to the floor. He bounced back up like a ball and headed for a large pot boiling on a nearby stove. I barely had time to react before the cockroach grabbed it and threw it in my direction. I moved just far enough away that I didn't catch the brunt of the water. My arm caught most of it, but thanks to the coat I was wearing, it caused only minor pain. Doesn't mean it didn't piss me off. I pulled the Magnum free from the shoulder holster and put a bullet in the vampire's brain. There was a quick shower of red, then heat and flame as he burned in front of us. We could hear the screams of pain as he died. Music to my ears.

"Is she all right?"

There was no answer. Nothing.

"Father Garcia?"

Still nothing.

"Father Garcia, you okay?"

I felt it. Power. Lots of it.

I looked over to him, only to see his 9mm drawn on Quinn

Rubio. He was also holding a large crucifix in the free hand. His eyes were staring right into Rubio's chest.

I felt the jolt of fear hit me. Somehow we'd gone from dealing with simple coffin bait to being eye to eye with the Master of the City. Quinn Rubio's power was electrifying and humbling. Even with the arsenal of weapons we had, Quinn had us out powered.

"Father, step away slowly. If one of us is going to draw on Quinn, and probably not live to tell about it, I want it to be me."

I did the most insane thing I could ever do. I pointed my Magnum at Quinn Rubio, Master of the City.

CHAPTER TWENTY

Quinn Rubio was dressed to the nines. Black suit jacket and pants, pink silk shirt, gold cuff links, wide black tie, dress shoes so polished they absorbed all light that landed on them. He glanced down and saw the pile of ash that just a few seconds ago had been a member of the walking dead.

"Where did he come from?" I asked Father Garcia.

"He simply appeared."

It was hard to read Quinn Rubio's face, but I could tell he wasn't pleased with what had just taken place. This vampire made even the bravest at heart stop in their tracks. He was a cold-blooded killer, older than time.

"You know, Mr. Isaac, killing my employees is bad for business. I have cooks running into the streets, and guests leaving the restaurant in a grand exodus."

"He attacked her," I said pointing to Gillian. "Not to mention he was illegal. Which is a violation for you. We might have to close you down and check everyone's records."

He looked pointedly at the two handguns still on him. "Are you going to shoot me as well?"

"Can't think of anything that would turn me on more. Besides, I promised you I would. I like to keep my promises. And this time, I'm not cuffed to a chair."

He shook his head lightly. "There is no need for violence. I can see I am well outnumbered."

"We need to talk to one of your bloodsuckers." Father Garcia spoke, holding the crucifix at arms length, the 9mm still drawn.

Quinn turned to meet him slowly. "Father, so glad to see you down here again. It has been such a long time. We have much catching up to do." To me, "I assume the Father has his license to hunt here? Or am I not the only one in danger of receiving a citation tonight?"

"I guess we all have something to lose tonight," Father Garcia said.

"I agree. All this excitement is bad for business. I do not care for the violence and drama I have just witnessed. Blood makes me queasy." Quinn looked over to Gillian. "Are you well, my dear?"

She shook her head as she wiped away a tear.

"Let the young woman go. She has been through enough for one night."

"She's free to go any time she wants," I said.

In one move, he shooed her out of the kitchen.

"Mr. Isaac, do you plan to keep that weapon on me all night? I am quite sure it must be growing heavy by now."

He was right. Either I killed him or dropped the Magnum.

"Now, for whom is it that you have come?" Quinn asked, looking in my direction.

"Evan Falkner. And then for you."

"Has Mr. Falkner done something wrong?"

"That's what we're here to find out," I answered.

He looked at the Magnum, still in my hand. "Please, Mr. Isaac, Father, I do not think the weapons will be needed. I am certainly at your mercy." Sarcasm at its best.

"I'm not here to make friends with you or your cockroaches. After our last meeting, you're lucky I haven't put a bullet through your heart yet, so if I were you, I'd be as useful as I could be. Otherwise, I have nothing to lose by killing you. This gun stays on you until we talk to Evan."

Something hit me hard, knocking me across the floor. My throat tightened. An invisible hand twisted me from inside. I tried to scream out in pain as the force continued to bend me. I couldn't make a sound. I fought for breath. Tears formed in my eyes. As if by magical force, I was lifted to my feet and slammed hard against the wall behind me, stopping only when my head hit the ceiling. My wounds from the night before cried out in pain. I could feel the force crushing me as I hung in the air about six feet off the ground.

"Never underestimate my power. Disrespect me again, and I will rip you into a million pieces." Quinn floated toward me. "There will not be enough of you to bury."

A violent rush of air zipped around the room. I looked behind him and saw Father Garcia on the floor.

"Your lives are in my hands whether you want to believe it or not. Your toy guns and religious trickery will not work on me, Avenger. Killing you is the mildest thing I will do to you. Do you understand? Never threaten me again."

His face was against mine. I could feel the heat of his breath. The power coming off his skin was so intense; it alone made me cringe with anguish, like electricity against my flesh. I wanted to say I understood, but the pain wouldn't allow me to answer.

"Understand?"

I tried to respond, but couldn't.

"Are we in agreement that the weapons are to be put away?"

I couldn't answer. I was being gutted from the inside out. Power. Ripping me apart.

"Do we have an understanding?"

I nodded the best I could. My vision swam as I fought to remain conscious. My life depended on it. The pain ate at me like cancer. My ears rang. Sweat beaded on my head. Everything spun. I looked past Quinn to Father Garcia, whose eyes were staring back at me blank, unfocused, eyes of a dead man. Blood trickled from his nose. His body shook in convulsions as he tried to grasp the 9mm that was just out of reach. Like me, the pain crippled him. I could see it wrapping around him like a cocoon.

The force dropped me. I slammed onto the floor. Jarring pain shot up my spine, knocking free the gasp of breath I had in my lungs.

I wiped away the blood from Father Garcia's nose the best I could. Bleeding was not something to do if you wanted to stay alive in this business. Slowly, he picked up the 9mm and put it to his head.

"Put your guns and crucifixes away, or he dies." Quinn said, watching Father Garcia.

"Okay, okay. I'll put it away!" I shouted. Father Garcia looked into my eyes, the 9mm at his temple.

I did as I was told reluctantly. I was willing to put the gun away if I was able to keep it. Win the little ones, and the big ones will follow.

"I did it. The guns are away. Please release him."

"So we have an understanding?"

"Yes."

"I hate to repeat myself. This night can go very well for you, or very badly."

"I said I understand. Please stop."

Quinn became the gentleman once more, as if nothing had taken place. He had made his point. His power was stronger than any of the weapons we had brought here. "Has Mr. Falkner done some-thing wrong?"

"Remains to be seen." I said. "Question for you. Who is Lyric? For real."

A low, deep laugh flowed from the vampire. "In due time, Mr. Isaac."

"I need to talk to Evan."

I put my hand on the Magnum again and did a quick inventory of weapons. I could hear the blood rushing through my ears; feel the pulsing of my heart rate. A combination of fear and hatred.

"I do not make idle threats, Mr. Isaac," Quinn said, never looking in my direction.

I moved the hand to my side, keeping my eyes on the cock-roach's back.

Quinn turned to face Father Garcia. "I have to hand it to you, Father. You have a lot of guts showing up here again. Forgiveness must really be good for the soul." He stopped and thought for a moment. "His parents do not know you are down here again, do they?"

"We can discuss morals and truth another time, Quinn. Produce Mr. Falkner, or we'll burn this building to the ground."

White teeth gleamed out of an equally white face. Sugarcoated evil tingling up the spine. "You know, Father, I was a man of the cloth before my demise all those years ago. Denying my flesh. Living in poverty. Trusting in prayer. Perception is such a distrac-tion for men like you and me. Now I do not pray for power and strength. I create it; command it like a sword. I live to watch men like you fall under the weight of unanswered prayers and constant persecution. I gain power from every soul I devour. It is quite addictive. I choose who lives and who dies, not God. He needs to thank me for not killing you two. Yet." Yet. That was a big word. "Please gentlemen, wait in my office. I will locate Mr. Falkner for you."

"I think we'll take our chances here. Just get Evan Falkner for us." I said.

Quinn let out a deep breath. "Are you always this difficult?"

"It's called staying alive."

Quinn shook his head and started to say something, then stopped. He took a deep breath and tried again. "Very well, Mr. Isaac. I will retrieve him." He bowed to me, more out of condescension than respect.

I jumped as my cell phone went off, and cursed under my breath. It's hard to be tough and cool when something that simple scares you. I took a deep breath and answered it. It was Kansas.

"Yeah," I said.

"You got Falkner there?"

"Not yet. Why?"

"Didn't think so. Listen carefully. We had our computer guru check out the information on Nigel with the undeadinbed.com website."

"And?"

"Seems Nigel and the doorman you were talking about are indeed the same person."

"You killed him, right?"

"That's where you come in." Sounded like he was running. "Nigel and Evan Falkner are one and the same."

My body went numb. "Come again?"

"Nigel is the name Evan used on the website. He got fired from The Coffin about three weeks ago for being aggressive with the female clientele. A woman was going to press charges against him, but her attorney dropped them after Evan agreed to counseling with a shrink, Dr. Lydia Petty. Quinn and the vampire community tried to sweep the whole thing under the rug. Seems your boy Vinnie was there that night, too. Price just called me. Our little serial killer just went to see his attorney, Veronica Powers. He has the son of a bitch at gunpoint as we speak. Get the hell out of there and meet me across the street at the SunTrust Building as soon as you can. Price won't be able to take on a vampire on his own. He'll get himself killed if we're not careful." A moment of silence, then, "The woman that was going to press charges against Evan was Sheri Charlesworth. The woman you turned to ash at the hospital."

"I'll see you there."

There were no good-byes. No need for them.

CHAPTER TWENTY-ONE

I slid the phone back in its belt case and looked back to Father Garcia. I sensed he already knew I had something to say. He knew me well. The room felt haunted, but alive. It was all very ironic to me. Here we were in a room with dead vampires, yet it felt alive with something. It was the "something" that worried me. I could feel my skin crawling with sensations, much like spiders moving over my flesh. It was power, lots of it. Worst of all, Quinn had evaporated into thin air. Gone.

"What is it?" Father Garcia finally said, growing impatient.

"Something with a lot of power is heading this way." I was already in motion. "Come on, we need to get across the street."

"What about Evan?"

"That's who we're going to go see." Father Garcia gave me a puzzled look, like I had just punched him. "I'll fill you in on the way."

"I'm sorry, you ain't goin' nowhere," a vampire said, coming through the door, his arms folded over his chest. "Quinn's orders mate."

I paused as more filthy cockroaches began to file in around us. Eight against two, not a fair fight, but rarely do I get to choose the odds. Even more rarely were they ever in my favor.

"If you move from the door now, I won't kill you. Mate," I snapped back.

"You sound as though you have a choice in who lives and who dies," another bloodsucker said, moving closer to me.

The daisy-pusher in front of the door had hair so golden it looked yellow, thin at the shoulders. He smiled and showed his fangs for effect. "Looks like Quinn ordered lunch for us."

Laughter broke out as I looked at Father Garcia. "You ready?"

He had already raised his 9mm and, with one quick release, pointed at one of the cockroaches to his right. He simply nodded while drawing a bead on the unfortunate undead.

"Are you gonna stand there, Avenger, or are you going to kill us?" a daisy-pusher to my left asked. I glanced at him and nearly choked. It was Evan.

"How in the hell did you get in here?"

"Told you at the club last night, I'd be back to kill you myself." He paused. "If you lived."

It was getting tough to keep all of them from getting behind us. Like real cockroaches, they were coming out of the woodwork. Filling the kitchen. Eight had become sixteen.

"I think he's as scared as his mommy and daddy were," a voice from the crowd said. The vampires laughed. "Only this time, he won't be able to run away."

I laughed humorlessly and shoved my Magnum in the face of the sunlight special I was most convinced he had made the remark. "You get to be the first to turn to ash."

His laughter stopped dead. He tried to leap. I pulled the trigger and felt the force of the gun do all the work. The bullet drilled into his skull. A small stream of blood trickled down before his body glowed orange and turned to ash. He looked for all the world like a giant cigarette.

Father Garcia opened fire. Vampire parts flew across the room. He turned and caught a second blood-sucker climbing up the wall.

Around me, I could see flashes of movement. Blurs of speed. Screams of fear, or excitement. I didn't think I really wanted to know which one.

I pulled the 9mm from my hip holster and fired with both guns. The kitchen filled with smoke, ash, and hellish screams.

Father Garcia and I were now back to back, moving in slow circles, trying to inch our way to the door. "We have to get out of The Coffin if we we're going to survive. Kind of ironic, huh?" Father Garcia shouted.

"Got any suggestions?" I asked him, keeping the guns drawn and my sights on the monsters. Beads of sweat ran down the side of my face. My hands were shaking with adrenaline. I liked the rush. It kept me sharp and focused, but this time I wasn't sure fear wasn't in the mixture. We were trapped, and running low on bullets. Fatigue started building in my arms. Holding weapons like ours got heavy after a few minutes. They don't tell you that in the movies.

"I think I have something for them." He reached in his pocket with his free hand and pulled out a vial of holy water. His hands shook as he looked around the room, catching the attention of every undead. Fear swept across their faces. They watched the vial intensely. Easing back, but trying to stay in control. Calculating the odds of being sprayed with the potentially deadly solution. For a vampire, the holy water would leave large scars, much like burn scars on humans. I gather it was not a pleasant experience for them. Father Garcia removed the cork and began to move slowly toward the door.

"We'll get to you before you ever have a chance to burn us," one of the vampires said as he rushed Father Garcia.

The blood-sucker was wrong. With one sweeping motion of his hand, Father Garcia sprayed the entire room.

The smell of burning dead flesh and the sounds of sizzling skin flooded the room. I found myself nearly gagging. From what I could tell, three of the cockroaches had gotten the worst of it. They were holding their wounds tightly. Hissing. Backing away. I kept my guns moving on the circle of vampires while Father Garcia opened a second vial of holy water and continued to move toward the door. We were only about ten feet from it. Moving. Splitting the wall of blood-suckers in half. Two of them still stood in front of the door, trying to decide on their next move.

"You will never make it out, Avenger," the shorter maggot in front of the door said.

"What makes you think that?" I said as I continued to ease forward. I put an ultraviolet bullet in his brain. The second cockroach moved to keep the ashes from hitting him and looked at me.

"You and your man of God can't do anything to us that will be any worse than what Quinn will do if we fail. Death is a better option." He flanked my move to the door.

"Father, can you handle things long enough for me to reload?"

"On the count of three, I'm going to get them wet again. You reload while they cook." He still had the 9mm pointed at no blood-licker in particular. They all held back as the gun waved back and forth.

I shook my head, still watching the vampire at the door. I wanted to look him in the eyes, but something told me he might be a little more powerful than I wanted to deal with. Committing to something like that can have grave results if you can't do it. If I fell under his power, Father Garcia and I were as good as dead.

The cell phone went off again. I knew it was Kansas without looking at it. He was waiting on me. This put me in another dilemma. If Kansas came across the street to see what was keeping me, he would more than likely be killed before he knew it. Still, I couldn't take the chance to answer it and warn him. I needed to keep things under control here. I was already going to have to drop one of the guns to reload the other. So many things to kill, so little time.

The cell phone continued to ring until it went to voice mail. I could only imagine what he had left as a message. I would no doubt have to make sure no children were present when I checked it. I knew Kansas. He was not the most patient man in the world. Cursing under his breath at an alarming rate and thinking of all the options he had to kill me, such pleasant thoughts. Note to self: Get better friends. Scratch that: Just get friends.

Father Garcia waited for the cell phone to stop ringing before starting his count. "Sometimes men of God are far too polite in critical situations," I grunted.

"One."

I quickly set the 9mm back in the holster around my belt and reached for the cartridge of bullets for the Magnum. It seemed to take forever. I tried to breathe, but found it impossible. It took too much time and effort. A bead of sweat went into my left eye; I had to blink quickly several times just to keep from going blind.

"Growing nervous, Avenger?" Evan said slowly, with a hint of confidence.

"That's the thing about you cockroaches. You always think you can outwit me. And you always get turned to ash," I countered.

"You seem tense."

"Just unsure."

"About what?"

"About which one of you I'll shoot first. I actually want to keep you alive if I can. You have a lot of questions to answer, and I want to be the one to beat them out of you."

He laughed. Father Garcia said, "Two."

I shoved the cartridge in the Magnum and heard the click, telling me I was ready to do damage. I breathed deep at last. A breath I was sure I wouldn't be able to exhale for some time to come. Which was fine as long as I was still be breathing at the end of all this. I readjusted the shoulder again, trying to ease the pain as much as I could. It was hurting bad enough now that it was slowly becoming a distraction, causing me to grit my teeth with each beat of my heart.

As Father Garcia said the word "three," he was lifted off the ground and sent flying backwards. One of the vampires jumped him and threw him to the ground, talon-like claws stabbing into skin, red circles of blood forming around the wounds.

I pulled my gun off of Evan and followed Father Garcia's body to the floor, trying to get a clear shot on the cockroach. I had to be careful with my aim; if I missed and hit Father Garcia, he would be as dead as if I shot him with normal bullets.

As my finger pressed the trigger, I felt the weight hit me. Evan had attacked. I heard the shot, but had no idea if the bullet found its mark. I hit the floor with a rude crash. Hot breath and sharp fangs met me. This was starting to get old.

I pulled the trigger a second time, feeling the recoil and the weight lift as one of the cockroaches quickly turned to ash. Smells of burning corpse covered the room like a blanket. The hair on my arm singed.

Claws dug into my ribs as one of the blood-suckers wrapped his arms around me, trapping my arms to my sides. I rolled as much as I could, freeing my hand. I still had the gun. More importantly, if I didn't get free, he would be able to suck me dry. I had lost a lot of blood from the night before. I really didn't want to lose any more.

I yelled to Father Garcia, unable to see if he was still alive. There was nothing. "Father Garcia!" I shouted again. Still nothing. Shit.

I heard an explosion. Someone either was coming in or going out of the door. My fear was Kansas had tried the door, found it locked, heard the talking around on the street about a gunshot, panicked and broke in. Yeah, I know. I did a lot of thinking while I was on the ground about to be chewed on.

"Kansas!" I shouted as I continued to try and free the hand with the gun. My other hand ran across the knife I had around my belt. I grabbed for the handle with stretched fingers.

Shots rang out around me. Vampires screamed. The room was a blur of chaotic motion. I expected to see Kansas above me, but I'd guessed wrong. I wasn't sure if I should be afraid or relieved, but one thing was for sure: the shooter wasn't Kansas. It was Angie.

CHAPTER TWENTY-TWO

S he stood with her gun pointed at the coffin-munchers and me. I closed my eyes and did something that I hadn't done in a very long time. I prayed. After all, the last time Angie and I were together hadn't ended so well. I had a gun in her ribs, that little thing with the lights going out and shots fired, yada, yada, yada. Hell hath no fury and all that.

I heard the gun go off, but felt no pain. The vamp above me went limp. I felt a spray of blood hit my face, hoped it was his. I rolled the maggot off me. It gasped for breath. Half of its back was now gone from the explosion of the bullet. She wasn't using ultraviolet ammo. Had he been a human, his death would still have been instant; instead, the cockroach was slowly healing and regaining strength. They have incredible healing powers, unless a shot takes out the heart or the head is removed, the vampire can survive and regenerate.

I brought the healing process to an end with a shot between the eyes. Mine did have ultraviolet ammo. This time the body jumped violently, and then shattered into nothingness in front of my eyes.

The other fang boy, Evan, now hung from the ceiling, hissing like some kind of snake. I hate snakes as much as I hate cockroaches.

I rolled away from Angie and balanced myself on my elbows, glancing at Father Garcia. I hoped to see him alive. It had crossed my mind Angie might just empty the place out, killing both humans and vampires. I had no doubt she was crazy like that.

She had dyed her hair pink, but not like the young girl we inter-viewed earlier-neon pink, so bright it almost glowed. I couldn't judge by her facial expressions whether she was friend or foe, but she had the coffin-munchers at bay for the moment.

I didn't want to point the Magnum at her. I didn't trust her, after all, she was one of the monsters, but I didn't want to burn any bridges prematurely. I kept my eyes on her and my hand on the Magnum. I had no problem killing her if it came down to that. Actu-ally, the best thing to do would be shoot now and ask questions later. I guess I was growing soft.

Father Garcia was alive, but not in good shape. His forehead bled as he crawled on his elbows toward the 9mm he'd lost in the attack leaving a thin trail of crimson liquid behind him. His knee seemed to be bent the wrong way, making mine ache in sympathy. I stood and moved toward him, keeping a strong grip on the Magnum and my eyes on Angie just in case the gunfight wasn't over.

I counted six dead. The others had gone out the door after Angie crashed through it; all were gone except Evan. Angie held my gaze for a quick second, then looked back to Evan. He inched across the kitchen, away from us, but didn't leave. It was almost as if he couldn't run, as if he were trapped by some invisible force. What-ever waited at the end of the escape path was apparently worse than staying inside with us.

Keeping her gun trained on Evan, Angie said, "See if he's okay." I took this as a sign Father Garcia and I weren't going to have to fight fur balls as well as cockroaches. Things were looking up. I glanced behind me to see where Evan was hiding.

"Just keep moving. Get him out of here," she added. For the first time, I got a close look at her. She was a death-dealing machine in painted-on pink leather. Pants as tight as skin, with small heart-shaped cutouts down the sides from hip to ankle. She was clearly not wearing underwear. A matching top, with only three of the five buttons fastened, baring a mound of flesh. Her lips glistened, pale metallic pink. She had on mirrored sunglasses, the ones corrupt cops wear. Her hair had been pulled back in a ponytail.

Father Garcia had reached his 9mm, but collapsed a second time. His body grew limp. He had lost a lot of blood; he was cold, and his breathing was shallow. He had been bitten, but it didn't look fatal.

He grunted in pain. "How ironic would it be that I came here to kill you if you turned all fangs and now I'm the one that has to be staked?" he gasped.

"Let's hope neither of us have to handle that one," I answered.

I wheeled around to meet Evan, the Magnum raised and ready to kill, all the while scanning the area for sneak attacks. Blood-suckers are freaky in that they aren't there one minute, and in front of you the next with ghost-like qualities only the dead possess.

"You okay?" I asked.

"Kill that thing. Worry about me later."

"Try to breath normally," I advised. What a hypocrite I was. Breathing normally was not something I had done for the last half-hour. Adrenaline sent my vital signs into uncharted territory. I don't care how used to this kind of stuff anyone says they are, they're lying if they say they can remain calm.

"That's the funny thing about blood." I added. "It can trick you into thinking you are more wounded than you really are." I wasn't sure who I was trying to convince.

"Let me take him out," Angie said as she moved toward me. "I can rip his heart out if you'd like."

"No, I'll take care of this myself. I need him alive for a few minutes anyway. Call an ambulance." I took the cell phone from my clip and handed it to her, gesturing to Father Garcia.

She snatched the phone. "How did you know I didn't have my own on me?"

I looked her up and down and grinned. "Believe me, there's no room for anything in there but your body."

She blew a kiss. "It's kind of twisted to know I'm being turned on by a 911 call. How do you do it?" Angie asked, a lusty smile on her lips.

"What?"

"Make me want to take you to bed with those eyes."

I smiled, but knew better than to respond. "No matter what I say, you'd twist it into something naughty. I'm not ready for naughty. I want violence, and vengeance."

Evan smiled coldly. "So Avenger, once again, someone dies on your watch. When I drank his blood, I tasted his fear of death." He laughed low. "Looks like you have a very important choice to make: you can either save him or kill me. A choice the boy never had when you and the great priest killed him in front of his family. Like me, you were convinced he was a killer, but all you had on your hands was his blood. I hope you make a better choice this time. You can't do both."

"Oh, I don't know, Evan. I'm pretty good at multi-tasking." I stabbed the knife in his shoulder. I wasn't ready to kill him just yet. I only wanted to wound him enough that he would be primed for old-fashioned torture.

Evan moaned with pain as he tried to rise off the floor. Blood trickled down his white shirt around the silver blade. "Making you suffer for what you have done is going to be my pleasure."

"I'll finish him." Angie pointed her Glock on him. Monsters usually don't carry guns. I was surprised to see her with one. Usually they simply change forms and go from there.

"No. This one is mine." I blocked his escape route and motioned

Angie to lower the gun. She kept her eyes on Evan, but began to lower the Glock slowly, almost reluctantly. It gave me the opportunity to take matters into my own hands. I moved into a position that I could keep an eye on Evan, but could see Angie in my peripheral vision. She seemed to be on our side so far, but trusting her only made me an easier target. "What the hell did you do with Lyric?" I asked, shoving the barrel of the Magnum in his chest. My finger twitched on the trigger, but instead of firing, I kicked him in the ribs. I wanted him to taste the pain and fear he inflicted on all those young girls. A quick death would be way too easy. "Where is she? Why does Quinn want her?"

"Torturing me will not give you peace, Avenger, and it most certainly will not keep her from burning in hell." Evan said, his breathing quick, twitching from the pain.

"Why does he want her?"

Evan laughed. "I wasn't aware he wanted her. The girl I killed was nothing more than a sacrifice for all vampires." He laughed harder, fueling my anger. "I was killing the disease."

I pulled the crucifix out of my shirt; it glowed as it came close to him. "Let me show you what I know about sacrifice."

"No!" he hissed, his injuries still too intense to allow him much movement.

"Broken ribs are just the beginning."

"You'll never get away with this. Quinn will bleed you dry."

"If he was going to avenge your loss, he would have stayed. Besides, I thought you liked torture. Isn't that what the club's all about?" I said as I placed the crucifix on the tattoo. It made a popping sound, like fresh meat in a pan of hot grease. Evan screamed in pain as the crucifix ate at his skin. I lifted the crucifix and kicked him a second time.

"She didn't die right away, you know," Evan said as I dragged him across the stockroom toward the large crate.

"Who didn't die right away?"

"Your girl. She didn't die right away. I killed her slow. She suffered like no freak before. It's funny how the blind have a way of sensing things that other humans can't. She could sense the danger, could taste the fear, but was powerless to run from it or fight against it. Kept bumping into things. Violence is quite arousing, wouldn't you say, Avenger?"

"So Lyric is blind, too?"

"What do you mean, too?"

"The girl we found tonight was also blind. You got a thing for blind chicks? Is that it, Evan?"

"I don't know who this Lyric girl is. The woman I fed off of called herself Anna. A spicy Hispanic love machine. If Anna and Lyric are one and the same, too bad, so sad. Maybe I'm not the only one into blind girls, huh, Avenger?"

"Run. I'll give you a chance. If you do, I can justify the shot." I wanted him to have the illusion of chance.

"I know my rights. I'll wait for the Vampire Council to bring me a lawyer."

"There are laws that say I can't kill you, but there's also rightful justice for what you've done. Your so-called rights as a living thing are all political. It has nothing to do with prejudices or embracing other cultures. It's all about money and covering up the death that your kind cause. You bring in a large percentage of the economy, but also bring in a large percentage of the crime rate." I smacked him with the crucifix. "I hate everything about it. I've seen the aftermath of what you've done. You don't deserve a fair trial or protective custody. You deserve to die, and I'm willing to make it as graphic and as messy as I can."

"I did things to her you've never imagined. It turned her on. Seems your girl was into pain, Avenger. Said she needed a real man to do it to her."

"You sorry son of a..." My hands grasped his throat; I could feel the warm sensation of taking life from him. I let go and shoved him backwards.

"Begged for her life as I drained her," he laughed. "Shoved her in that dumpster like the trash she was."

"Ambulance is on the way." Angie shut the phone and handed it back to me. Small red speckles on the smooth pink leather, signs of cockroach blood. "Move a little and I'll slice his heart out," Angie added, standing in the doorway. Her no-nonsense personality had started to shine. Somehow, I knew she hated these things as much as I did. Comforting to know. "You may have obligations to the law, but I don't."

"I don't think so. I think I have something better in store. He knows that when Quinn finds out he failed, he's dead anyway. And I'm sure Quinn will do things we can only imagine," I answered. "Keeping him alive only complicates his world."

"What do you have in mind, baby?" Angie asked. I couldn't see her eyes, only my own reflection in the mirrored glasses.

"Let him feel what it is like to be blind and fight for his life." I opened a bottle of holy water and brought it to his face.

"You can't do this. It's against the law. You'll be dead before I will. I want Ms. Powers here, now!"

"Shut your pie hole, or I'll cut your guts out right here and now." Angie, moving with animal-like quickness, had the vampire by the throat.

"You'll never get away with this," Evan said, batting at the hand at his throat.

"Why not? When we're through with you, you won't be able to talk about it," she said with a vindictive smile. "I'll cut your tongue out."

I dragged the wounded cockroach to a stockroom that led off from the kitchen. It was filled with cases of beer and liquor, empty aluminum cans, and a coffin hidden in the back. Most of the cockroaches had coffins hidden in the event of an emergency. Working overtime can be hazardous to their health. Evan began to fight against me; his strength built with every passing second. It wouldn't take long for him to gather enough strength to overtake me. I would be left with no choice other than to stab him again. Once inside the stock room, I shut the door to keep Evan contained.

"Bring him close by so I can keep an eye on him," I said to Angie, looking at Father Garcia. "I don't want any of Evan's friends to get any bright ideas."

She had the strength of ten humans. To move a human a few feet was nothing. I only hoped she handled him with care.

In one quick move, Father Garcia was within reach again. And so was Angie. She was like a kid on Christmas morning, ready to rip and tear.

"Kill him. Don't leave him at the mercy of the bleeding hearts in this town. I promise, God will forgive this," Father Garcia said from behind me.

Angie held the vampire's head still. I lifted the vial of holy water and poured it in Evan's eyes, turning his face into a melting horror. He screamed in pain. The stench was so thick; I had to hold my breath just to keep from heaving. Angie struggled to keep him in her headlock, stumbling occasionally with each jerk and convulse of Evan's body.

"How does it feel to be blind?" I asked.

"They'll kill you for this."

Water mixed with blood from his melting eyes. Angie released her grip, and Evan hit the floor. His hands were tight against his face as he continued to scream.

"I don't care about anything except avenging the deaths of young girls at the hands of undead killers. I have no remorse. I have no second thoughts. The holy water can rot out your sockets for all I care." I watched as crater-like tracks ran down his face where the water had left his eyes. His face was red with flowing blood and melting skin.

Outside, I could hear the ambulance siren approaching. I was torn. I wanted it to get here quickly because I wanted Father Garcia to get medical attention, but it was cutting into my torture time.

"Tell me how you killed the others, Evan. Confession is good for the soul."

"What others?" A pool of blood formed around his head.

"You know who I'm talking about. The other girls you carved up and killed."

"I ain't killed nobody else." He moved across the floor like a caterpillar. First rolled up like a ball, then springing out full length, then returning to the ball, again and again.

"I'll kill you so slowly, it will take days."

"I didn't kill anyone else. Just the one girl."

"Don't lie to me, Evan. I swear the police will never find your body. You did to them what you did to your own sister, didn't you?"

"Quinn will take you down, mate."

I lifted him up and leaned him against the wall. "Go ahead, Evan. Run for your life. Run and get Quinn. You'll save me the time. I'll give you the same chance you gave Anna last night. Now, tell me you killed the others."

He swung at me, hitting nothing but air. He tried to stand and run, only to hit one of the shelves and fall backwards. His hands frantically searched for the way out. His skin melted away from his face like candle wax. "My eyes! I can't see, you bloody lunatic!"

On one of the shelves in the stockroom I saw a case of Jack Daniels. I quickly walked to it and pulled out one of the bottles. It was heavy in my shaking hands. My anger began to consume me.

I opened the bottle and returned to Evan, who had already slid back down the wall and slumped on the floor. His screams were starting to give way to a mewling sound as he swung wildly at me. From time to time, he would bite into the unknown like a rabid dog, hoping to catch anything. I watched him move in pain as the stinging holy water ate away at his skin like a cancer. All I could think about were the dead women I had to deal with after his escapades. Call it poetic justice if you will, but he was getting better than he deserved.

"Not so exciting from the other end, is it, Evan?" I stood over him. "Where's the rush you were talking about? I thought you were into pain. Is this how the women screamed? I'm giving you the same compassion you gave each and every one of them."

"You're out of your mind, mate. You're a dead man."

"Shut up." Angie kicked him between the legs.

I began to pour the Jack Daniels over his body. He screamed when it first hit him. "No more holy water."

"It's not holy water, Evan; it's a very nice alcohol. I hear that liquor is very combustible." I emptied the bottle.

"I've heard the same about vampires." Angie giggled as she moved behind me and put her arms around my waist, the butt of her gun now pressing against my stomach, pointed at Evan. She squeezed me playfully. "Never killed one like this before. Hold my hands; let's do it together."

I could feel her hot breath on the back of my neck, every curve of her body pressed tight against me. Excitement filled her muscles as well as mine as we stared down at Evan; she was twitching with energy. The hug was making me nervous; I needed my full range of movement in the event that Evan regained strength.

"He's got a lot to answer to before he dies," I explained. Then to Evan, "Tell me, how did Dr. Petty set you up with all your lovely dates?" It was a rhetorical question. I already knew the story.

Angie let go of her death grip, but was still close enough to make the hairs on my arm to rise. She was more powerful than I had ever given her credit for.

"What are you talking about?"

"All your victims were her patients. All in the same support group as you. When you ran out of friends there, you began to pray on dates from the Internet, right?"

"I don't know what you're talking about. The only person I killed was that Anna chick. I don't know anything about any other girls."

"Maybe a little flame will help him remember." Angie grabbed a book of matches from a nearby shelf. "Ready to talk, creep?" She bent down and peered at him, flicking the matchbook with a fingernail. His hands still covered the eyes that were no longer there.

"You are out of your mind!"

"Why were you talking to Dr. Petty tonight, if you are so innocent? She was giving you information on your next girl, wasn't she?" I asked him.

"What the hell's going on in here?" Kansas.

I turned to see his eyes wide with confusion. Sweat ran down the side of his face. His white shirt was hanging out of his pants. He looked at the dead vampires littered along the floor.

"Really, what's going on here?" he repeated.

"It's Evan."

"Seems to be what's left of him. Tell me you didn't do this." His voice was strong and loud. "The paramedics are trying to get through a crowd out front to handle all this. People are talking about shots being fired in here. For God's sake, tell me they're wrong."

"They attacked us."

Kansas looked down at Evan, then back up to me. "How did this happen?" He paused. "You know what, I don't want to know. You can explain it to the Vampire Council when they arrive. I sent you down here to talk to Evan because I thought you'd behave yourself. I should have known better. That's what people get for believing in you."

"Vampire Council? You aren't really thinking of turning him over to them, are you?" I shouted.

"No, I'm handing you over to the Council. You did all this in a vampire establishment. How do you expect me to sweep this under a rug? You're looking at life at best. I told you the other night your attitude was going to get you put away. Now it will."

"They tried to kill me!" Evan shouted from the floor.

"Shut up," Angie commanded.

"Who's your S&M deputy here?" Kansas asked, looking at Angie with curiosity. I think the pink leather was scarier to him than the vampire with no eyes.

"Angie. Who the hell are you?" she answered.

"This is a crime scene. Get lost."

Angie stared at him through the mirrored glasses. I was growing concerned that she might just bite his head off. Kansas didn't know she was a fur ball. If I knew Angie wouldn't kill him, I'd just let him think she was human and watch the fun, but I knew Angie would hurt him bad if he pushed her.

"Go," he said again, pointing to the door.

Uniformed cops now started to gather. The paramedics wheeled a stretcher inside to tend to Father Garcia. I was thankful to see them, but knew the added distractions were not good. "Until the Cockroach Counsel arrives, our coffin crispy is technically not under arrest. Don't you think we should do something about that before he kills someone else?" I said to Kansas.

Putting a vampire under arrest was not like putting a human under arrest. Cuffs would not hold the supernatural. He had to be placed in a coffin with a blessed crucifix on top. Until Kansas made that happen, I was very uneasy with the situation at hand.

"When we get a coffin here, we'll take care of it. In the mean-time, enjoy your last minute of freedom."

"There's a coffin in the store room, and since all police officers are required to wear crucifixes while on duty, finding one won't be a challenge. Besides, Father Garcia and I have extras if needed."

"Yeah, that's another thing. What's he doing down here? I tell you to not do something and you let it go in one ear and out the other," Kansas screamed, his arm pointing toward the door. "And don't tell me how to do my job. I know how to contain these things as well as you do. I'll arrest him. Don't worry. I won't tell you again: get your slut out of here."

Angie grabbed the extended hand and pushed it to Kansas' back, sending him to his knees. Ahh, now he knows what she is. I smiled despite myself. "Don't point your finger at me again, or I'll break your arm."

Two officers nearby pointed their guns on Angie as the paramedics hustled to get Father Garcia outside as quickly as possible.

"Whoa, whoa, whoa," I shouted to the officers. "It's okay. Everyone calm down."

Angie released Kansas' arm, and he popped back up to meet her smiling gaze. The redness in his face showed his embarrassment. The guns were slowly lowered.

"You're going down on assault charges, sweetheart." Kansas said, but not pointing. He learns fast.

"Angie, it's okay. Wait outside." I said, trying to remain calm.

She gave me a confused look. She was like me, she lived for this.

"Please," I added.

She nodded lightly and began to walk toward the door.

"She saved our lives," Father Garcia said from the stretcher, looking over to Kansas.

"I don't care if she saves the world. I want her out of here," Kansas retorted. "Put her in cuffs," he said to the nearest officer. "Make sure they're silver cuffs. She's a fur ball."

Angie gave him one last glare. The mirrored glasses enhanced the effect. She looked over to me, gave me a small smile, and blew a kiss. I smiled back, even though I didn't mean to. In an instant, she was lost in the crowd. I pitied the officer that tried to place her in cuffs. He was about to be in a lot of pain.

Kansas leaned down to Evan. "Shit, what did you do to him,

Paul?" He looked up at me in disgust. "I won't be able to save you from the Council on this, you know."

"Doesn't matter to me. In a few hours, I'll be dead anyway." I lit a cigar and waited for the Cockroach Council. I had one more thing to do: kill them when they arrived.

CHAPTER TWENTY-THREE

Like ghosts, they arrived without warning. I could feel them behind me. Evil has a very distinct vibe to it. It made the hair on my arms stand at attention, my skin crawl with goose bumps. No one else registered their arrival, but I was drowning in a pool of power, unable to catch my breath.

I turned to see Dieter Procnow and Maximilian before me. Dieter had dressed in a charcoal gray suit, light gray vest, white shirt and deep blue tie. Maximilian wore a black tux with a gleaming white shirt and a pink carnation boutonniere, accessorized with, I'm not making this up, a black top hat, white gloves, and a cane. The top hat was purely decorative, while the cane was more functional. He walked with a limp like a Caribbean pirate.

"Playing dress-up tonight, fellas?"

Maximilian looked in my direction, but never spoke.

"I couldn't resist." This to Dieter.

"Who is this?" Maximilian said, looking down at Evan. "I am unable to make out his identity through the grotesque disfigurement."

"It is the product of Mr. Isaac, I am sure," Dieter answered, his words slurred, serpent-like.

"I'll tell you what it is, Dieter. It is the product of blood sucking cockroach scum. This is the maggot that's been killing all the women over the last few weeks. Now, we're going to arrest the good Dr. Petty as an accessory. Then, I'll be back to kill the two of you, so don't go too far."

"You must be so proud of your diligent work, Avenger. I am sure the mayor will see to it that you receive the key to the city. Too bad you'll be enjoying it from the grave," Dieter said to me.

"Mr. Procnow, Maximilian, thank you for coming down here on short notice. I wouldn't have had the department call you if I didn't feel it was urgent," Kansas said, extending his hand. He was playing diplomat tonight.

Maximilian looked at the hand and snarled, moving past Kansas as if he was not there. "I was at a ballet across town, Detective." Maximilian rarely came out of hiding. He was a recluse among the vampires; only a few knew anything about him. "I had front-row tickets."

"I am sorry for the inconvenience."

"Do you know how hard it is to get tickets to Coppélia, Detective?"

"Again, I apologize, Maximilian, but this is a matter of great importance. We are confident that we have the vampire responsible for the serial killings in the area over the last few weeks. I thought you would want to know."

"Such time and effort just to catch the killer of common street whores. But I guess all in all, it is a good thing for the community to have this man off the street."

He looked over to me. "Detective Kansas, may I ask why Mr. Isaac is here in the first place? I thought the police department and the Council agreed that he would be locked away for his actions."

"My eyes! I need a doctor!" Evan shouted from the floor.

"You have my word. Paul will be placed under arrest after this is taken care of," Kansas said, looking down at Evan.

"So have you promised before? And now I find yet another victim of his vigilante behavior. No matter what crimes Evan may or may not have committed, no civilized being could believe Mr. Isaac's actions are justified."

I grabbed him by the coat. "Civilized? Look at that thing on the floor. Think about what he's done, and tell me about being civilized. Mutilation and killing is all you monsters know. He killed a blind woman. He got what he deserved. He should know what it's like to have to live and die like that."

Kansas pushed me off of the elder bloodsucker. "You're under arrest, Isaac. I can't help you this time. You did this to yourself." Other officers grabbed me from behind.

"Go ahead, Kansas, let them put you in their hip pocket. But you know as well as I do they'll turn on all of us the first chance they get. They kidnapped and poisoned me, yet they walk free and I'm under arrest. What I did to Evan was in self-defense. Quinn Rubio sent him in here to kill Father Garcia and myself. Ask Maximilian about his so-called daughter, Lyric."

"Shut up, Paul."

"How much are they paying you to look the other way?"

"I said, shut up!" Kansas hit me across the jaw. I tasted blood.

"You're nothing but a sell-out. You spineless coward."

"Mr. Isaac has apparently had a most stressful week, Detective. We in the vampire community are most concerned with his actions, and will press charges for this." Maximilian met my gaze and continued. "As for kidnapping, I assure you that there has been nothing of the kind. I have no idea who this Lyric is, except perhaps a figment of Mr. Isaac's delusional mind. But I do recall a rumor of a missing young man in the district where Mr. Isaac killed Vinnie the other night. A vampire activist, I am told."

I pulled away from the cops holding me and put the Magnum

against Maximilian's chest. "I'll shoot you on the spot," I snapped. "To say I owe you one would be an understatement. Now, tell me why the Council wants Lyric. Tell me, or I'll end it all for you here."

"Don't be so sure of that, Avenger. Sometimes the most unlikely person can come to your rescue if they still find you of value. The enemy of my enemy just might be you."

"Put the gun down," Kansas said, his gun now to my head.

"Maximilian, please tell them I didn't kill all those girls," Evan whined.

"Mr. Procnow, please see to it that Mr. Falkner is disposed of," Maximilian growled.

"I promised myself when you got here, I'd kill you," I said to the two vampires in front of me, my Magnum still on Maximilian. "I'll make good on that promise."

"Do it, Avenger. Save your friends the aggravation of having to kill you once you turn", Dieter said as he walked over to Evan.

"You can't just kill him here," I said to Dieter, looking to Kansas for support.

"And why not?" Maximilian asked.

"Please don't kill me. I only killed the one. I'm sorry. Please, Maximilian, have mercy!" Evan cried.

"He killed those women, did he not, Avenger? Is that not what you said a moment ago? This is the vampire that killed the women of the night?"

"Yes, but he must be tried in a court of law."

Dieter grabbed a large knife and walked toward Evan. "Not under vampire law."

I looked back to Kansas. "Do something. You can't let them have jurisdiction over this. He must be tried in our courts."

"The Council has the option to deny your courts if we feel the accused will not get a fair trial." This from Maximilian.

"Not if the victim is a human, it doesn't."

Kansas dropped his gun and caught my eye. "If they kill that thing, they destroy all the evidence against you. We kill two birds with one stone. Otherwise, they will kill you too. You know that as well as I do."

"You know they're cooperating far too easily. Something is wrong here."

"Please tell them I didn't do those things. Tell them!" Evan begged. Dieter stood over him now.

I jabbed Maximilian with the Magnum. "You can't kill him here."

Maximilian laughed. "Are you trying to defend Mr. Falkner? After you burned his eyes out?"

"No, I want him dead as much as everyone else. Probably a little more. But you seem to want him dead a little too quickly. And I know it's not for the good of the community, so what is it?"

Maximilian nodded. Dieter drove the knife into the vampire's heart. Blood sprayed the floor. Dieter cut the heart free and tossed it to the side, then looked at me. "See, Avenger, you aren't the only one that can kill."

"And I'm the one under arrest?" I said to Kansas.

"Let it go, Paul. There's nothing we can do about it. Besides, we all got what we wanted."

"And what did they want, Kansas? Dead men tell no tales. Don't be so sure this is over."

"With his death, your secrets die as well, Avenger," Maximilian responded.

"So many secrets of your own to hide, right, Maximilian? Tell us who Lyric is to you. Why does the Council want her so bad?"

"Drop the gun, now!" Kansas shouted as other officers pulled the Magnum free. I had a gun drawn on me again.

"Who you find is not as important as when you find them, Avenger. Sunrise is only hours away. If we find her before you do, we have no need for you, dead or alive. Kill Piel, and you still have a chance to cheat your destiny. Opportunity rarely knocks twice. If you fail this time, there may not be anyone there to stitch you up", Maximilian said to me.

Kansas' cell phone went off, causing me to jump. Second time tonight. "Kansas." One hand kept the gun trained on me as he talked.

"A little jumpy, Avenger. Not good for an executioner to lose his nerve. Especially when threatening the life of a thousand-year-old vampire. People will start to doubt your ability to do your job. If they lose faith in you, who will be there to console them? You will be nothing more than a relic trying to relive glory years", Dieter added as he walked behind Maximilian. I guess some things never really change.

"I'll be the one that drives the stake through all your hearts, mark my words."

"Looks to me as if you are making the same mistakes you did with that young man you killed in cold blood a few years ago. Innocent blood on your hands again. The answers are staring you in the face and you cannot see them. A quick rush to judgment is your modus operandi. That is what I like about you: you are a distraction from the obvious," said Maximilian.

"Maybe I've filled in more blanks than you think."

"So you have, Mr. Isaac. But as in all good tragedies, this will not end well for you."

My whole body was shaking. "Kansas, I need to talk to you."

Kansas ended his call and lowered the gun as if the life had suddenly been sucked out of him. If he had heard anything I said, it wasn't showing on his face.

"Everyone move!" he shouted as he pushed through the officers. "Price will be dead by the time we get there." He looked back to me. "I need your help, or they'll all die."

"I need my gun back."

"There's no need for it, yet. We're not killing vampires. We're killing werewolves."

I stared at Maximilian, unable to do anything more than that.

"You better not keep Detective Price waiting. Death waits for no one," the monster purred.

CHAPTER TWENTY-FOUR

I crashed through the kitchen door, nearly knocking over a waiter in my path. The restaurant was empty of patrons. It looked like the rapture had taken place. Half-eaten plates of food and half-filled glasses of wines sat on the tables. Solitary candles flickered, unaware of the evil around them.

"Kansas." My leather trench coat hung heavy and bulky as I ran. "Kansas, what is it?"

He didn't look back. "Werewolves are attacking the SunTrust Building and trying to get in Powers' office. Price's men can't hold them off any longer. I should have left you here to fend for yourself. "

"Piel. He's found Dr. Feelgood again," I said, more to myself than to Kansas. Once again, I wasn't ready for this fight. I had anything and everything to kill vampires with, but very little to kill shape-shifters. "We're going to need silver."

"I know. Here." Kansas handed me an extra Browning. "Silver nitrate bullets. But that doesn't mean you should kill everything that moves over there."

We hit the street. Other officers joined us in our run. My heart pounded with panic and exhaustion, a recipe for a heart attack. This night just kept getting better. Loud music poured over us like syrup. Crowds parted as we moved through them. I hit someone along the way, felt cold beer spray me.

The SunTrust Building sat across the street from The Coffin, towering above Church Street like a giant gargoyle. By looking at it, you could tell something was wrong. The oversized glass doors leading into the lobby had been shattered; glass littered the floor in pebble-sized green pellets. Another crowd had started to gather there, with police pushing them back.

Kansas and I moved into the lobby and began to look around. I could hear the crunch of broken glass as more and more officers entered the building. They would not be prepared for what was upstairs. I could see it in their eyes.

"I have a bad feeling about this. Things are going to get worse before they get better," I said to Kansas as we surveyed the damage. "Most of us will probably be dead by the time this is over."

"The L.T.F. is on its way, but I can't wait for them to get here." L.T.F. was short for Lycanthrope Task Force. "If we don't stabilize the area, Price and his men will be dead by the time they show up. I need your help. Most of these men have never been in a real lycanthrope situation before."

Against the back wall, I saw a dead officer, his throat ripped out. Maroon liquid pooled around him. He didn't look real. More like a prop in a very good haunted house. But I knew better. He was a warning of what was upstairs.

"We'll move up the stairs. The elevator makes us sitting ducks; we could use the element of surprise." Kansas said, looking back at us. "Make sure you have silver nitrate bullets in your weapons."

I already dreaded the climb. I wasn't in the best of shape, and I smoked too much. By the time we made it to Powers' office, we would all be too tired to fight anyway. Being killed at that point would be more like putting us out of our misery.

From above I heard howls and shots. I tried to keep the dark thoughts from entering my mind, but they continued to ooze in.

We reached the tenth floor before we found the next body. He was facedown on the stairs, blood dripping from beneath him. Thank God Kansas didn't roll him over. I wasn't in the mood to see someone I knew yet. I wanted to have as clear a mind as I could.

Fifteenth floor. More shots, more howls. Fewer screams. I pushed forward, trying to keep up with Kansas and not get knocked down by the overzealous cop behind me. I wiped sweat from my forehead, tried to catch my breath. My legs felt as though they were on fire. I thought about those stickers that say "No Pain, No Gain" and laughed. If that were true, I was gaining more than I needed. I figured I'd puke before I made it to the eighteenth floor.

Kansas stopped and looked back at me, his face red. "Glad I'm not the only one about to pass out."

"If we die up there, at least we'll get some rest." I hunched over, hands on my knees, and gasped for air for a few seconds, wiping sweat away from my eyes.

"If you two don't get a move on, they'll all be dead before we see any action," the cop behind me said.

"Listen up, Sparky, the last thing we need right now is for you to try and make this your blaze of glory. Save your strength. You're gonna need it in a few minutes," I snapped back.

"Let's go," Kansas said. And we were off again.

Our pace slowed with each additional step. We rounded the door to the seventeenth floor, and I peeked in to see if I saw any movement. It was a ghost town. I wasn't sure if that was a good thing or a bad thing. We kept moving.

A couple more howls. Shots rang out. They were much louder and closer now, making us jump. Another ten steps above me was the doorway to the eighteenth floor. The door itself had been ripped from its hinges and lay crumpled on the stairs in our path. Kansas stepped around it, gun drawn and close to his body. "The nightmare is about to begin, Martin," he said to the mouthy officer behind me, motioning for us to stop with his free hand. For the moment, he was our eyes and ears. I motioned behind me as well, and in a few seconds all footsteps had come to stop.

Kansas began to move again, out into the hallway of offices. I followed, along with the eight men behind me. "Don't shoot me in the back of the head," I said to Martin.

I entered the hallway and began to look around for any signs of Price and his men. It looked like a war zone. Walls were completely missing in some places; the ones remaining were painted with blood. Six dead officers and two naked men, whom I assumed to be fur balls, sprawled in the hallway. I thought back to the night at Feelgood's office and cringed. I knew what these things could do. I had seen it firsthand.

From behind me I heard a scream, followed by a growl and a thump. I turned to find one of the fur balls on top of one of the officers. It had the policeman on the ground, ripping into his back with talons of incredible strength. Teeth sharper than razors tore into flesh. Blood gushed from open arteries. The other officers began to shoot. I rolled away from the monster, firing two shots of my own. It hit the ground, dead.

"Shit, what was that thing?" Martin screamed as he moved away from the dead man.

"It's a werewolf. What did you think you were going to find up here?" I asked.

"Not something like that. They don't pay me enough to kill those things." He looked back at the body again and threw up on his own feet.

"Get back down the stairs then," I commanded.

"I'll be okay in a second." He was still bent over.

"No, you won't. You're going to get yourself killed-or worse yet, one of us."

He looked at me with a deadly stare. "Who do you think you are? Technically, you're under arrest. You're not in charge."

"But I am. Now get back down there if you can't handle this, Martin," Kansas joined in.

Martin looked at him and back to me. "I said I'm okay. I just wasn't expecting something like that."

"Weren't you trained on these things at the academy?" I asked.

"Yeah, I was. So what? I don't see you leading the way."

"I'm not the one puking on my shoes, either."

We began to move fast down the hallway, following the sounds around a blind corner. If the fur balls didn't know we were there before, they did now. We had fired our weapons and killed one of their own. Things like that seem to draw attention. "God, how many of them are there?"

"Price!" Kansas shouted. "Cover me while I see what's hiding around the corner," he said to me. He was making a great effort to keep his voice as calm as possible, but his face showed the fear. Couldn't blame him. I probably had the same look.

We didn't have to wait on whatever was hiding behind the next corner. It came crashing through the wall on top of us, hitting the two officers behind me. Three more wolves began to attack. Blood rained down. Body parts flew through the air in a spray of horror. The officer on the other side of the mess shot a hole in the chest of the monster closest to her. I took one of the other two in the head. Martin flanked the third, trying to get off a shot.

Kansas was shooting around the corner. I could see shadows of movement on the walls. Howls filled the narrow passage, blending with the explosion of bullets.

"Kansas, get down!" I heard Price shout. Price was alive!

Kansas pulled back around the corner where the remaining few of us waited. Bullets peppered the wall across from us. I could hear the crashing of bodies. I hoped they were furry bodies.

Silence.

"Price, you okay?" Kansas shouted.

"Come on around, the coast is clear," he shouted back.

We moved as one body around the corner and came face to face with Price and one other officer. My heart sank. I wasn't sure how many police officers had been with Price, but the reality of what took place here sunk in with the number that was left. "Jesus, Price, how many of these things are there up here?" I asked.

"I don't know. They just keep coming."

"Where's Dr. Petty?" Kansas asked.

"That thing's after her." He motioned with his head.

"What thing?" I asked. "If it's Piel, it could be anything."

"It was a...spider or bug or something. I tried to stop it, but there was too many of them."

"Spiders?" I asked.

"No, the rest of them are werewolves. One spider."

"And Powers?" I asked again.

"She's dead, I think. She's in her office." He swallowed hard. "Werewolves busted in and attacked everybody."

"Is it Piel?" Kansas asked. "I never heard of were spiders."

"That's what I was telling you. Piel is a freak, even among the shape-shifters. He can change into anything he wants. And now he has the good doctor with him. We'll have to find him-fast." I moved down the hallway past the two detectives at a swift walk. I wanted to find Piel as quickly as I could. I knew he could just as easily be waiting for us in ambush around the next corner.

The hallway seemed to go on forever, leading back to the stairwell where I first entered the building. I looked up the stairs and back down, knowing that the monster could be hiding in either direction. I strained to hear anything. Motion. Screams from Feel-good. I had no visual on either her or the spider. Kansas, Price, and the remaining officers moved into the stairwell and looked to me for direction.

"They're moving up." I said. Kansas nodded to me, and we crept up the stairs.

"Help me!" someone shouted. Not Feelgood.

"It's Powers. She's still alive." Price said.

The sound of more werewolves approaching could be heard in the distance.

"Shame. I hoped they had already gotten to the blood-sucking lawyer." I turned in the direction of the shout and met Price's gaze. He never did like the monsters, but for different reasons than me. To him, they were just too damn scary. I couldn't blame him for that. I thought the same thing, but my revenge and hatred ran a little deeper. It had become my motivation.

"You two go help her. The rest of us will hunt the spider," I said to Price and Kansas. I knew I wouldn't get too much flack from Price. Kansas was a different story. He was always afraid I was trying to take over, and he didn't take kindly to it. I didn't blame him, really. I wouldn't want someone who wasn't even a cop giving me orders if I were in his shoes. However, his specialty was solving cases. Mine was killing things.

"No, I'm going after Piel too," Kansas retorted. See, told you so.

"Help!" Powers again.

"Look, Kansas, the pissing contest will have to wait. Right now, we have lives on the line. I'm the monster killer, not you. You can't leave Price with those things again. If nothing else, send him out of here and save the girl."

"You kill vampires, Isaac, not were...whatever's. This is my man to capture. Alive, if possible. If it's up to you, you'll just go up there and blast him."

"Your conscience is going to get you killed one day, Kansas.

You can't treat these things like humans. They aren't wired that way. There is no negotiating with them. There's life and there's death. There's no in-between." I started up the stairs. "There's no time for this. If I can get Piel to come with me quietly, I'll play by the rules. Otherwise, one of us will die." Kansas huffed, but then like a good Boy Scout moved back out of the mouth of the stairwell and toward the shouts of an injured vampire.

"Remember, you're still under arrest," he called over his shoulder.

I ran up the stairs, on pure adrenaline now. My legs threatened to give out on me, but I had to find and kill the monster. How, I was still working on.

"Keep your eyes open," I muttered to the officers below me.

"For what?" Martin asked.

"Anything that is big, hairy, and can eat you."

There were signs that the monster was still moving above us. Noises found only in nightmares. Screams. Metal bending. Things breaking. But to my relief, no more bodies. No more blood. No more death.

Ahead of us, I saw the monster. It reached out in all directions with tentacle-like legs, one of them holding Dr. Feelgood. I took a deep breath. The monster hulked over us like a skyline.

I brought the Browning up. "Let her go, Piel. It's over."

The spider swung a long leg at me. I dodged and rolled out of the way. Shots went off behind me as Martin and the other officers moved to take position. My ears rang with the sound. I stayed huddled for a few extra seconds. Bullets had to land somewhere. Note to self: Shoot Martin in the knee if we lived through this.

"Jesus, what are you doing?" I shouted.

"Killing it!" Martin shouted back as he fired two more shots.

"Get out of here before you shoot us all." I knocked Martin's wrist upward.

The spider moved toward us, striking out again, this time

sending the female officer spinning across the floor. Her gun skittered away. Shit. Being unarmed against a hellish creature like this was not a good thing. I moved toward her. Martin took another shot at Piel, hitting the monster in the body. If Piel was allergic to silver, it wasn't showing.

Piel threw Feelgood against the wall and covered her in a sticky substance. I wasn't sure what it was at first, then realized it was a webbing of some kind. Martin took another couple shots. Both hit, puncturing the carapace of the spider. The monster moved toward him, leaving me a clear lane to the gun and the female officer. She was back on her feet, with little damage done.

The were-spider continued to attack. Large fangs punctured one officer's shoulder, followed by decapitation. I moved in from behind as the bloodbath continued. The monster devoured the officers one by one until only I, Martin, and the female officer remained.

I kicked the gun back to the woman and hoped that she was able to get to it before she lost her head. Physically speaking.

"Piel, come and get me! I'm the one that killed your little pet last night." I wanted to take it back as soon as I said it. "Your turn."

I held the gun on the spider as it turned to me. Yeah, I was sure I wanted to take it back now. The last thing I wanted to do was piss him off any more than I already had.

Through the hallway door, I saw more movement. Angie. She was moving with animal-like speed, changing into a fur ball right before my eyes. I had never seen the transformation take place. Human features giving way to claws, fur, and teeth. It was a horror show all its own. My eyes saw it, but I still found it hard to believe. It was graphic and gross. Not to mention that it looked like it would hurt. I placed my finger on the trigger of the Browning. One threatening move by her and I'd end her misery.

She drew closer, placing herself between the spider and me. Teeth gnashing together, the hair stood up on her neck.

I saw Martin draw his gun on Angie. "Shoot her, and I shoot you."

He glanced at me, confused, but still held the gun on Angie. "You've got to be kidding me! Didn't you see what those things did down there? She's gonna die."

"You heard me. Shoot her, and I'll kill you. I think she's here to help." I had a clear shot at Piel and took it before moving toward Feelgood. I felt stupid trying to save her life after all the shit she had pulled over the last few days.

Angie jumped on Piel's back and began to attack. Spider chunks flew. One leg swung up and threw her off. Angie went spinning across the floor, yelping in pain.

I struggled to free Feelgood's wrapped body, only to find the silk impossible to break. Piel smacked me with a leg, hard. I saw stars. My vision blurred. I lost my grip on Feelgood.

"Davenport, shoot it!" Martin shouted. Ahh, Davenport. Now the woman had a name.

Angie was back up and attacking again.

Davenport moved next to me. "I'm gonna try to get to her. Keep distracting that thing," she said, moving toward Feelgood. "If it comes after me, kill it." This about Angie. She slid next to Feelgood and became tangled in the sticky web, but never lost her momentum. She grabbed the doctor by the webbing and began to pull. I wasn't sure if Feelgood was alive or dead. I couldn't see her face, couldn't hear her screams...if there were any.

A spray of blood, and Davenport hit the floor. What was left of her. Piel had bitten her head off. The body kicked a couple of times before falling still. A pool of red liquid spread, and pulsating spray shot from the opening. I tried to swallow, waves of nausea rolling over me. Forget dying by the hands of stake magnets; it would be a spider instead. She tried to help, and I got her killed.

Angie was thrown a second time, landing near the stairwell. I reached for my Magnum and began to fill Piel's underbelly full of silver nitrate bullets. A woman had just lost her life trying to save mine. I took it very personally. The son of a bitch was going down.

The spider backed away from me and moved toward Martin. I felt a blast of power like a gale-force wind as Angie moved past me in hot pursuit.

I quickly reloaded and shot the spider again as it attacked Martin, who had made it to the entrance of the stairway before Piel got to him. Martin's hands got tangled in the web, leaving him unable to defend himself. Angie bit at one of the spider's legs.

Piel sank his fangs into Martin's right shoulder. The screams will haunt me for the rest of my life. Popping noises followed by tearing and ripping sounds. His arm was instantly amputated, and Feelgood's body fell to the floor, the white webbing now covered in glistening red. Blood flowed down the side of Martin's body and began to run across the floor. He fell to his knees, screaming.

Piel began to devour Martin as we watched in helpless horror. Splatters of flesh hit the wall. Sprays of blood painted the floor. Screams of horror filled our ears. Bones crunching, bullets signing as he tried in vain to stop the attack. It seemed to go on and on and then...silence. Martin was dead.

Piel whirled back toward the cocooned body of Feelgood. I held my breath. Afraid to yell, afraid not to.

I pulled the silver knife out of its sheath and began to move toward Feelgood's webbing. Piel was on top of me before I had a chance to stand. I instinctively brought the knife upward and into the spider's belly. From above, I felt Angie attacking again. I have to hand it to her, she's persistent.

The spider stopped and hovered as I continued to slice as much of its underbelly as I could. Freeing a sticky, yellowish substance. Whatever this stuff was, it was nasty.

For the first time in my battle with Piel, he seemed to be hurt enough to back off. The spider wobbled a few steps away and fell to the floor. Angie continued to rip at the monster from above. Piel had an incredible healing ability; the bullet wounds were practically healed already.

I turned to Feelgood, the knife still in my hand, covered in the yellow...stuff, and began to slice into the webbing. My hands were working through the wet webbing, covered in blood and now spider guts. I fantasized about a hot shower. The webbing covered me like a new layer of skin, sticking to the knife. Dulling it quickly. I had to wipe it clean on my pants several times. I glanced back at Piel and Angie, making sure I wasn't about to be blindsided by anything.

As Feelgood broke free, she looked toward the stairwell where Davenport's headless body lay, then with apprehension toward Piel. Paralyzed with fear, she couldn't tear her eyes from the monster.

Piel was face down, turning back to human form. It had been a fatal blow through the heart.

Feelgood and I stared at each other for a moment. "We got your killer."

"What do you mean, my killer?"

"Evan Falkner. Seems he's the one that killed Anna Martinez. As soon as you step out of this building, you'll be arrested as an accessory to murder."

"Me? What are you talking about?"

"You've been feeding him the patients from your group. Your way of helping out the cockroach community."

"You're insane. I had nothing to do with it. I was trying to save them, not kill them. I went to see them at the hospital every evening. You can check with Dr. Montgomery if you don't believe that."

I let it all sink in. "Dr. Montgomery?"

"Yes, Dr. George Montgomery. He and I worked with the group. Why? Is he your next suspect?"

"Run," I said.

"You have to believe me."

"I do. Now, run."

She sprinted for the stairs. A thin layer of blood and webbing still covered her, but overall, she was fine. The blood didn't appear to be hers. I had mixed feelings about that.

Piel was on his knees, bent over as if trying to breathe. Anger spilling from his eyes. For the second time, I had kept him from killing Feelgood. His hands pressed against his wound, blood flowing between the fingers. "She feeds the vampires your victims, yet you kill me. You're no different than they are. You don't hate the vampires, you hate yourself."

"I don't think so, but I don't have the time to go into it now," I answered.

Angie began to change back to human form as well. Animal features giving way to human ones. Her cinnamon skin started to overtake the fur, glistening with sweat, naked and smooth. Her bright pink hair was wet and clinging to her.

"I'll kill you both," Piel said, watching her.

I could see the flesh knitting together. He was healing quickly; my time was running out. I already knew battle lines had been drawn. One of us would die. He wouldn't leave me with a choice. I could see the strength entering his muscles again, a warm new energy.

"Kill me. I die at sunrise anyway," I said sarcastically. Or at least I wanted it to be sarcastic.

"Why would you want to save her, after all she's done? Don't lose your life over that bitch."

"Like I said, I have nothing to lose. I'm a dead man."

"I can give you back your life."

"Really. Do tell."

"The poison running through your veins can be cancelled out with the lycan virus. It will keep you from dying and becoming one of them."

"Sorry, I have no desire to bark at the moon either. I'd rather just die if those are my options." I leveled my Browning on Piel. I wasn't sure in human form if he would be more vulnerable to the bullets or not, but I was willing to try.

"You don't understand. The lycan virus won't turn you into an animal; just keep the vampire poison from killing you. You'll be better than all of us. You'll have my virus running through your veins, giving you strength, speed-and immunity to the poison inside you."

Angie flanked him without saying a word.

"You try anything and I'll kill you, bitch. You've betrayed me for the last time," he said without looking at her. Then to me, "Let me help you. We can take over the vampire district together. I have no beef with you. It's the vampires and their associates that must pay for the evil here."

"And why would you be willing to help me? How do you know I wouldn't betray you?"

Piel's laugh was sinister. "Haven't you ever heard of the old saying, 'The enemy of my enemy is my friend'?"

"Yeah, a few times tonight, in fact. I'm not your friend, Piel. If you don't kill me, I assure you, I will kill you."

"And her?"

I continued to watch Angie out of the corner of my eye. "I still don't trust her. I mean, what's her motivation in helping me? It makes no sense. The best-case scenario would be to kill you all. That way, I'm sure to get the right one."

"By sunrise, the hunter becomes the hunted. You will become the very thing you hate the most. I can help keep you from that."

"So can a stake through the heart. And I have a long list of people and monsters that will be willing to do that. I'm not afraid of dying, Piel. There have been plenty of nights that I put a gun to my temple and fantasized about it. I've lost my parents, seen more corruption than I can shake a stick at. And no matter how many monsters I kill, the pain never goes away. In fact, it feeds on the violence and killing. If I die, there will be others like me to take my place. You'll never be safe." I felt my finger growing stiff against the trigger.

"I can take him out right now," Angie said, causing me to jump. I had forgotten she was there for a second.

Piel laughed again. "Sweetheart, you can't kill me. Neither of you have bullets that can kill me. Slow me down, make me bleed, perhaps, but not kill me. I'm far too powerful for this." He looked at me. "Besides, if you kill me, you'll never find Lyric. I know who she is, where she is, and why the vampires want her. Always have."

"In a few hours, it won't matter."

"She's the key to the murders, you know. That's why they want her. She saw things."

"What do you mean?"

"She's a witness to one of the murders. Maximilian needs to keep her quiet. Her testimony could cause his house of cards to tumble to the ground. You were a pawn in his game. Flush out the threat for them, and then kill you. Perfect." More laughter. "They've gone to great lengths to cover their tracks and make you the scape-goat. They get you either way."

"Sorry, I don't buy your lies. I've seen what you do in your club, and there is no way you'll live either way. If not me, someone else will hunt you down and kill you. You are no better than the other monsters here. And no more untouchable." With that, I put a bullet in his neck.

Angie was on top of Piel with animal speed and strength. Piel started to stand, pushing her off of him. I fired another shot, driving Piel backwards toward a large glass window. Another couple rounds drove him toward the window. He staggered backward, his eyes showed the horror of things to come. He lost his balance and crashed through the window to his death nineteen stories below. "Silver couldn't kill him, but he's the same as anyone else when it comes to the laws of gravity," I said to Angie as she peered out the hole in the window.

"Pity," she remarked.

The outline of his body was a black dot among the neon lights. But like everything else in my world, when one nightmare ends, it simply melts into the next.

CHAPTER TWENTY-FIVE

I looked back to Angie and hoped that my fighting was over. Her caramel body glistened with sweat, dampening the bright pink hair that draped across her breasts and played with her nipples. Her curves caught the moonlight as it poured into the room. I could feel her power like electricity. It mixed with erotic heat, animal-like, primal. I wanted her and wanted her now, a craving of unspeakable proportions. Now was not the time.

"Why?" I was still trying to catch my breath.

She smiled at me. The same smile that she'd had at the Lunatic Moon. She walked toward me, slowly, hips gyrating with pulsing rhythm. "What?" she purred. "Never seen a naked girl before?"

I had a sneaking suspicion that she knew the answer to my question, but wanted me to ask it again. "Why did you come here and help me kill him?" God, I couldn't keep my eyes from her exposed breasts. All I could think about was putting them in my mouth and sucking them, feeling them in my hands. Unlike her lycan form, she was clean-shaven. All over. Think of anything else. Think, think, think.

"Most of the wolves wanted him dead. But none as much as I did," she answered, now only inches away from me. I could smell her; feel the power growing stronger. I could hardly breathe. "Piel had them under his control. They did as they were told."

"Why?"

She ran her fingernails across my chest. Chills shot down my spine. "My brother was the alpha male before Piel showed up. Piel killed my brother when he wouldn't step down and be submissive. I vowed to kill that son of a bitch when I could. I was avenging my brother's death." The last word was mere breath. Her lips brushed mine so lightly that it made me shiver. Her hands now worked their way across my chest, exploring and capturing every nerve her fingers graced. I ached for her. My body grew hard. My embarrassment grew just as fast. I could feel my heart pounding harder than it had all night, and that was saying something.

"Thank you," I said. There was no way of saying it without it sounding anything but stupid, but I had to say it.

"Not a problem." Her mouth locked on my lips; her wet tongue forced its way inside my mouth. Her body melted to mine. The softness of her belly and breasts pressed against my shirt. I wanted to rip it off and feel our bodies touching skin against skin. There was a power between us. It wasn't the power of her beast this time, but pure animal magnetism. My hands moved along her curves, fingers exploring and tingling with excitement. She had a certain softness to her that fed into the hunger. Her tongue pressed against mine, soft yet forceful. She purred as she licked along my lips with erotic passion.

I was torn between my fate and my desires. There was a certain bitterness to it all. Whether I lived or died, I had already come to terms with myself. I had found Evan and placed him under arrest. I had killed Piel, leaving me with nothing but time to find Lyric and use her to get to Quinn.

I wanted vengeance against those that had killed me. I wanted to look into their eyes as I drove a stake through their fucking hearts. Somehow, I had to live long enough to see that. But now, there were other desires. If this was truly going to be my last night on earth, why not indulge myself with this beautiful woman?

I looked into Angie's eyes and saw the longing and the desire I'd felt in her hands and body. She wanted the same things I did, but probably for very different reasons. Her scent was strong, like a fresh picked rose. I drank her in.

"Is what Piel said true?" she purred.

I pulled away enough to see her face in the glow of the moonlight shining through the broken window. "What do you mean?"

"About becoming a vampire. Are you going to die tonight because of them?"

"Yes. A poison that will kill me at sunrise. Some sort of shapeshifting shit that turns me into a monster."

"I know about the poison." She continued running her hands along my chest.

"What do you mean, you know about the poison?"

"Quinn got it from Piel. It was supposed to be a mixture of lycan virus with some sort of vampire shit. I didn't know what it was exactly, but Piel had been working on it to take over the humans without being detected. After he killed the vampires, of course."

"So it's true, then."

She shrugged. "I can help you. If you trust me, I can keep it from killing you."

My heart stopped. "What are you talking about?"

"The poison won't work if the victim has lycan virus already in their system."

"So I have a choice of either being a cockroach or furry?"

"No. They cancel each other out. You would be a carrier of both, but truly neither. You would have the strength and power of all of us, but stay as you are." She slid back into my arms. Her pink hair flowed across my skin. Fingernails traced my stomach, moving slowly southward.

"So what are you saying?" I wanted to push her away, but I couldn't. I wanted to throw her down on the floor and take her all in. I wanted to be inside her, my tongue licking her skin, my hands feeling her breasts and erect nipples. I needed her. And I wasn't sure I could keep from giving in. She seemed to melt with each passing move, daring me, tempting me, wanting me.

"Some lycan viruses are easier to catch than others. That's why the werewolf is most common. It is easy to catch; a light break of the skin can do the trick. Other viral forms are much harder to catch. Rats, leopards, and others take a bit more effort." Her fingers had found their way inside my shirt and were moving over my chest. I could feel the heat from her hands as they touched, fingers spread wide, taking in everything. Stopping at my nipples, making them instantly grow hard. She pinched lightly, making me grunt, a combination of pain and pleasure. I liked it. We were more alike than I wanted to admit.

"Meaning if you infect me, you could save my life?" I grabbed her arms, tried to make her stop playing hand games under my shirt. I needed to know what she was implying, and if she kept this up much longer, I would lose control.

"That's right," she said, looking up at me like a little girl, her wide smile framed by wanting lips.

"And why do I believe you? After all, you are one of the monsters, no matter how beautiful."

"You believe me because you know I would never do anything to hurt you."

"Really?" It was said with a certain sarcastic flair.

"Yeah, really. I could have killed you already if I wanted to. I could have infected you if I wanted to. After all, you were the one holding the gun against my stomach at the Lunatic Moon." Those eyes were so full of lust and innocence, a deadly oxymoron. "It'd be a shame if this was the last night you got to kill vampires."

"If it is my last night on earth, I will spend it killing the Master of the City. Fuck Lyric, fuck the cockroaches, and fuck humanity. I'm going to clean the city with blood on my hands. Quinn, Maximilian, Veronica Powers, and my good buddy Dieter will all die tonight. I'm not going to end up a blood-sucking vampire. Father Garcia would see to that by morning. I'm not going to be furry either. I'll be dead. Plain and simple. My tombstone will read 'Here lies the biggest sap that ever staked the undead.'"

She began to move those lethal fingers again, kissing lightly on the exposed skin as she lifted my shirt. I began to shake with desire as her tongue worked with her full lips against my stomach. Her hot breathe wrapping me with pleasure. I wanted to push her away, but I couldn't. Things were going too far to stop it. My mind told me I needed to go. I needed to kill the cockroaches responsible for making this my last night on earth. I needed to do a lot of things, but I needed the touch and feel of Angie more. Unlike the death I dealt with, she was comforting, warm, and here.

I pulled her back up to me with one quick move. Her eyes met mine, more animal than human. There was no more thinking, no more holding back. My hands moved across her full ass, fingers searching, scratching, wanting. It was smooth, muscular, bucking softly with each caress.

My hands moved upward and around to her large full breasts. I skimmed my palms over her hard nipples as she sighed with need.

"Please," she cried. Her hands slid down into the front of my pants, massaging me so hard it almost hurt, but my hunger overrode any thought of pain. "Please fuck me," she added. Her breathing became faster with each touch of her nipples against my palms. Her tongue moved back into my mouth, her body melting into mine.

I could feel myself rubbing against her thigh like a horny dog, no longer in control. I lifted her up, and she instantly wrapped me with her legs, continuing to grind against me harder and faster. Her jaw was clenched tight, lips apart, trying to catch any breath she could. Her desires were now more animal than human.

I carried her to the wall behind us and pinned her. She moaned, dropped a hand and, with speed so quick I never saw it happen, my pants loosened and hit the floor. Her hand tightened around me, working like a piston. "I want you so bad," she cried as she looked into my eyes.

I could smell her musky scent as she worked herself against me, mixing with the sweet smell of her perfume. Her breasts pressed against me like pillows. I began to shake with desire, flooding over me with such a force that I was going mad.

"Hurry up and fuck her. We still have a killer out there," a voice called out from behind us. It was Detective Ezekiel Kansas.

CHAPTER TWENTY-SIX

Kansas and I found Price standing over a body that had been fished out of the SunTrust Building. Police officers took statements and tried to restore order in the growing chaos. I think every officer on the force was here, plus the onlookers, news crews, and cockroaches that framed the area just outside the yellow tape. It looked more like a battlefield than a crime scene.

Price gave us an emotionless stare. "There doesn't seem to be any rhyme or reason to how they're separating the bodies. Police officers lay next to the monsters. I find the general thought of it appalling, but then again...."

"It's not like they can catch the lycan virus. All the bodies are back to human form. It's impossible to catch it while the shifter is in human form. No one really knows why," Kansas said, looking at me as though I had done all the killing.

The night air felt thick as I walked past the carnage. All eyes seemed to be on me. "Why is it any time there's a dead body around, the first thing the police do is look at me?"

"Because usually you're the cause of it. And it appears tonight is no different."

"I didn't have a choice in the matter. Either I threw him out the window, or you'd still have a big insect to kill."

"Spiders are arachnids, not insects."

I rolled my eyes. "Whatever."

Angie was taken to a nearby squad car and given a blanket to wrap in. Catcalls and whistles were at an all-time high as she moved through the crowd. Lucky for them, Angie wasn't affected by the comments. If she were, they would be in little pieces. That was the thing with being a fur ball, I guess: being caught naked came with the territory.

"So run this by me one more time," Price said to Kansas as we pushed through the crowd.

"Lab came back with fang prints on the first victims. Anna Martinez's wounds are different." Kansas looked up as reporters called out to him to answer questions.

"But the way she died was different. She wasn't subdued with magic like the others. That's why the wounds are different." I lit a cigar.

"The fangs were different. We have the killer of a girl, not a serial killer."

"But it has to be him. He killed them, I know it," Price insisted. "Have the lab check it again."

"Damn it, Frank, he's not the killer. We fucked up, okay?" Kansas said as we made our way to Dieter Procnow, who was standing with Veronica Powers.

I drew deeply from the cigar as we approached. Screw the rules of protocol, I wanted to track down Quinn and Maximilian, watch them bleed before the sun rose. I looked at Dieter and Powers. "Here's my grand dilemma. Before me are two of the cockroaches that are responsible for my death, and I have to decide whether to kill you here and now, or wait. If we still have a killer on our hands,

I might have to alter my actions. I want the killer more than I want revenge. Go figure." I blew the smoke in Dieter's face, then turned to face Veronica Powers. The normally beautiful woman was now covered in dried blood. Hers, I was guessing. "Hell, you look like shit. And I'm loving every minute of it."

She started to say something, and then regained her composure. "Thank you for saving our lives, Mr. Isaac. I regret that so many had to die needlessly tonight."

I pulled my Magnum from its holster and placed it against her temple. "If I die tonight, so will you, you bitch."

"Paul, no!" Price shouted as he tried to get between me and the coffin crispy.

I could feel the cold steel of Kansas' gun pressed against my temple.

"For some strange reason, you seem to think I'll care if you put a bullet in my brain. Little do you know you'd probably be doing us both a favor."

"Paul, I swear to God, I'll blow your brains out right here. Put the fucking gun down."

"Do it, Avenger. End all the pain here and now. She was the one that stuck the needle in your vein", Dieter added, with a cynical laugh that gave me the chills.

"You don't want to do this," Price pleaded. "Father Garcia is going to be all right. You don't want him to have to see you in prison, or worse." He hesitated for a second. "Think of him if nothing else, for Christ's sake."

Everything was moving in fast-forward. Everything Price was saying was in a vacuum a million miles away. "Nothing matters anymore. I'm not afraid of dying by a bullet to the brain. In fact, I prefer it. Quick and painless." I pressed the gun harder. "Where is Lyric, Veronica? Tell me, and I won't stick a crucifix up your crotch. I have the advantage now. They can't do anything to me that's not going to happen in a few hours anyway. Who killed those girls, and where do I find Lyric?"

"I don't know what you're talking about, Mr. Isaac."

"Just as I suspected. Still a cold, heartless bitch, even in the eyes of death." I shoved her again. "Who the fuck is she, and why does Quinn want her?" I pulled out a crucifix.

"Paul, I won't ask you again. Put the fucking gun down, now," Kansas said again. "You're already under arrest. Don't complicate things further."

"She knows who the killer is." I kept my eyes on Veronica. "I want to hear her say it."

"You truly have lost your mind," she answered.

"She knows, Avenger. Don't be a fool. Intimidate her enough, and she will talk", Dieter whispered in my mind.

"Paul, please put down the gun. We'll get to the bottom of this. I promise," Price pleaded.

I gripped the crucifix so tight, I thought it would cut through my skin. Against my better judgment, I lowered the gun. "This ain't over, bitch." I backed off, but only a little. "I don't follow the law. I'm far more interested in finding the killer, by any means necessary. My Achilles heel is time, and I'm not willing to waste it by being handcuffed in the back of a squad car. Sure, I could kill you. It would feel good. Real good. I could probably even get the little bottom dweller, Dieter, as well. But all I would accomplish is killing a cockroach that had a hand in killing one human, me. If I keep my cool, I might be able to find the serial killer and stop a cockroach that's killing a lot more."

"You're under fucking arrest, Isaac," Kansas said, his gun still at my temple. Typical.

"Come on, Kansas, you know as well as I do I'm not going to kill her. Not yet, anyway," I said as I looked at Powers. "Call it interrogation of the undead."

"You really are the crazy son of a bitch everyone says you are," Powers said as she fell into Price's grasp. He looked horrified. He didn't like the monsters any more than I did, and I honestly think he believed he could turn into one by simply touching them or drinking after them, like you can a common cold. I liked that about him. The more afraid of them someone was, the less chance they would grow soft in their cause.

"You are a disease," she added.

"A couple of days ago, it was okay to fill me with a slow poison, but now that I'm the one threatening to take your life, I'm the crazy son of a bitch. Figure that one out."

"Just cool down a minute," Price said, pulling me away.

"Price, she's one of the cockroaches that poisoned me. Not only that, but I believe she knows more about the killings than she is telling us."

"Yes, and just a few hours ago, you were accusing Evan Falkner and Dr. Petty. You are grasping at straws. I doubt that you even have a poison in your veins. Have you seen a doctor to confirm it?" Dieter asked.

"Kansas, please put the gun down," Price said, softer than I'd ever heard him speak.

Kansas reluctantly lowered his gun. Things were slowly getting back in control.

"I am going to give the Council a full report on this, Detective Kansas. I'm sure they will be grateful for your cooperation in his arrest," Dieter said as he looked at me. *"You're a dead man. Tick-tock,"* he added for my benefit.

"Can I be of any assistance?" a familiar voice from behind us said.

"Dr. Montgomery." I did a double-take. She was dressed in a formal blue gown-a far cry from how I usually saw her.

"Whoa, look at you! I'm not used to seeing you in anything other than scrubs and somebody else's blood," I quipped.

"Hello, Paul. Glad to see you're okay." She turned to Price. "Heard someone was thrown out a window."

"That's right. Not much of him left." Price said, looking back to Piel's dead body.

"How are you?" she asked Veronica Powers.

"You two know each other?" I said.

"It's not illegal to talk to vampires, Paul," she said, never taking her eyes off the cockroach.

"Here to rescue me again from the mystery man?" I said, half smiling, half serious.

She turned to me and smiled, but it felt forced. "It doesn't seem as though the night calls for a rescue. No, I was at the theater earlier. I heard about all of this. Knowing that time was running out for you and your situation, I thought you might need help. I didn't know if I could be of assistance. Gunshots seem to draw a crowd. Usually it means someone needs medical attention."

"Put your hands behind your back, Paul," Kansas said.

"Have you found Lyric yet?" Dr. Montgomery asked.

"No, not yet." I looked at her. She was acting strangely.

"Why, do you know where we can find her?" Angie was dressed in silver leather pants and a matching top. Where she got her clothes, I don't know, but God bless them.

"No, why would I?" Dr. Montgomery asked.

"Put your hands behind your back," Kansas commanded. I delayed the move.

"Just a question, nothing more." Angie answered.

"And the answer is no. I was just worried about Paul. I knew he didn't have a lot of time to find her."

I looked at Dr. Montgomery, waiting for her to elaborate, while the staring contest between the two continued.

"Give me your hands, Paul," Kansas barked impatiently.

"Wait a minute, Zeke," Price said as he lowered his cell phone from his ear. "There's someone who is adamant about seeing Paul."

"Well, they can see him in his cell later on tonight," Kansas said through gritted teeth, thumping me on the back. "Give me your wrists!"

"Detective Kansas, I'm asking you to hold on a minute." It was rare for Price to use Kansas' title. "As far as I know, I am still in charge here. And although I don't condone Mr. Isaac's actions, I think I need to pull rank on this one." I couldn't tell if he was as angry or not. It didn't matter right now. If I could get out of this without violence, he could remain pissed off at me as long as he wanted to.

Kansas muttered a couple of profanities under his breath to no one in particular. "I'll see to it that you rot in hell," he finally said to me, just before the sucker punch. I knew better than to come back with a smart-ass answer. Unlike Price, there was no doubt about Kansas' anger.

"Surely you are not going to let Mr. Isaac walk free from here, after what he just did?" Dieter commented.

"Surely you aren't going to tell me how to run my investigation, Dieter?" Price replied. I smiled. One more for the good guys. I could feel the blood trickling down my nose.

In the crowd, I saw another familiar face. Gillian. You know, the girl from The Coffin. "Paul, this is Gillian Whitehead. She works over at The Coffin," Price said.

"Yeah, I know who she is."

"Be nice," hissed Price.

"I'm sure that came across a lot harsher than I had intended, but after the last few days, I'm not in a let's-be-friends mood. I have been kidnapped, drugged, and poisoned by cockroaches, and attacked by shape-shifters. God would be in a bad mood after all that."

"She says needs to talk to you about something. Says it's important," Price said, eyeing the two bloodsuckers next to him. To

Kansas, "Detective, let's get statements from Ms. Powers and Mr. Procnow. I have no doubt in that Ms. Powers must be quite shaken by what happened here tonight."

Price looked at Kansas and me, then at the vampires. He frowned. Sure, he hated me, but it was clear he hated the monsters worse. Babysitting daisy-pushers was the last thing he wanted to do tonight.

"Please tell me you have no plans to let this man just walk away from here, Detective Price." Dieter hissed, looking at me, through me. "The Council will have your head. There is no way you can cover up all the death Mr. Isaac has caused tonight."

Price ignored the threat. "Detective Kansas, please escort these two over there while we talk," he said, nodding to an open space in the crowd.

"You can't be..." Kansas started.

"Please, Detective Kansas," Price snapped irritably.

He waited as Kansas and the two blood maggots moved away before turning to Gillian. "Go ahead, honey, it's all right."

"Mr. Isaac," Gillian started. Her voice was soft and shaky.

I took another drag on the cigar. It helped me think. I answered her by not answering her.

Gillian cleared her throat and began. "Mr. Isaac, I want to thank you for saving my life."

I thought of things to say, but nothing profound came to mind. "You're welcome." See.

"I want to return the favor."

"I'm listening."

"I know where you can find Lyric." Her eyes were now wide and scared.

"Okay, you have my attention."

"She's been staying at my place, hiding from the vampires."

"Hiding from them? Why?"

"She saw something. She went to a Tortured Skin party and saw something. She used to hang out with vampires, went to their parties all the time. She was one of the pain freaks. She let one of them cut her. Now he calls to her all the time. She has no free will from it." Gillian kept looking back at Dieter and Veronica, who were being led farther and farther away. Like Gillian, I could sense the bloodsuckers watching us. "He wants her back."

"What did she see?"

"The vampire killed a girl. He tortured her for the pleasure of it. One of the girls you found."

"What was his name?" I asked.

"She wouldn't say. She just saw him kill the woman. Then she ran away. She thinks the vampires are out to kill her. I promised I wouldn't say anything, but I'm afraid the vampires will kill her. I don't want her to die. I don't want to die."

I wasn't about to tell her she was right. It wouldn't do anything at this point other than freak her out even more. "Where can I find Lyric?"

"She went back to the freak show. Says she can't help herself. It's her addiction. I tried to stop her, but she wouldn't stay put. I'm so scared. If they find her, they'll kill her."

"You mean the Tortured Skin club."

"Yeah." She started to cry. "Here's the address where she said she'd be."

"Thank you, Ms. Whitehead. I'll find her for you." I chewed on the butt of the cigar for a second while I thought everything through.

I nodded over to Detective Price. "He'll keep you safe. You know as well as I do what these things are capable of. Don't leave his side."

I didn't have to explain. That was a good thing.

"Here," Price said, handing me back my Magnum. "Don't let Kansas know I gave it back to you."

I nodded.

"I hope I've done the right thing," Gillian said. The emotions in her face told me how scared she was. Again, I wanted to say something profound, but couldn't think of anything.

"Ms. Whitehead, thank you."

Note to self: Send flowers in the morning if still alive.

CHAPTER TWENTY-SEVEN

I walked back toward Angie and Dr. Montgomery, swimming with emotions, some good, others not so good. I locked eyes with Dr. Montgomery as I threw the cigar butt to the ground. Angie tried to swallow me with her eyes, taking in my emotions. It had become clear that she had the ability to ride on my senses and make them her own somehow. I can't explain it. Detective Price took Gillian to a nearby squad car, which gave me an opportunity to work outside police boundaries.

"Dr. Montgomery, I think we just got a huge break in the killings." My body was shaking with hatred and anger.

"Thank God. What did you find out? What did she say?" she asked.

"I know where to find Lyric, and better yet, I know who's been feeding the cockroaches the young girls."

I allowed the comment to sink in as I stood in front of her. "That's wonderful, Paul." Her expression vacillated between a fake smile and pure terror.

"Do you think so, Dr. Montgomery?"

"Of course. Why wouldn't I?" Her guilt glowed on her face like sweat.

"Why are you really down here, Dr. Montgomery?"

"I told you, I was at the theater. I came down here after hearing of shots, to see if I could be of any help."

"That's a nice story, but I don't think it's true."

She began to breathe quicker, fidgeting with her hands. "Are you accusing me of something, Paul?"

"At first it didn't make sense. I allowed Piel to throw me off track for a little bit, but in talking to a certain vampire earlier and then seeing you here, all the lights went on. You said something that fucked you over, Dr. Montgomery."

"I don't understand."

I placed the Magnum under her ribs, out of sight, as I continued. "When you met me a few minutes ago, you asked about the poison in my system. I never told you about that."

"Sure you did, at the morgue the other night," she countered.

"No, Dr. Montgomery, I didn't. I never mentioned it at all. The feeder isn't Dr. Petty, it's you."

"You really are losing it, aren't you? No wonder you're seeing a shrink. Now take that thing out of my ribs."

"Or what?" I asked.

"Or I'll get the police involved."

"Go ahead, Dr. Montgomery. Go ahead and get them involved. Tell them how you came down here tonight to kill Gillian. You knew Lyric had told her all the dirty little details. Except I kind of interrupted the party by having a shoot-out with Evan. Whoops." I grinned humorlessly at her. "It would've been a good plan if it weren't for me. That's why a certain other cockroach showed up instead, isn't it?"

"You give yourself way too much credit, Paul."

"Let me tell you a few other things I've put together, Dr. Montgomery." I lit another cigar.

She stopped and twirled around, the frustration and panic showing in her face. There was an urgency about her now.

"You're gonna need to get to your blood-sucking cockroach before I do," I added as I drew on the cigar.

"I don't have time for this, Paul. I have other appointments."

"I thought you said you were down here to help?" I blew the smoke in her face. She tried not to cough. "I've been looking at the records of all the victims in this case, and you know what I found out, Dr. Montgomery?"

"Oh, please do tell, Mr. Isaac."

"We've somehow become formal. I'm okay with that." She began to walk toward her car again. I followed. "They all had a few doctors in common."

"I know. Dr. Petty treated them all. So why aren't you arresting her? She seems to be everywhere the dead bodies show up."

"True. I was thinking the same thing, thanks to Piel, but they had another doctor in common. Your husband. He was the staff psychiatrist in the psych ward where all the victims were being held on Baker Acts."

She stopped again and turned to face me. "My husband? You think my husband had something to do with this?"

"Maybe at first, but after a little thinking outside the box, everything began to move back to you."

"How so, Mr. Isaac?"

"You had access to his records. You knew all the passwords to his computer. And worst of all, you were having an affair with a cockroach. Maximilian. That's why the vampire at the morgue the other night didn't kill you. Maximilian was protecting his woman. And you were protecting him. At the morgue, the new vampire grew strong because the crucifixes on the wall that were supposed to keep them from gaining strength weren't crucifixes. They were simply crosses. A cross will do nothing against a throat ripper, and I'm betting you knew that. You were his inside link to the victims." I paused for effect. "Better yet, his food source. You have to be out of your mind to be messing with him. How long do you think it'll be before he turns his fantasies on you and kills you? It's just a matter of time."

"Preposterous. I'm not having an affair with Maximilian-or any other vampire, for that matter." She began to move again. Angie tagged along behind me, but so far was behaving herself.

"Really? Consider yourself a religious woman, don't you?"

"What?"

"In all the bits of small talk we had at the morgue, I remember you saying that you grew up in a Catholic church. You used to wear your mother's crucifix around your neck. Vowed never to take it off so she'd always be with you."

"I'm sure you have a point, Mr. Isaac."

"Oh, I do. Show me your crucifix, Dr. Montgomery."

She stalled, felt for the crucifix as if she thought it would magically appear. "You're grasping at straws."

"You don't have it because it would cause issues with your new squeeze. I can condone you having an affair, but not with a cockroach."

"From the whispers I've heard around here, Mr. Isaac, I'm not the only one getting close to the monsters." She looked at Angie.

"You're the only monster here, sweetheart," Angie growled.

"Excuse me. I have to go now," Dr. Montgomery walked to her car.

"You two had me fooled with the little game at the Lunatic Moon, too. I couldn't for the life of me figure out why someone would've called you to come and get me the other night. It just didn't make sense."

"I'm sure you're going to explain it all to me." She gave a fake smile as she hit the unlock button. Her car chirped a couple of times in synch with flashing head and taillights. "But do it quickly. I have places to go."

"Again, I thought you were here to help out."

"I don't appreciate being accused of things I had nothing to do with. Especially from a hate filled, outdated executioner like yourself. While we are pointing fingers here, Paul, let's talk about the incident a few years ago with you and the great Father Garcia. Tell me how it felt to shoot a boy in the streets in front of his parents. You and Father Garcia killed that boy without an order of execution. He lost his license to kill vampires, and you will be forever known as Saint Avenger. You two killed him for revenge of the new laws, nothing more. And you know it."

"He was thought to have been a vampire that had killed two women that night. By law, he was to be executed."

"Thought to be. That's the point. You seem to work a lot on suspicion. There was no due process, no order of execution. You both got out of it on a technicality, but neither of you can escape the memories of it. And you call the vampires the monsters."

"Split hairs all you want. You can tell it all to the families of the girls Maximilian killed."

"Those women were going to kill themselves anyway. There was no hope for them. He simply gave them the completion they desired. If I didn't give the girls to the club, the vampires would have gotten them somewhere else on their own. Besides, they didn't go there kicking and screaming. Amputation is what they wanted. What they needed to feel complete. At least he didn't kill normal women, good women, from better families. It was the best-case scenario. I don't see the big deal. They were only runaway heroin prostitutes and strippers. Forgettable people."

"God, you're both monsters." I sighed. "You and Maximilian."

A thought struck me. "The other night at the hospital. When the cockroach came to life... you did it, didn't you?"

"You think I brought her to life? I'm not God, Paul."

"But you do carry the powers of a vampire servant. Maximilian can feed and work through you, you can't deny that."

"You'll have a tough time proving that one."

"You planned to have me killed the other night in the hospital. That's why the monster didn't kill you. The two of you were working together. You weren't trying to keep that thing from getting out. You were trying to keep me from getting out."

"You're insane."

"Why didn't you kill me, instead of bringing me home?"

She swallowed hard. "All right. You want the truth? I did want you dead. Maximilian is my lover. I knew you were a threat to both of us alive. You'd attempt to kill him one day. I wanted you dead to give us both some peace. Now, if you will excuse me." She opened the door.

"It was Maximilian that gave me the gun that night."

She laughed for real this time. "Maximilian gave you a gun? Don't you think he would have killed you if it had been him?"

"You'd think so at first, but if you connect all the dots, it makes sense. He could have killed me the first night. The night he and his merry men kidnapped and poisoned me. Killing me wasn't part of the plan-yet. He wanted me to kill Piel because Piel was a threat to the cockroach world. He was bad for economics, not to mention the fact that he made a great scapegoat for Maximilian's murders.

"I was supposed to kill Piel, bringing an end to the whole threat, and then get arrested for his murder. With the attention on me killing Piel, the cockroaches could cover up the murders by making them second-page news. In the meantime, Maximilian would kill Quinn. But instead, things grew more complicated."

"By 'complicated,' you mean you failed. It's a good story, but why would I have saved you that night?"

"Because with Piel and Lyric both still alive, I was still useful to your boyfriend. Lyric saw him kill one of those girls. Her testimony could bring the whole empire down. And if I killed Piel, it still linked nothing to your cockroach lover."

She laughed again. "Like anyone is going to believe a heroin junkie over a prominent figure in the vampire community. Maximilian sees their weakness as disgusting."

"Really? Why does he walk with a cane?"

"What is that supposed to mean? Anyone with a cane or a limp is a killer?" She was nearly screaming now.

"He's a forsaken cockroach. They can rejuvenate wounds and cuts. Cut off an arm or leg, and they sprout a new one." My face was inches from hers. "Unless the vamp puts silver on the wound or burns it. In that case, the leg will never grow back. Truth is, Maximilian has the same disease as the patients that saw your husband and Dr. Petty, only his grew out of control. He got off on the pain to himself, and finally felt complete when he amputated his own leg and sealed it in silver. But after a while, it wasn't enough. Soon it grew into cutting others. Erotic at first, torture later, murder last. Quinn, Veronica Powers, and Dieter wanted this covered up as quickly as possible. They turned Vinnie over to me that night, hoping I'd go after Piel for the murders. The blood of those girls is on your hands, Doctor."

Dr. Montgomery started the car. "Have fun proving it all before the sun rises." Tires barked as she pulled away. There would be time to bring her in. I was going after a much more dangerous monster.

I'd never be sympathetic to the vampire cause, but when my fellow humans feed them like animals at the zoo, I lose all respect for them as well. Not all monsters have fangs or change shapes.

CHAPTER TWENTY-EIGHT

The Tortured Skin party was about half an hour away, in a warehouse off of Orange Blossom Trail, an area of town known for its nude dancing, prostitution, and drugs.

"Lovely part of town," Angie said sarcastically as we passed a group of streetwalkers.

"Yeah, you'll never find it on a postcard. It's growing in cockroach activity right under everybody's noses-but as long as the money continues to fill the right pockets and the victims don't pile up, no one's going to do anything about it."

If I failed before sunrise, there was a very good chance I was a walking dead man. My own health and safety meant nothing to me right now. The only thing that mattered was finding Maximilian. Price was already working with the judicial system on getting an order of execution for him, but I didn't have time to wait. We'd work on formalities later.

I parked the 'Cuda about a block from the warehouse and looked at Angie. "You ready for this?"

She looked over at me, eyes glowing. "Never more." A faint smile slid across her face.

"You don't have to do this if you don't want to. The last thing I want to do is get you killed," I said.

"The last thing I want to do is see you die. Let's end this. Besides, Maximilian and I have a few scores of our own to settle."

With that, we were walking toward the nomadic sex club just ahead. I wanted to smoke another cigar to calm my nerves, but I didn't want my hands occupied with anything other than the Magnum, not even for a second. Maximilian was nearly as powerful as Quinn; he would be the first master vampire I had killed in years, the first since they had gained rights and protection.

As we got closer to the warehouse, I could hear the repetitious bass thumping inside. I could pick up voices, but not conversations. My body tensed.

"Don't hesitate killing anything in here," Angie said, eyes on the door. "Being scared might be an advantage."

"I'm about to enter the nest of the most perverse monsters known to man: a Tortured Skin party, where it's all about blood, sex, and pain. I don't think scared covers it."

"It's a trick of light that makes them think they're safe. Just like the tourists that go down to Bat Town. Once inside, there's no coming back out."

"Couldn't have said it better myself." I checked the Magnum for bullets.

"We won't be able to just walk through the front door and execute Maximilian. There will be incredible security. Especially if you're not on the list, and I highly doubt you made the list."

"Having a reputation as a death dealer tends to leave me off most party lists. You, on the other hand, will have no problem making your way through the front door if you want to."

"Meaning?"

"You're one of them. And when a woman looks like you do, you can go anywhere you want with minimal questions. Beauty has its advantages. No male would be upset to see you walk in there. After all, it is a sex club under all the secrecy. You sell that well."

She kissed me on the lips, slowly and seductively. "If I didn't know better, I'd say you were flirting." Angie didn't wait for an answer, she just kept walking.

Around back were three guards holding weapons of some kind. In the dark, I couldn't tell make and model, but I'm sure they would kill all the same.

I looked at my watch. It was three-thirty. "Only two hours before the sun rises and all good little cockroaches are snug in their coffins. My window of opportunity is running out in more ways than one. The daisy-pushers will be gone within another hour."

"I know how to take care of this without firing a shot," Angie said, looking at the three men and smiling.

Before I could ask the question, she was undressed and walking toward them with that stripper walk that she seemed to pull off a little too well. I felt sorry for them. I had been on the receiving end of that walk, and I knew how intoxicating it was. She was a deadly spider getting ready to snare her flies. For the first time, I felt ashamed to be a man. We were all so visual, so stupid. Show us boobs, and we drop our defenses. I laughed to myself as I watched that butt glow in the moonlight.

The three saw her approach and looked a little puzzled. Under any other circumstances, the decision would have been easy. Shoot to kill. But with a beautiful naked woman approaching, things weren't as black and white. After the initial shock wore off, they smiled.

The trap had been set. They were no longer thinking with their heads. Good for us, bad for them. Soon, bad things would be happening to them.

Angie was talking to them, moving her body seductively, interrupted only by the playful laughter of the three men. I continued to watch the surroundings for any others that might be moving in the night. It was a good bet that the fang fritters knew we were coming. I would be surprised if the news of Piel's death hadn't hit here yet.

There was minimal noise from the three men as Angie swiped her hand across their necks with razor-sharp claws. They grabbed their throats as crimson fluid cascaded over their hands. As one, they dropped to their knees, then fell face-first to the ground.

She turned and motioned me forward, smiling at her conquest.

"And you wonder why you can't get a date," I said as I made my way across the darkness to her, stepping over the dead men. I wasn't sure I was joking.

She pointed to a doorway ahead of us. "Let me lead," she said. I started to protest, and she added, "I'm easier to heal than you are if there's trouble on the other side."

"You're right about that, but I can't let you lead the way. If anyone dies here tonight other than Maximilian, it should be me. I have nothing to lose. And I want to be the first face these monsters see. One in particular."

"Are all of you the same?"

"Excuse me?" I looked back at her.

"Male pride. Are you all the same? If I was a man, you wouldn't have thought twice, would you?"

I shrugged. "It's not pride. I just don't want to be the cause of anyone dying here tonight that shouldn't." I didn't wait for her answer. It didn't matter anyway. I wasn't about to let anyone else hinder me, or die for me. "This is personal."

"Maybe it's personal for both of us. The last thing that either of us need is to let our hatred for Maximilian and this place cloud our judgment. By the time this is over, there will be enough blood to spill for us all."

With that, she moved through the door into a world only found in hellish nightmares.

CHAPTER TWENTY-NINE

The back entrance of the warehouse/club was nothing more than a long hallway of trash and junk, left over by the last occupants of the building. I hadn't expected it to be anything more. For all I knew, the main entrance might have been just the same. After all, no one was here to see the latest in fine decor. Everyone was here to feed their inner demons, mostly through graphic violence decorated as sex.

By the looks of the place, it had been a theatre of some kind. I could see the lights of the main room and shadows of people moving, dancing, and drinking. The music was so loud that you felt it more than heard it. It vibrated through my body with such force; it made me lose my balance from time to time. If we had been detected, it wasn't showing on anyone's face.

Angie stuck close to me, her hands and eyes showing the animal inside. Part of me still didn't trust her. Just because I wanted her didn't mean that I believed she was loyal to me. I cringed when I thought of what we might have done in the SunTrust Building if

Kansas hadn't shown up. No matter how beautiful she was, inside she was still one of them.

I had filled the Magnum with ultraviolet bullets, but I also brought silver bullets. By the time I got out of here, I figured I might need to kill more than blood maggots. The crucifix inside my shirt was vibrating from both the music and the evil in the room. Fang-heads and holy objects seem to clash. Go figure.

I'd also brought three wooden stakes and a hunting knife with a silver blade. The ax would have been far too cumbersome, even though I wanted something to cut Maximilian's head off after I killed him.

The hallway snaked through the debris. Liquids splotched the floor; I didn't want to know their origin. Some things were best left unsolved.

Just offstage, I got my first taste of what Tortured Skin was all about. In a makeshift room, a woman dressed in black leather had a naked man tied to a wall, spread-eagle. She was sticking long, thin, needle-like objects into his skin. The man jumped and screamed with each penetration. I wasn't sure if he was a willing victim or not. My first guess was yes, but...

"Silver pins," Angie said softly to me as she looked at the act. "Lycanthrope."

I looked at her and asked the question with my eyes.

"We are allergic to the stuff. If not properly administered, it can be deadly. She's giving him his pain."

"On purpose?"

"Yeah. The more the pain, the more the pleasure. Lycanthropes enjoy it far more than any of the others here. We can endure the most and heal the quickest. An addiction to those that indulge in it." She continued to watch, mesmerized by the act.

"You're into this, aren't you?" I'd already wished I could have taken it back.

"Not like this. There is a thin line between pleasure, pain, and death." Her eyes were all mine now. "I like the first two. The third, not so much." She looked back to the scene before us. "They come here to feed the pain as well as the pleasure. Alarming methods and practices to Middle America, but it doesn't make them monsters. Some are here for the release of the torture. Others are here to apply it. The better the scar, the better the experience. Calling cards and bragging rights to their friends. Businessmen come here to be dominated without the judging eyes of their community. They come here to feel complete."

"How do you know so much about this place?"

"My brother was a member. I came with him a few times, just to watch. Sometimes voyeurism is quite erotic on its own. I never participated, but I wasn't grossed out by it, either." Her voice was very matter-of-fact.

A large man walked toward us, hair long and flowing, wearing only black leather pants, Kasey. Apparently he had survived the shooting at the Lunatic Moon. Somehow I didn't think that was a good thing. I pulled the Magnum up slowly as he approached. He saw us; there was no doubt.

Angie pushed the gun back down. "No. He knows about us coming here." She stayed in the darkness behind me.

I was suddenly very nervous. She had teamed up with the monsters. I would have to kill them both. I began to formulate a plan. "He's still alive."

"He's going to help us."

"Help us? How?"

"He's going to tell us where to find Maximilian and Lyric, if they're still here."

"So that's how you knew where the fun was tonight," I said, sounding far more accusatory than I'd meant to.

"Piel used to oversee all of this. In fact, the show you saw at the Lunatic Moon was for Tortured Skin members only. I just couldn't let you know at the time. We had planned on killing Piel that night. We didn't think you'd be showing up."

"What do you mean, you didn't think I'd show up?"

"We had a bet that you'd kill Kasey and his men before they got you to the party."

I wanted to finish the conversation, but Kasey was now next to us. The dancing lights, pulsating with the beat of the music, flashed across his face. The woman continued to stick her shape-shifting pincushion. If she knew we were there, she never let on.

"Paul, good to see you," Kasey said, dry and without emotion. I wasn't buying the fact that he was sincere. He had several piercings of his own. I was guessing his weren't silver.

"You, too." Equally as dry.

"I hear that you killed Piel tonight."

"Word travels fast."

"When you throw the leader of the shape-shifters out of the SunTrust Building, people are going to talk. Even the vampires are impressed. Most importantly, Maximilian."

"Is he still here?" Angie asked.

"Yeah, he's here. I don't like getting into vampire politics," Kasey said to her. "Especially when you bring him with you. Kind of dampens the trust factor."

"If we don't kill him, it will only be a matter of time before he starts killing your kind as well," I added.

He looked at me with those cold, animal eyes. "I could say the same thing about you. Your love of who we are isn't exactly something that makes me comfortable. So don't tell me you are here out of the kindness of your heart. Are you here to save humankind? Or to prove you have the balls?"

I got the impression the man didn't liked me.

"Maybe it's both."

"Do you have what we need?" Angie asked him.

He nodded. "Behind that set of boxes. Make it quick. I'm not here to baby-sit either of you. I won't get involved, no matter what happens. Enjoy the costumes," he said as he walked off.

"Something I should know?" I asked.

"The shape-shifters know me. They've wanted me to come here for a long time, so me being here won't set off any alarms. The vampires are too arrogant and into themselves to care. But you are another story. No one here likes you, or trusts you. I needed a way to get you in without the place turning on you."

"Stop. You're making me blush," I replied.

"It's time to get dressed for the party," she said as she led me behind the stack of boxes.

CHAPTER THIRTY

"Oh, hell no," I said as I looked at myself in the mirror leaning up against a barren wall. "I look like something out of S&M Monthly." The black leather pants were complemented with slim leather straps across my torso, and a leather hood over my face that covered everything but my eyes. It felt as though it were about a thousand degrees inside the hood, probably just pure panic regarding my outfit.

"Look, you said you wanted to get in here and find Maximilian, didn't you?" Angie said as she primped. She had on a shiny black leather cat suit that fit her like a second skin. It reflected my image, making things a lot worse for me.

"At least your outfit fits you. That's something you'd normally wear."

"Come on." She led the way to the main area of the Tortured Skin party. "And one more thing-keep your mouth shut. If you don't, we both die tonight."

I'd do my best, but I made no promises.

We worked past the few stalls, all occupied with perverse sexual acts. No one paid any attention to us. Voyeurism was an added turn-on, so seeing us was nothing unusual.

We hit the main floor of Tortured Skin. Angie pulled on a leash that attached to a dog collar around my neck. It felt as if every eye in the room was on me as we made our grand entrance. The music was blaring so loud, I couldn't even think. A part of me was convinced it was to drown out the screams from the rooms we'd yet to discover.

Kasey stood about twenty yards from us, sipping a drink. His eyes laughed at me. The monsters had finally found a way to humiliate me before I died. Nice touch.

There were roughly two hundred people on the dance floor, most of them nude. Others were going in and out of various coves of the building, doing things that I was sure I didn't want to know. I saw two male daisy-pushers carrying a young nude girl, still bleeding from the neck. She was at best unconscious; though something told me she was probably dead. Under other circumstances, I'd be on them like a bum on a ham sandwich. But tonight, we had priorities. If I found a way to live through the night, I would be back for them.

Above us, I noticed three vampires with large hooks in their backs, swinging in large circles like a demented wind chime. Others were gathered around the device, waiting for their turn. To my left, a woman was tied to a wheel, which spun as others threw knives at her.

"So nice to see you again, my night wolf," a tall blood-licker said to Angie. He smiled and looked her over like a piece of meat. He was six foot tall, with close-cropped blond hair, very pale. His bright blue silk shirt hung unbuttoned across his body, brushing his black leather pants and thigh-high boots. Dried blood decorated his chin and mouth.

"Alec, so nice to see you again. Where's Fredrick?" Angie said sweetly. She walked the extra few steps to him, like a well-trained puppy. It was a walk that I'm sure had a great payoff once a woman mastered it.

"Oh, you know that bitch. He never comes to these things with me. Sometimes I get so lonely, I can't help but stray."

"You're such a naughty boy."

"Come to indulge yourself?"

"I'm here on beck and call," she said dryly.

Alec looked at me and smiled. "Ah, I see you brought your own dinner with you?" His laugh sent ice down my spine.

"You know I did, baby."

"Mind if I join you? To say he looks delicious would be an understatement."

"Maybe later. Right now she has been asked to join Maximilian." This from Kasey. He had come out of nowhere to stand beside Alec.

"For a snack or a fuck?" Alec asked.

Kasey looked at Angie, then to me. "A little of both, actually. Then again, it's none of your business."

Alec looked over to Kasey. "I would have ordered take-out tonight also, had I known it would come in such beautiful packaging." He looked at me as he stroked Angie's hair. "Later, then, my night wolf. I will be calling on you and your toy, if it is still alive."

It's talk like that that makes me hate them so bad. They look at us humans as objects, possessions. There is no living with them, as the bleeding-heart liberals want to believe. We are just food for them. And we aren't even allowed to protect ourselves. I just don't get it.

Angie led me past Alec and Kasey and into the crush on the dance floor. Pulling violently at the leash around my neck. I heard it pop a couple of times. I followed like a good little sex slave. If I didn't act submissive, we were dead.

Alec looked at me, trying to draw me in with his eyes as we passed. I quickly looked down; avoiding the mind rape.

He stopped me with a brush of his hand. "He avoids my eyes. Why?"

I could feel my heartbeat pick up.

"He's not for you. I already told you," Kasey said.

"He is a freak." I could feel his power. He wasn't a master vampire, not as old as Quinn Rubio, but still packed a punch. He was old. Five hundred years or more, I'd guess.

"Yeah, so?" Kasey asked. God, I hoped this ended well.

"He smells of death." He was within inches of my neck. I tried to keep from tensing up. "Yet he vibrates with power. Odd."

"He vibrates with fear," Angie said as she stepped between Alec and me. "He's a virgin freak. He's never fed your kind before. A little white mouse in the nest of vipers."

"Do you lie to me because you think I'm stupid, or because you think you are so beautiful you can get away with it?" Alec asked as he jockeyed to move next to me again.

"Why would I lie to you?"

"Someone has fed from his delicate skin." He pushed my head aside, exposing the wound Jonathan had left. "That's how I knew he was a freak. Who has beaten me to him? Whom shall I envy?"

"It's his first as a willing subject," Angie replied.

"Ahh. And what if Maximilian bleeds your toy to death?"

"He will be Maximilian's toy soon, not mine. What he chooses to do with him is not my concern."

"Control has never been a strong characteristic of his. If I can't feast, perhaps I could play."

"That's up to Maximilian," Kasey said, pushing me past the stake bait.

"But I'd leave no marks. Nothing that would cause his delicate skin to bruise in black and blues. After all, as you say, it's only a little white mouse."

"So it is," I heard from behind. It was the same voice as the one at the Lunatic Moon. Power rolled over me in hot, invisible waves. Maximilian.

CHAPTER THIRTY-ONE

"Angela, how odd to see you here tonight." Maximilian played with her pink hair. I could feel her tense with the touch, as if he had shocked her. It was power. I could feel it too.

"She's here as my guest," Kasey said as he walked next to Maximilian.

"Also odd." Maximilian never looked at Kasey, but instead continued to play with Angie's hair.

"Odd? How?" Angie finally answered, lightly grabbing Maximilian's hand, stopping the petting. She held his hand in hers and smiled her best fake smile. We stopped before a door.

"You said you were here to bring me a gift, did you not?" Maximilian said, breaking away from Angie's grasp to unlock the door. "I just so happen to have a room where we can indulge in our fantasies and pleasures." He cracked it slightly. I could see the dancing candlelight inside, casting shadows, distorting shapes. "And I have a few intriguing things for you, as well." I was beginning to panic.

Intriguing for fang fritters is usually a buffet of virgins, throats laid open for the tasting.

"It all seems so delightful. Erotic. Exciting." I jumped, hoped no one saw it. Alec was still standing beside me. His power had been overshadowed by Maximilian's. He was looking me in the eyes. I dropped my gaze, keeping him from catching it. His hand lifted my chin. "You seem shy," he purred. "Perhaps I could relax you a little. I promise I won't bite." His laugh toyed with my spine.

"Alec, please control your libido. I find it tiring at best." Maximilian looked at me, then back to Angie. "So which is it, Angela? Are you here as Kasey's guest, or mine? And him," Maximilian looked back at me, "is he Kasey's gift, or mine?"

"I'm your wolf to call if you wish, now that my brother is dead. I wish to settle his debts to you. As for the human, he is yours for the taking."

"So you say, yet you have not allowed me to feed from your blood, given in to my desires, opened your mind to me, watched over me while I sleep. These are the things your brother did for me willingly."

"Piel has kept me from being with you, and you know it." She walked to him. "If you desired his blood, and mine, you should have protected us better." Bitterness rose in the words.

"I hear he is dead," Alec commented as he stood next to Maximilian. "I hear you killed him. Is that why you are here? You are no longer under his thumb?"

"Of course."

"You do not sound confidant, my night wolf."

"I saw his dead body myself. I am very confident he is dead."

"And where is the great vampire executioner?" Maximilian looked at me. "I have also heard he was there tonight."

"Dead. I killed him." Angie answered.

"I can feel truth and lies, my sweet night wolf. You toy with me." He moved close to her again, kissing her neck lightly. "You smell of lies."

"That's why I have come here. I killed him. I need your protection." Angie commented.

"Protection? From whom?"

"From the police. Murdering the executioner tends to draw attention."

He looked at her, then to me again. Only his eyes were animated; the rest of him was as unmoving as a stone. "Alec, Kasey, please leave us. Angela and I have much to talk about."

"And the gift, what about it?" Alec asked.

"Take it with you," Maximilian said as he opened the door farther and motioned Angie inside. "You seem far more interested in it, anyway."

"But I brought him as a gift for you." Angie stopped short of the room.

"Why do I need it when I have you?" Maximilian added.

"Feed off of it. Take it as a token of my appreciation," Angie answered, not budging. "As my apology for not being here sooner."

"I have already fed. He is of no use to me. By the bite marks, it looks as though you have brought me nothing more than leftovers." God, did everyone recognize the marks? "Besides, I would rather feed off of you, given the choice," Maximilian said as he ran his hands down her shoulders and grabbed her hand. He placed a soft kiss on it. I could see her shudder. "I find your scent to be most intoxicating."

"I'm not here for that."

"But I thought you said you were here to settle your brother's debts. You asked me to make you my animal to call at night. To protect you, did you not?"

"I did, but I'm here to warn you of great danger."

"Danger? Do tell."

"It's Lyric. I think she has talked to the police. They're on their way here."

Maximilian stopped moving. "You brought a warm body to feed on, just to tell me of this danger? Odd, again." He smiled at her. "My sweet wolf, do not fear me. I mean you no harm. Please enter and we will talk. You can tell me of this danger." Maximilian looked at me. "We do not need him."

"And I don't enter without him," Angie responded.

"It is not a choice I have given you."

"I'm simply asking you to allow it. I wish no harm to come to him at the hands of the other vampires here. He was hand-picked for your pleasure." She looked down the hallway. "I don't want him fed on or fucked with."

"Why would you be so protective of him? If he is just a freak slave, it should not matter," Maximilian said. "We both know the city is infested with freaks just like him."

"I don't find it very respectful of you to throw away a gift I bring you in good faith. Is that how you will treat me in years to come? As nothing more than a piece of warm meat to pass around and discard at will?"

Maximilian laughed, touched her hair again. He stroked her cheek like a small child. "Very well. Bring your gift with you, my night wolf. I will never discard you, nor will I deny you of any wants."

"Thank you." Angie pulled me by the leash. "Come on, slave." I heard the door shut and lock behind me. It was as if my tomb had just been sealed.

The room was large with dancing candlelight and that's when I saw it. How could I miss it? A young girl was tied to an over-sized bed, her arms and legs bound to the four corners, a gag in her mouth. Blood stained the white comforter. I stared into eyes that still screamed for help, eyes that still held the torture and pain inside. Begging to be released. A deep slit ran from ear to ear, like a smiling death mark. Fresh blood glistened atop old, dried tracks.

Angie noticed her too. She turned to Maximilian, fear glowing in her face. "What is this?"

"Lyric. So you see, we are not in any danger."

"What did you do to her?"

"I hope that is a rhetorical question."

"It's not."

"It is a sign of madness, my night wolf. You see, when I lost your brother to Piel, the madness rose in me. I could no longer control it. I lost my food source. I was forced to look elsewhere. They needed the pain. I needed the pleasure it brought. Their blood fed the disease in me. Your brother's absence was too much."

"You mean when my brother was taken from you, you had no other food source?"

"Oh, there is always a freak out there willing to allow us to feed. But without my wolf to call, I was unable to control my lust. You know as well as I do that a lycan's blood is the purest of all blood, absent of disease. Without your brother, I fed on the whores, the underworld. But all I truly fed was the disease itself, which grew with each feeding." He picked up the cane that leaned against the wall. "You denied me that stability by not taking his place. All the killings could have been avoided."

"So you seduced Dr. Montgomery into giving you the castaways of society to feed on."

He laughed. "No, no. The sweet doctor was more than willing to help. An aging beauty with a loveless marriage and thankless employment, she gave me the women in exchange for eternal youth. Freaks with the same sickness as myself, they begged for the pain. I gave them what they desired most: perfection."

"Perfection? How could cutting them up, bleeding them, and watching them die be perfection? You did it for your own pleasure."

"You are wrong, my night wolf. They sought the amputations.

You can ask anyone. Like me, they saw the appendages as imperfec-
tions. I used silver on my own wound in order to complete the task."

"But you did more than amputate. You killed them."

"I am a vampire. It is what I do. And they were impure. Still,
they did not suffer. And I left the bodies where I knew they would
be found. Everything comes with a price, my night wolf. It was the
only thing that kept me alive. The more I devoured, the more it
devoured me. Now Lyric will pay the ultimate price for my
madness."

"Why her?"

"She knows too much. Secrets must be kept under lock and key.
Besides, she is a cutter herself. Practically masturbates at the sight
of my knives."

"Let her go. You must stop this. I am here now. Feed from me."

"Very well. I will let her go if your allow your gift to me to take
her place."

Angie stiffened. "You don't understand. All of this must come to
an end. They will find you and kill you for this. They are on their
way here now."

Maximilian laughed. "The humans do not understand death as
we do." He moved to Lyric and pulled out a large knife, stained
with blood. Lyric twisted in the bindings, watching the knife with
both excitement and horror.

"Please, Maximilian, don't do this."

"It is your choice, my night wolf. You may substitute your gift
for her at anytime." He brought the blade down to Lyric's arm and
began to cut along her shoulder. A stream of blood grew from the
wound, following the blade. Lyric screamed from behind the gag in
her mouth, pain overtaking pleasure. "Somehow, I do not think your
pet will enjoy the cutting as much as she will."

"You sick bastard."

I began to slowly reach for the Magnum in my boot. I couldn't
play submissive little slave anymore.

Maximilian licked the blood as it trickled from the wound. "Do not fear, my love. She enjoys this more than you know. Show her a blade, and she is yours for the night."

"Maximilian, I beg you, please let her go. Don't do this."

"You know, my night wolf, if there is one thing I hate, it is a liar."

"I don't understand."

"I do not believe in your loyalty. I do not believe in your reasons for being here. And most of all, I don't believe that Paul Isaac is dead."

I pulled the Magnum from my boot. Maximilian's power hit me and threw me against the wall. It was the same power I had felt when I tried to go against Quinn at The Coffin. I couldn't move a muscle. I couldn't breathe, couldn't talk.

The vampire moved with ghostlike quickness, dropping fangs into Angie's neck. Maximilian lowered her to the floor as she fought his magic. I had to get to her.

Maximilian rose from Angie's body and looked at me, his face dripping with saliva and blood. "What kind of fool do the two of you take me for? To think I did not know who you were, Avenger. You cannot out-think me. You cannot kill me." He took the Magnum. The only weapon I had, now in the hands of a vampire. "I will kill both of you. But first, I will let you watch me kill the only person who could have saved your soul."

He returned to Lyric and began to cut into the flesh of her arm, just below the shoulder. Maximilian sawed deep and hard into the arm as if it were a large branch of a tree. Flesh and blood mixed and collected on the serrated blade as it bit and chewed through the arm. Lyric writhed in pain. The blade cut without mercy. As steel met bone, she screamed. Horrific sounds of grinding filled my ears. I was unable to stop it, or the monster; I was paralyzed, forced to watch and listen.

The blade ate through the other side of the arm. It gave way without a fight. The sheets on the bed were now soaked in a red sea. In my worst nightmare, I'd never imagined anything like this.

"Now you see where I find my pleasure, Avenger. It is not the killing or the blood that I lust for, but the pain and the horror."

He turned from me and began to move toward Lyric again. His dark magic continued to hold me, rendering me unable to help Lyric, unable to prevent the torture. Angie remained motionless.

Maximilian took the large knife and moved to the leg on the same side as the missing arm. "Enjoying the show, I hope," he said with a lascivious grin. Like a knife cutting through a loaf of warm bread, the blade chewed its way into the white flesh. Blood gushed from the wound, spraying into the air as the knife cut into arteries. Screams struggled to escape the gag. I tried to close my eyes, but the vision somehow followed me into the darkness. I could still see the blood pouring from the wound, still hear the cracking of the bone, the cries of pain and helplessness. The fear and anger still welled inside me.

When I opened my eyes, he had severed the leg, discarded it beside the bed. Maximilian was drinking from the wound in large laps, like a cat with a warm bowl of milk. My stomach rolled with each lick. I swallowed hard as heat rushed through me.

The monster turned to me and smiled. "I can save some for you if you would like. This time tomorrow, you will not find this nearly as repulsive."

I was still unable to speak. Maybe it was the magic. Maybe it was the horror. Either way, I was silent.

Lyric was silent as well. I prayed that she had passed out from the pain-or better yet, that she had escaped into death. Ironic. Only hours ago, I was trying to keep her alive.

"Oh, do not be so arrogant, Avenger. Did you not do much the same thing to our dear friend Evan earlier? Holy water to the eyes. Nice touch. Torture seems to be the one thing that keeps you alive. We are not so different, you and I. It is just that I embrace it, and you deny it." He was within inches of me, the large blade still dripping with unimaginable things. "She is dead now. I have drained her of all the blood. That's the thing about humans; they cannot take the pain, making this little game a lot shorter than I care for."

I looked down at Angie, who was crawling along the floor, holding her neck. Maximilian had ripped a huge chunk of flesh from her. I could hear her labored breathing.

Another figure sat in the shadows. A boy. His face glowed in the candlelight. I recognized him. He was the boy I thought I had killed the night I was kidnapped. He had been bound and gagged, cut and tortured. Death had come slow.

"The boy?" Maximilian caught me looking. "A shifter. A nice touch, no? I placed silver nitrate in his veins. He died from the inside out. I must shed all witnesses, you understand." He laughed, and his power released me to the floor. "You see, Lyric complicated things. I had kept my secrets away from the Council until she caught me in one of my little operations. With her dead, my secret is safe. The Vampire District cannot afford the press, or so Quinn would say. He is appalled at my work. But he tries to suppress what he is. We are vampires. We are at the top of the food chain. You are nothing more than dinner to us."

I looked back to Angie again. She would heal in time, but for now she was weak from the blood loss.

Maximilian looked back down at her. "She is bound to me now. She will answer to my call." He limped his way to her and stopped her forward progress.

"Let her go. She has nothing to do with this. This is between you and me." I tried to stand.

"On the contrary, Avenger. You see, she has as much to do with this as any of us. If she had allowed me the blood I needed, I would not have gone mad. Not to mention the fact she, like you, came here to kill me." He sat the Magnum on the bed and moved back to Angie, towering over her. There was a moment of hesitation before he kicked her hard in the ribs. She rolled on her side, grabbing the injury with her hands. Blood from the wound in her neck smeared her face and chest. "The wonderful thing about shape-shifters is the abuse they can take. Humans bruise and die far too easily. Shape-shifters can take the abuse again and again, and far more of it. They have an incredible healing ability." He kicked her again. She grunted from the impact. This time the movement was less; she was losing her ability to fight.

He looked up at me. "Tell me, Avenger, how does it feel, knowing you only have hours to live?"

I remained silent.

"Beg me, and I'll kill you." A rush of power threw me against the wall. I had to count to five before I could breathe again. He ripped the leather mask from my face.

"At least tell me about the poison in me. What is it? I'm not afraid of dying, but I want to know what killed me. What did you stick in me?"

"We got it from the same source that made Piel a shifter."

"You mean military," I answered.

"Correct. They are working on ways to make soldiers more reliable. Able to take a bullet and keep on fighting. Problem is, with the laws in place, turning someone into a vampire, even with consent, is illegal. The military scientists have found a way to isolate the vampire DNA and inject it into the bloodstream, leaving no trace of a bite."

"Is there really an antidote?"

He laughed. "I am sorry, Avenger, but I'm afraid not. You would have died whether you found our precious Lyric or not. Surely, this does not come as a surprise. Did you really think we would let you live?"

He looked to Angie. "Come to me, my wolf." His hands reached out to her as if pulling her inside out.

She began to writhe on the floor. "No," she cried, as she began to change from human to wolf.

He took the Magnum and emptied the bullets on the bed next to him, methodically, dramatically. This was his moment, a moment for which I was sure he had waited for a long time.

"You see, Avenger," he said, producing another bullet from his pocket, "after I have turned you to a vampire, I plan to kill Quinn Rubio and become the new Master of the City. I will be the most powerful vampire in the new world when I am done. You, on the other hand, will have no alliances in the vampire community and will be a wanted man in the human one. You will truly die alone."

"The more things change, the more they stay the same," I said.

"Oh, on the contrary. I will not follow the façade that Quinn set up. I do not care if the tourists come here or not. I do not wish to gain their money, only their power. Vampires can feed off of many things, not just blood. For some of us, it is sex and lust. For others, it is fear. For me it is power. I will rule the police and the politicians excepting, of course, the ones that will be arriving here in a few moments. They will be slaughtered."

Maximilian put the bullet in the Magnum and walked toward me. "Afraid of death, Avenger?"

"Somehow, I don't believe you will kill me. That would take all the fun out of it for you."

"You catch on very quick. I am impressed. Here is your weapon back, Avenger. You have a choice to make. In the gun is one bullet. A silver nitrate bullet. You may use it to kill yourself if you feel the need. Or you can use it to kill Angela; she will rip your throat out otherwise. Your third option is to put the bullet in me. I will not die from it, but it will weaken me so that I will be unable to kill anyone else tonight. I will never heal from it, just like the leg." He pointed to his stump. "The choice is yours, but you had best decide quickly." Laughter filled his voice. "I think I hear sirens."

He turned to face Angela, now in full werewolf form: large and powerful, jaws ready to rip and tear, teeth sharp and menacing. The Angie I knew was no longer in those eyes; she was nothing more than an extension of Maximilian's sick mind. And the only way to free someone of a vampire's mind tricks is kill the source.

I brought the Magnum up on Maximilian. If I could kill him, I could save Angie as well as the police that were quickly moving into a trap. I thought about Kansas, Price, and all the others on the force that had families, families that loved them and depended on them. I wasn't about to let this cockroach hurt all those people.

Angie was on me before I could fire the shot. Teeth sank deep in my shoulder. The pain was blinding. I felt a mixture of hot breath and blood. My blood. The wolf brought us both to the ground in a hard crash. I broke our fall. Lucky me.

I tightened my grip on the gun. If I couldn't get Angie off of me, I'd put the bullet in her. Not a choice I wanted to make, but if I killed Angie, she would at least be free of Maximilian's spells and torture. It was the humane thing to do.

"Feed on him, my night wolf," Maximilian said from above. He was saying other things too, but I was a little too busy to hear them. For the first time in my life, I was doing what I could to keep a monster alive, even as it ripped my shoulder from my body. She had saved my life. I felt I should at least try to do the same for her.

My hands were wrapped around her throat. I tried to brace myself the best I could. A human was no match for a monster like this. A mixture of saliva and my blood dripped on my chest. The Magnum was just to the side of her head. All I had to do was turn it slightly and pull the trigger. But I wasn't willing to do that just yet.

I pushed with my left hand and arm on her throat. With the right hand, I turned the Magnum. Not to her head, but to Maximilian's chest. Blood was streaming down the length of my arm. I felt it giving way to the weight of the monster on top of me.

I felt the Magnum's explosion. I saw the bullet hit Maximilian in the throat. Both hands grabbed at the wound: blood painted his long white fingers. His face was hollow, looking into nothingness. The power behind those orbs was at least temporarily gone, leaving nothing but the corpse in front of me. Like a receding wave on the ocean, I could feel the power being pulled from the room.

Angie howled madly above me. Her body grew limp and fell on top of me. Getting out from under her was high on my priority list. I glanced at the ultraviolet bullets on the bed. I had to get to them and finish Maximilian before he regained enough strength to kill again.

Maximilian was down on his knees, as if praying. Blood streamed through his fingers. I could see the wound slowly healing itself. The silver would keep the wound from healing as quickly, but it would still heal all the same, leaving nothing but a nasty scar.

I dragged myself to the bed, using my good arm, feeling the trails of blood running down my shoulder and across my chest. I refused to look at the wound. It would only distract me. The bed seemed a mile away. My head was growing lighter by the second as blood loss began to take its toll.

As I reached for the bed, I felt my stomach growing weak. I was going to puke. There was no doubt about it. Between the numbing pain in my shoulder and the loss of blood, my stomach had had enough. I hurled.

"You will never be able to kill me, Avenger. I own your fear. I feed off of it even as you begin to die," Maximilian said in a hoarse voice. I couldn't look up. I didn't have the strength. I could feel him growing stronger again. His power was beginning to flow through the room once more, like a cascading waterfall, flooding my every sense.

Pulling myself up on the bed, I grabbed for the bullets with fingers now uncoordinated, slick and sticky all at the same time. Slowly, I tried to put the bullets in the Magnum. It was all I could do to keep from blacking out.

"I will bleed you myself, before you die." I felt a cold hand reach for my throat, and I was lifted to my feet. "But before you die,

I want you to know I am going to kill Angela slowly and painfully. I will cut her from limb to limb, as I did with Lyric. And when the police arrive, I will kill them as well. I will kill them all."

I continued to fumble bullets into the Magnum. From the angle I was being lifted, I couldn't see the gun or my hands, only feel the touch of the bullets.

"Do you really think your bullets will harm me? I am a master vampire, not some scavenger like you are used to killing. The pain will only make me stronger." With a crashing blow, he knocked the Magnum from my hands. Bullets flew. My body was growing numb. The pain felt almost hollow. My ears began to ring.

I brought my elbow across the bloodsucker's chest, felt it give way. I had space between my neck and his fangs. Using his own strength, I twisted my upper body and jammed my fist into the open wound in his neck.

I ripped flesh out of the wound. Blood and meat filled my hand, jamming under my fingernails. I fell to the floor. The cockroach screamed in pain, mixed with a harmony of gurgling noises.

I dove for the Magnum, only to feel the force of his foot in my lower back. I could feel my spine tingling with pressure, popping at least one rib for sure. Hands reached out for my shoulder.

Lifted and thrown, my body rolled across the floor, landing next to Angie's body. If she was still under Maximilian's control, I had two monsters to deal with. See, there is never a nice, pleasant choice when you kill monsters for a living.

I felt another presence in the room with us now. Familiar. Powerful. Ancient. Quinn Rubio.

CHAPTER THIRTY-TWO

"Quinn," Maximilian said.

"You have embarrassed the vampire community long enough. I will no longer hide your lies," Quinn spat. The vampire looked around the room with disgust. "The death you have brought shall be on your hands, not ours. The blood you have spilled has nothing to do with us as a community."

I began to scramble back across the room, hoping to find the bullets. They had scattered like marbles. In the low light, it was practically impossible to find them. Then one caught the flickering candlelight. One less than I needed, but...

"You continue to rule the vampires here as if they were part of humanity. We are far more than that. Humans are nothing more than a source of food and pleasure. You cannot colonize us into cattle." Maximilian moved slowly around the room. He almost seemed relieved that the old vampire had confronted him. "I thought I would have to hunt you down to kill you. I never dreamed you would come to me to die."

"In the old days, we were hunted and killed for what we were. We now have an opportunity to walk freely among the humans. Grow as a society with them. Yes, we are superior to them, but there is a delicate balance that must be maintained if we are to survive. They outnumber us."

"That is your problem, Quinn. You live in the past. Seize the day. Live for the moment. I may be mad, but I still know the reality of your vision for us. Numbers mean nothing. It is power and control that will survive."

I continued to crawl slowly to the bullet, keeping my eyes on the two vampires. I was now behind Quinn, with Maximilian on the other side of the room, giving me the smallest of advantages. Master vampires can move from one spot to another without being seen. Whether it was magic or just incredible speed, I still wasn't sure, but the result is the same. One minute the cockroach with teeth can be yards away; the next, at your throat.

"You want to bind us to their cultures, make us accountable to their laws. Not all of us think becoming citizens with the humans is a good thing," Maximilian added.

"There are plenty of willing participants here to feed us. They come to us with necks exposed. We no longer have to fear being killed while we slumber. We are undead, not uncivilized. Being dead does not exclude us from law and order, ours or theirs. You have jeopardized everything that most of us have built here. You challenge my authority and power with your carelessness. I will not allow you to do so any longer."

"Your authority should be challenged. You have sold our way of life for trinkets, nightclubs, notoriety, and money. You have made the vampire community nothing more than a sideshow at a circus. I did not survive eight hundred years to be a monkey for the humans. I am a vampire. I will never serve human laws. They are food, not business partners."

"You were a sick man in life; a rapist, a murderer. Being a

vampire has not changed that. Your actions stand to hurt the growth of all vampires here. I will no longer sweep the deaths away. You must be stopped. You must be punished."

A rush of power hit Maximilian, knocking him backwards into the wall. I used the time to put the bullet in the Magnum. Question was, which fang fritter would I take out?

Maximilian's body was raised into the air by Quinn's magic. I could hear and feel the pain. Pain I knew well. I trained the Magnum on Quinn Rubio and held my breath. My finger refused to pull the trigger. I wasn't sure what Quinn Rubio was capable of, what he had done in his past, or what he planned to do, but I was sure of all those things with Maximilian. Maximilian was my killer. He was the evil of here and now. My bullet would kill him.

Maximilian fought back with magic of his own, spilling it over the two of us like a blanket. My throat collapsed, my head pounded. Quinn appeared to be in pain. Power and magic flowed through him.

Maximilian moved toward him. "Rise, my wolf," he said as he gestured to Angie.

Angie rose from the floor and moved toward Rubio, baring the same sharp teeth that had bitten into me. In one animal-like movement, flowing and graceful, she was at Quinn Rubio's throat.

I could feel my body giving way to the blood loss, the poison, the power. I had to kill Maximilian, or more innocent would die tonight. I could hear the distant wail of the sirens moving closer. Kansas, Price, and countless other officers would be here soon. They would all die if I didn't stop this now. I forced the Magnum on Maximilian. It was heavy in my hands.

Maximilian looked in my direction just as I pulled the trigger. His mouth moved, but no words came out. A look of surprise painted his face. The bullet found its mark in his chest, exploding the heart.

He didn't turn into a pile of ash. Instead, he began to burn from the wound. Smoldering heat glowed as he howled in pain. The power and magic began to fade once again. Quinn floated to his feet. Angie fell to the floor.

Blue, green, and orange flames began to roll across the blood-sucker's body. He screamed, eyes locked on Quinn's. Dead skin filled the air, painting a sea of smoke. Chills ran down my arms as the wave of power evaporated.

Quinn picked up a large cleaver that was sitting on a wooden crate not far from Lyric's body, moved to the wounded Maximilian. "You will never be at my throat again," he growled. And with that he brought the cleaver down on Maximilian's throat, severing the head.

I collapsed on my side. The spinning room overwhelmed me. Outside the room, I heard crashing doors. Yelling. Movement. Chaos. The good guys were here. Entering a building filled with monsters, a room with a master vampire in it.

The black silhouette of Quinn Rubio floated across me. He looked at me and smiled his sinister smile. "Good work, Avenger. The vampire community, as well as the human community, owes a great debt to you."

I pulled the trigger. It was empty. I hated him for what he was. What he had done to me. Stopping Maximilian didn't change that. Quinn was just another type of evil, no better, no worse. They were all blood maggots. They had taken my mother's life. My father's life. Now they had taken mine.

"Mark my words, I will kill you." I laid my head on the floor. I couldn't hold it up any longer. Angie was now back to human form and moving to me, her eyes full of horror and pain.

"Paul? I'm sorry, so sorry." She began to cry.

"Kill him. Then kill me." I felt her lift me on her knees. I could smell her sweet scent. I was cold and numb, shaking uncontrollably. Death was close. I could feel my heart slowing, my vision fading. I wasn't sure if it was from the poison or the blood loss. In the end, it didn't make a difference.

"What does not kill you makes you stronger, Avenger."

"Go to hell," I answered.

"The sun will rise soon, Avenger. I must go. I am truly sorry for your demise. I do not expect you to understand the politics behind this. I had to do what was best for my people. The poison was none of our doing. We were nothing more than victims of his madness, as you were." Quinn Rubio vanished.

The door opened. Price stood there with his mouth open. Others gathered behind him, only shadows now. Shadows.

"Paul," I heard in the distance. I wasn't sure who it was. Blackness ate at me. I couldn't stop it. "Paul," I heard again, more distant. So this is what death feels like.

CHAPTER THIRTY-THREE

I woke to the sounds of machines, beeping, breathing, and humming. I was cold, very cold. My eyes opened to unfamiliar surroundings, sterile and plain. My body felt extremely heavy, as if someone had sucked my energy from me. The smells, the sounds, the feel of the room told me I was in a hospital.

My mind raced to put together the impossibility of where I was. I had been poisoned. Then it hit me. I should be dead, or at least undead.

I ran my tongue across my upper teeth. No fangs. Could it be another cruel joke from those that had tried to kill me? Make me a vampire but somehow remove my fangs? Of course it was possible. It would be quite typical, actually.

Death. I had nothing to compare it to, but somehow I guessed this was not what it felt like. For one, I was in a hospital room, not the morgue. None of this was making any sense.

The possibility that I was in Hell came next. Given my life, Heaven was just not an option. Which left only one place. Could be that Father Garcia had found me and staked me, cut off my head, cut out my heart, and now I was just in a waiting room in Hell somewhere, waiting for admittance. I felt my neck with my fingers, but couldn't feel any type of scar or wound. I opened my gown and looked down at my chest. There was no visible wound, just a stabbing pain that came with lowering my neck. My shoulder was throbbing now.

Pulling the gown open a little more, I saw the large bandage and remembered the Tortured Skin party. Angie had attacked me. Well, not Angie, per se, it was really Maximilian, but Angie had done the mauling. The wound didn't seem to care who did it or why.

I lay back in the bed and tried to figure out what had happened to me. I was hooked up to all kinds of monitors and IVs. Not knowing where I was scared me the most. In my profession, it was a good idea to know where you were at all times. I had no idea whether to kill what came through the door next or thank it. I decided to kill it. Just to be on the safe side.

Detective Kansas came through the door, smiled at me as he drew close to my bed. "Finally coming around, are you?"

"Okay, so God has a sense of humor. Not only did he send me to Hell, but he sent you to keep me company. How wonderful."

Kansas laughed.

"Where am I?"

"Florida Hospital. They're taking real good care of you."

"But I thought..." I trailed off as Angie came through the door. She was actually dressed normally for a change, in a bright yellow blouse and tight faded jeans with holes in the knees. Her caramel skin practically glowed. Her scent was intoxicating. She had a large latex balloon with a teddy bear on it that read "Get Well Soon."

"You thought you'd be dead by now," she finished and smiled. She tied the balloon to the foot of the bed and watched it float upward until the string grew tight. Then I noticed two sets of floral arrangements on the table next to me. There was an arrangement of wildflowers in a small white basket, and an arrangement of roses-six black, six white. Odd.

"Yeah, something like that."

"Seems like you are the luckiest man on earth," Kansas said, looking at the flowers.

I looked at him, but didn't say anything. My eyes did it for me.

"The things I saw in that place..." His words trailed off. "The girl, Lyric, she was tortured like nothing I have ever seen before. Just when you think you've seen the sickest thing ever, someone comes along and tops it."

"You mean something."

"Well, yeah, I guess so."

"And Maximilian? Did you find him?"

"Yeah, what was left of him? You killed him yourself?"

"I had a little help."

"Whatever. The point is that you're alive and okay."

"What about Dr. Montgomery?"

"Dr. Montgomery was found in her car, a gunshot to the head. There were plenty of arrests at the warehouse where the Tortured Skin party was. We still need your side of the story to give to the Vampire Counsel, but truthfully, it's nothing more than paperwork. You got him," Kansas said with a half smile. "The Vampire Council has forgiven all your actions. I got it straight from Quinn Rubio. No charges will be filed."

"Montgomery shot herself?" I asked in disbelief. "I didn't think she'd have the guts."

"Or someone shot her. That's what we're trying to find out."

"How long have I been here?"

"You've been in a coma for two days now. The doctors didn't think you were going to make it. You lost a lot of blood, and your system was shutting down. Then something amazing happened.

Your body began to heal itself, just like a shape-shifter, but much, much slower. With a wound like yours, a human would take months of healing and therapy, but the doctors expect you to be up and around in a week or less." He stopped, took a deep breath. "Seems that the vampire poison that was supposed to make you undead got cancelled out when Angie bit you. The lycan virus and the vampire poison have created a bond in you."

"Define bond," I said, not really wanting an answer.

"You have the DNA of a vampire and the host virus of a were-wolf running through your veins, but neither will kill you or change you. Or at least, no one thinks so."

"What do you mean by 'think so'?" Panic set in. The thought of being one of them was beyond any nightmare. I looked at Angie. "I don't want to be what she is. I kill things like she is. I can't be a monster. I refuse the idea."

"The doctors have never seen anything like this before. A vampire toxin bonding with a lycan virus is unheard of. A couple of university doctors will be down later tomorrow to do tests and see what they find."

"Great. Now I'm an experiment. Just the thought of having vampire crap running through my veins gives me the willies. I can't stay here. I won't be one of those things." I looked at Angie.

"I'm not a thing. I am what I am, and I've come to terms with it. I didn't choose it any more than you did. I'll have to live with this for the rest of my life." Angie sat on the far corner of the bed. "I'm sorry for the bite. I hope you can forgive me one day." Her head lowered, eyes looking at the floor.

"I'm sorry. It's all too much to take in right now." I looked back to Kansas. "Quinn, Veronica Powers, and Dieter were all in on trying to kill me. Have you killed them?"

"Trouble is, there's nothing we can hold them on unless they admit to poisoning you. And I don't think they will do that."

"So he goes free while I live with this." I wanted to crawl out of my skin. "Somehow I picture this as being icing on the cake for him. Not killing me, but instead having me live with vampire blood in my veins. I'll find him and kill him myself." I tried to lift myself out of the bed.

"Like I told you, we are working on it. You know vampire politics. They're never easy. Let us handle this. It's our job. You get some rest. You've been through a lot. There are a lot of people praying for you, wanting to see you. Father Garcia has been here with you over the last twenty-four hours. We sent him back to the church to rest about two hours ago. He's worried sick about you."

"I'm not up for visitors. Besides, he was probably here to keep a very big promise."

"And Angie has never left your side. She feels responsible for what has happened to you." Kansas turned to leave. "I'll notify the nurses that you're awake."

Angie hopped off the bed and looked at me. Her eyes were still glassy with tears she refused to let fall. "I'm glad you're alive."

"Thank you." It was all I could say to her. The words just weren't there.

"You just had a very lucky break. You cheated death. I'd make a few changes in my life if I were you," Kansas said.

"You're right." Changes were needed. I wanted to visit my parents' graves. I had so many questions for them, questions I'd never get answers to, but I needed closure. I needed to let go of the anger, find more motivation for living than simply killing. This kind of life was cold and lonely, just like me. I was so afraid of being a monster that I didn't see I already was one. I didn't have fangs or grow fur, but I was a monster all the same.

Angie kissed my cheek lightly. "We'll all be here for you."

I picked up the card in the wildflower arrangement. It was from Father Garcia and Sister Mary. The card had Psalms 23 on it, and a handwritten note: "Get well soon. God be with you." I smiled.

I opened the card from the second arrangement. It was a blank card with a handwritten note.

What does not kill you will make you stronger.
From one monster to another,
Get Well Soon.

Q.R.

ABOUT THE AUTHOR

James C. Gillen is creative mind behind the award winning Paul Isaac Vampire Series, including Tortured Skin, Crimson Madness, and Sins of Retribution from Hydra Publications. He has won the Florida Writers Royal Palm Award for Best in Horror, Best in Horror at Imaginarium, Finalist with Book USA's Best in Horror.

James lives in Orlando, Florida with his American bulldog, Pursey. He's also a graphic artist and bass player for a couple of local jazz big bands. He enjoys riding motorcycles and spending quality time with his family.

ALSO BY JAMES C. GILLEN

The Paul Isaac Vampire Series

Crimson Madness

Sins of Retribution

www.ingramcontent.com/pod-product-compliance
Lightning Source LLC
Chambersburg PA
CBHW060852250626
47159CB00008B/2709